I0762088

SOUND OF THE SINNERS

This edition first published 2020 by Fahrenheit Press.

ISBN: 978-1-912526-84-0

10 9 8 7 6 5 4 3 2 1

www.Fahrenheit-Press.com

F 4 E

Sound Of The Sinners

By

Nick Quantrill

A Joe Geraghty Novel

Other books in this series

Book 1: Broken Dreams
Book 2: The Late Greats
Book 3: The Crooked Beat

Fahrenheit Press

For Alice... not as good as The Beano, but one day...

PROLOGUE

1989

Too slow to register the crunch of footwear on gravel behind him, a flash of light in his eyes and a blow across the face sent him falling into the arms of the second man. Carried over to the open boot and thrown inside, the lid pushed down to lock him into a space as small and dark as a coffin. John Gove listened to the fading echo of boots on concrete, the sound of car doors opening, then closing. The engine started, his head jolting back as the car pulled away from the kerb. The car increased in speed, as did the nightmare scenarios playing out in his head. No one would hear a scream for help.

The car cornered, slowed, pulled off what felt like a main road, each bump and jolt sending pain through his body. Slowing further, his head hit the back of the boot as the road inclined slightly. Another corner and another incline, the car coming to a stop. Forcing himself to think, he was in a multi-storey car park, it would be empty at this time of night. Hands frantically searching for a release catch, not finding one. He stopped and listened as the engine was killed, the sound of doors opening and the men making their way towards him. The boot opened, light from a torch flooding his vision, involuntarily forcing his hands to his eyes, leaving him unable to fight off those lifting him out.

Thrown to the ground, blood mixed with dirt in his mouth, a foot on his head pushing him further down onto the cold concrete floor. A hand grabbed his hair, pulling him upright. Silence settling around the empty car park. Another blow, this time to the back of his head. It connected sweetly, his senses going like the jackpot on a fruit machine. He rolled over and vomited. Hearing laughter, he tried to move out of range, but was too slow. A kick to the head landed, leaving him unable to move, gasping for air. A pair of hands pulled him back up. There was something familiar about the two figures, something he couldn't focus on for long enough to make sense of. He was thrown back to the floor, blows coming in until he collapsed in a heap, blood and broken teeth swirling around in his mouth.

The men stepped closer. 'You know who this is for?' the first one said.

It was about more than the violence being inflicted. It was something more dangerous than pain which would eventually pass. It was about guilt and shame. It was about accountability and responsibility. An eye for an eye. 'It wasn't my fault,' he said, struggling to speak.

'It's payback time.'

He shook his head violently, self-preservation kicking in. 'Please.' The heavy boots kicked out, pushing him closer to the edge of darkness. Another burst of blows, his body being trashed and shutting down. No more time to think, no more time to beg for mercy. Hauled to his feet, he stared at the men.

'You know how this has to work, John.'

The voice sounded different, his vision and hearing not clearing enough to pinpoint where it was coming from. But actions always have consequences, he knew that much. There was a tab to pay and it was being called in. Nothing happened for a moment, maybe it would be ok. Maybe there was a chance. A punch he didn't see coming snapped his head back, sending him skidding backwards, no chance of keeping his balance. Falling, his head cracked like an egg, bouncing up off the concrete floor, just enough time to realise this was the end.

ONE

The crematorium door creaked as I closed it behind me, mourners turning to glance in my direction, the service already underway. My flight into Humberside Airport from Amsterdam had been delayed, Marieke dropping me off at the airport with a promise to pick me up tomorrow. Taking a seat to the rear, it was the larger of the two chapels, a crude measurement of someone's final tally of friends and family.

Staring at the order of service sheet, the news still hadn't fully sunk in. Don Ridley, 1949 – 2019. You can count the number of people who really change your life on one hand and Don had been one of them for me. He'd picked me up several years ago when I'd been at my lowest after my wife's death in a house fire, seeing something in me worth saving. If there was such a thing as being a natural private investigator in a city like Hull, he'd said I was one. It had all ended sourly when I'd pursued a case that had delved into his past, throwing up things I hadn't been able to turn a blind eye to. Now it was too late to repair the damage. A hit and run a week previously had ended his life, the minister describing it as a tragic accident.

I stared at the photographs on the sheet. The first showed him as a young police officer, the hair style and car he was leaning on dating it in the mid-1970's, pride and expectation etched on his face as he embarked on his new career. It had been a journey that had taken him into the detective ranks, confronting the worst humanity could throw at him before retiring and starting up the agency.

In reality, the business had been a three-way partnership with Sarah more than playing her part. She'd been the glue that held us together, mediating between me and her father, keeping the peace and signalling the way forward.

Flipping the sheet over, I stared at the second photograph recognising his back garden and the people in it. It had been taken a decade previously and showed him laughing, his granddaughter, Lauren, at his feet in a splash pool. Next to him, his daughter, Sarah smiled as she leaned into the shot. Looking up, I scanned to the front of the chapel looking for them, Lauren a teenager now and growing up fast.

I let the service wash over me. Looking around, I recognised some of the faces. Many were Don's former-colleagues in the police. I spotted Gerard Branning, a former colleague of Don's we'd used for background help on cases, sometimes swapping information, sometimes just exploring theories together. Others were Don's distant family, some were friends made along the way. Looking for high ranking police officers, they'd be here out a sense of duty. Lauren stood up and read a poem she'd written at school, voice cracking as she did so. Reading it showed more bravery than most ever do in their life.

A hymn and a closing prayer brought the service to an end. Heading for the door, I took a moment for a quick glance and nod to the coffin at the front of the room. Standing outside, I drew in the cold air and blinked against the sunlight. The gathering split into groups making small talk, others checking messages on phones, or lighting up cigarettes.

I spotted Branning talking to a small group of men, all in their sixties and seventies, all old enough to realise it was funerals which increasingly brought them back together. Edging closer, I could hear them discussing drinking plans for later in the day. They'd pay their respects at the wake before retiring to share memories and stories, mourning giving away to laughter, anecdotes and old jokes dusted down for one more telling. Branning noticed me moving towards him, quickly turning his back to me. The message was clear.

Instead, I headed towards Sarah, a mourner I didn't recognise offering his condolences to her. As she thanked him and he moved away, I took my chance. There was a split-second's hesitation before recognising me despite the beard and longer hair. It didn't need a psychologist to analyse the reasons why I'd changed my appearance, but she still paused for a moment to take it in. We hadn't seen each other for five years. Caught in the moment, I couldn't decide if a hug was appropriate or not. Sarah made the decision for me as she guided me away from the crowd by the elbow towards a quiet corner.

'I wasn't sure whether or not to come,' I said, 'but I wanted to be here.' She didn't respond, leaving me grasping for the right words. The last thing we needed between us was silence. 'It seems to have gone well,' I said, offering a meaningless platitude.

Sarah looked to the floor. 'You can't begin to guess how many times I've heard that today.'

'Sorry.'

'I'll be glad when it's over.'

'Sure.' I could still remember burying my own father, how it hurt and never really left you. 'How's Lauren coping? That was some poem she read out.'

'Important time coming up for her with exams.'

'Doing ok with them?'

'She's staying on track.'

I was pleased to hear it. 'How about you?'

'Keeping busy.'

I nodded, understanding. There was an edge to her answer, much more to be said, but now wasn't the time or the place.

'What about you, Joe? Working?'

'Just out on building sites in Holland for a mate, mainly around Amsterdam.' She looked surprised by my news. It was a life that had quickly become routine. 'I've picked up a bit of the language. It's pleasant enough.'

'Good to hear.' She looked across to Lauren. 'I need to get back to her.'

I put my arm out to stop her leaving before quickly lowering it again. 'I'm sorry to bring this up here, but there's something we need to talk about.'

Sarah's face hardened. 'I don't want to hear it.'

'It's important.'

'No.' She started to walk away.

I paused for a moment, unsure of how to react. 'I've still got the same number,' I shouted after her. 'We need to talk.'

She stopped, turned back and walked towards me, closing the gap quickly. The look on her face made it perfectly clear what she thought of me. I was worse than something she'd scrapped off the bottom of her shoe.

'Don't you think you've done enough damage, Joe? Stay away from us.'

TWO

I drove east out of the city, the sprawling docks a reminder that the place was always at the mercy of water, that it took as much as it offered. I passed the imposing Victorian facade of the prison knowing some of the inmates would be the worst humanity had to offer, and some would merely be trapped by circumstances. There was often little in between, the house gambled on red or black. It didn't take a lot to tip the balance if you sailed close to the wind.

Turning off the main road, I passed the large chemical plant and headed into the village of Paull on the banks of the Humber. I knew the village well, a childhood staple for family walks. Reaching a fork in the road, the main street at the front took you to a lighthouse via a school, a village hall and a pub. Edging left, I took the residential back street which opened up into the road linking to a small market town three or so miles away.

Pulling over, I pinpointed the place where Don had died. An overgrown ditch ran parallel to the road, deeper than it looked at first glance, a keeper of its own secrets. It was a road little traffic used. Kicking out a stone underfoot, I pulled my coat tighter around me, discarded crime scene tape caught on the branch of a tree the only visible marker of what had happened. Accidents would happen and it wouldn't take much to knock a person out of sight. Equally, there wasn't anything to say that's all it was. It would have been icy underfoot, no lighting. What it really meant was dying alone, cold and scared.

A vehicle came to a stop behind me, its tyres softly crunching on the road surface underneath. Watching DI Coleman get out, the dark overcoat gave him the easy air of an accountant or solicitor, but the crumpled suit underneath belonged to a man used to working long hours without respite. He stared at me for a moment before heading over. It had been a couple of years since our paths had crossed. He'd put me to work on his behalf in Amsterdam, giving me little choice but to get involved.

'How did the funeral go, Joe?'

'I thought I might have seen you there.'

'I wasn't able to make it.'

Coleman had the decency to at least look embarrassed. Clearly it hadn't been his choice to make. 'Made an arrest yet in relation to Don's death?'

'You don't change.'

'And you didn't answer my question.'

'With respect, police business isn't anything to do with you.'

I didn't dignify the comment with a response. We both looked around at the desolate patchwork of fields, both of us probably thinking the same thing. A cat ran into the road, stopping to stare for a moment, surprised to see its territory invaded.

Coleman broke the silence between us. 'No arrest yet.'

'You've had a week.'

'We're still investigating.'

'Sounds like an excuse to me.' Coleman bristled at the suggestion, unable to hide his irritation. 'Sounds like you don't expect to make an arrest?' I'd needled him, gotten under his skin.

'There's a team working on it. Don't forget that Don was one of us.'

If I was supposed to take some comfort from the fact Don's name still had some pull within the police force, I wasn't feeling it. 'What about witnesses?' I asked. 'What about camera footage from the area?' Maybe they'd picked something up, a vehicle on the main road, tracked its route.

'I'm not going to talk about that with you.'

It was frustrating, but Coleman had every reason not to be open with me, or show any trust. I'd crossed the line in the past, and as much as it had always been in good faith and sometimes chimed with his agenda, I was trouble to him.

'How's Sarah bearing up?' he asked.

'I wouldn't really know.'

He read the situation for what it was, letting it go. 'Tough time for everyone.'

'You're not wrong.'

Coleman looked me over properly. 'You're in good shape.'

I told him the same as I'd told Sarah. Despite that, I was closing in on fifty and hadn't felt this low since injury had ended my rugby league with Hull Kingston Rovers. I felt like I was drifting through life again, lacking the purpose Don had once given me.

Coleman cocked his head slightly. 'Sometimes a fresh start is the right thing to do. Honest work is good for you.'

I smiled at the barb about honest work, but let it pass. His eyes went to my car. 'My brother's,' I said, stopping him going any further. 'Named driver if you want to check the insurance?'

Coleman waved the suggestion away. 'What was your relationship with Don like of late?'

Back to business and the question had a simple answer. 'There wasn't one.' His eyes bored into mine, searching for a lie, but the truth was always an easier sell. 'There's nothing to be sensitive about,' I said. 'We haven't spoken for the best part of five years.'

'So why are you back?'

'For the funeral.' I straightened up and looked him in the eye. 'It's Don we're talking about.'

'Don't say it, Joe.'

'Don't say what?'

'A police investigation isn't a participation sport.' The mood changed. He angled himself towards me, wanting to take control of the conversation. 'There's nothing here for you. If you're happy with your new life in Holland, you should pay your respects and head back there and get on with it. Leave things here to us.'

'You've come out here to warn me off?'

'I came out here at your request, as a courtesy to you. I can make sure you're informed of any progress we make. What I don't appreciate is a distraction.'

'I'm a distraction?'

'As things stand, Don's death is a tragic accident until the evidence tells us something else.' Coleman took in the wide-open space. 'It's desolate, but the facts are the facts. Don was a dog owner and he came out here regularly to let it off the lead. It's possible he had good reason to be out here.'

Looking around, it still didn't feel right to me. It wasn't the kind of place you took a dog for a walk, but I held my tongue for now.

I watched Coleman head back to his car, climb in and drive away, no more to be said. He'd delivered the message he felt was necessary. It settled things in my mind, too. Taking my mobile out, I carried it for emergencies, something I'd had for years. It was cheap and basic, but it did what I needed it to. The message from Don had been timed two days before his death when I'd been out of signal range. Listening again, his voice was hesitant and quiet, but he'd asked me to call him back, leaving his new landline number. Explaining it was a professional matter, not personal, my best guess was that it related to the days when he'd worked for the police. Something in his voice betrayed a reluctance to call me. It had hurt him to do so, but his words were clear. Without directly telling me what he wanted to speak about, I understood he didn't have anywhere else to turn, no one else he trusted. Don had called to ask for my help.

THREE

Main Street in the village ran parallel to the water, a glass-panelled barrier ran alongside the pavement, acting as a flood defence device against the Humber's high tides. A transit van pulled up onto the pavement outside of the pub and flicked it's hazard lights on. I watched as the driver jumped out and started to drag heavy boxes inside. Turning away and looking out across the water to Lincolnshire, the petroleum plants and refineries felt close enough to touch. Further east, a vast spread of tidal mudflats and salt marsh before the open spaces of Holderness and Spurn Point.

The village lighthouse stood unused, a relic of a bygone age. It was modest in size, railings running around an outdoor viewing platform, but still imposing enough to dominate all it overlooked. Down the side ran a short length of cottage-style houses, the end one being Don's home. Walking up to the door, drawn curtains left me unable to see inside. Stepping back, I looked the small house over, wanting to put myself in his shoes for a moment, try to get a feel for what his life had become, how he'd chosen to live it. The front garden was neat and tidy, looked after by someone who enjoyed spending time on it, the paintwork recently touched up.

It would be easy enough to get inside, but it would be crossing a line. Turning away, I decided it would save. I walked to the waterfront, heading along the uneven path underfoot in the direction of the nature reserve, the mudflats acting as a magnet for wildlife. I'd walked maybe 500 yards away from the cottage, but it felt like I was the only person in the world. I walked as far as the old low lights that had been similarly rendered redundant. Examining them, they looked like mini-rockets, one red and one white, both rusted and fenced off to stop unwanted access. A dog bounded up to me, breaking the spell. I watched as its owner took a ball out of her pocket and threw it, apologising for bothering me. We both watched the dog chase after it for a moment. Treading carefully so I didn't slip on the mud, I headed back.

I walked towards the village pub, it was where people would talk, the heartbeat of the community. I was drawn to them like a moth to a flame. Pushing at the door, the warmth inside hit me immediately. The television bolted to the wall was switched off, a poster for a Peaky Blinders fancy dress night above the bar. It looked like a million other village pubs. It was rough around the edges with frayed fixtures and fittings, but battling on as best it could. Once it was gone, it wouldn't come back. The place was empty, no drinkers in. A woman in her fifties appeared from behind the bar, a box of crisps under her arm.

'You're quiet.' I said, heading across the room.

'There's a funeral on in Hull.' She placed the box down and looked me over. 'A local from around here.'

I found a stool and pulled it up at the bar. 'Could I get a coffee?' and watched her disappear to put the kettle on. Thinking, I wondered which doors Coleman and his team had knocked on in the area, who they'd spoken to. There was something else. They'd eventually access the call list on his phone and want to know what he'd said to me. The harder question I had to answer was figuring out what Don felt I could help him with. Once I knew that, I could work out what my next move should be. I had a head start over Coleman, though.

A mug of coffee was placed in front of me, a carton of milk nudged in my direction. 'You didn't go to the funeral?' I asked before stirring some sugar in.

'Thought it was best left to family and close friends, that kind of thing.' She sipped at her drink. 'Did you know him?'

I nodded, lifted my mug up and suggested a toast. 'To Don.' She followed suit. 'A good man.'

'He came in here regularly?'

'Most nights for a bit of company, I think, after he'd taken his dog for a walk.'

'What did he like to talk about?'

'Family, the usual stuff,' she said, counting them off. 'His old job, the news, Brexit. Always had an opinion did Don.'

I smiled, saying it sounded about right. I wasn't up to speed on Brexit, mainly because it wasn't a big deal where I was living. I also tried to avoid the news as best I could for my own sanity.

'Are you a journalist?'

I sipped at my coffee and shook my head. 'No.'

'You're certainly not police, you scruffy bugger.'

I raised my mug and smiled, but didn't push it. I rocked on the stool slightly, wondering just how much she would tell me. 'Did Don ever talk about his work?'

'Sometimes,' she said. 'In passing. Not the details. More just that he felt some things shouldn't be allowed to stand.'

'Something was eating at him?'

'I'd say so.'

'Any idea what it was?'

She shook her head. 'Not sure he really had anyone he felt comfortable enough to share it with. He didn't want to burden his daughter, quite understandably, but there was a falling out with his former business partner. Maybe he could have helped?'

She was staring at me, a thin smile on her face. The woman had known who I was from the moment I'd walked in and she was the one in control of the conversation. I put my mug down on the bar. 'You got me.'

'You should have introduced yourself.'

'It seems we never got to that stage.'

'I've seen photographs of you together.'

That surprised me. I wasn't sure I even had a photograph of Don, certainly not one of us together. The woman's words forced me to look away for a moment. It was difficult picturing Don living in such a place, talking to people so openly. I had to push all that to one side, not let it cloud my judgment. I took a breath, watched the steam at the top of my mug float upwards, composing myself. 'Have you had the police around?'

'They sent a PCSO just after it happened.' The disappointment in her voice was obvious.

'That was all?'

'She wanted to know if anyone had seen anything out of place recently, that kind of thing.'

'What did you tell her?'

'There was nothing to tell.'

'Did Don mention anything he was looking at in particular, maybe an old case?' I was rolling the dice, as we both knew what my question really meant, what I was really asking her. It was her choice if she wanted to follow me down that particular path. Sometimes it was easier to decide something was none of your business, lock it away at the back of your mind, safe from being thought about again. Ignoring that option had cost me plenty over the years. Truth was, I couldn't blame her if she didn't want to speak. Sometimes not getting involved was the right thing to do.

She disappeared from behind the bar and returned with a business card, holding it out towards me. 'This is for you.' I took it from her and looked at the details. The name on it, Natalie Okorie, wasn't familiar to me. My heart sunk a little at the words underneath it. Okorie was a freelance journalist working for The Northern News Alliance. I didn't know them, had never heard of them. I flipped it over, but it was blank. Turning it face up again, I looked again at the website address and mobile number. There was nothing else on the card.

'She brought it in yesterday, saying you'd be dropping by today. Looks like she can read you like a book.'

'Did she say what she wanted?'

'She wants you to call her.'

FOUR

The Queens was the place I'd always done my best thinking, something I could count on not changing. The pub wasn't busy, just a handful of people as the daytime drinkers turned into the night crowd. A couple of faces glanced at me, double-takes as the penny dropped. None of them felt the need to speak to me, though. It wasn't that kind of place. It had been a second home back in the day, but driving across the turning for Westbourne Avenue, I hadn't felt the need to detour and see the flat I'd once called home. Ordering a glass of water and a packet of crisps, I picked up the day's newspaper from the bar and took up residence in what had been my favourite corner, not wanting to be disturbed.

Flicking through the newspaper, most of the names and faces had changed since I'd last read it. Glancing at the headshots of the journalists, they all looked implausibly young, starting out on their careers. Maybe the city wouldn't contain them, or maybe they'd be like the old-stagers I did recognise, dedicating their careers to the place.

The lead on the front page was about the launch of *Hit The North*, an arts festival featuring installations and events stretching from Hull to Liverpool across the M62. It was part of the legacy programme following the city's moment in the spotlight as the UK City of Culture in 2017. I'd missed it all. It was little more than PR drivel, blandly telling me it would celebrate all the things that made the North great, unique and challenging. From the Industrial Revolution to the popular music it had given the world, a parade at the weekend would snake through the Fruit Market and the Old Town, paying homage to the great people who'd been forged by it, as well as what would come next.

The Fruit Market area had been under-development as I left the city. It had been a riot of barriers and building materials, ripped up pavements and vague promises about retaining the original feel of the area. Repurposed warehouses had been filled with shops selling designer goods and expensive places to eat and drink. Some parts were still under-development, partly-finished or yet to see building work properly started. I looked at an advert for apartments in the area, the imagery showing airbrushed young professionals and families living a glossy lifestyle. The high cost apartments would create a sizable return, the sweetener for developing the less-profitable aspects of the scheme, standing out like over-whitened teeth.

The photograph of the team organising the festival contained a face I did recognise. Grant Piercy had played professional football, a small town hero for Hull City, before moving on, his career just missing the serious money introduced into the game by the Premier League. The inside page told me Piercy was now the key player in Hull's regeneration work around the Fruit Market area, an earlier adopter of using and promoting culture as a wider driver for change.

I pushed the paper to one side, unable to concentrate, Sarah on my mind. Don had hinted more than once that we'd be well-suited, but it had never happened. I hadn't wanted to mix business with pleasure, neither of us prepared to make a move, or show our hand. Maybe it was a missed opportunity, maybe it had never been anything of the sort.

Placing Natalie Okorie's business card in front of me on the table, undecided about calling, I had a decision to make. It tied in to the decision I had to make in relation to Don. Stay or leave, and it wasn't an easy one to make. Part of me knew the police were best placed to look into things, part of me knew not to trust them. My passport and travel documents were in my pocket. I'd paid for a return flight, but could stand the financial loss if I didn't make it.

Glancing at my phone, I thought about Marieke, how she was waiting to hear from me. It was coming up for a year since we'd met, mutual friends introducing us. She'd shown me around Amsterdam, parts of the city tourists would never see, made me feel like I belonged. It was an ongoing process and I'd promised to show her my city in the near future, though I wasn't sure I recognised it myself.

'Well, look at you, Joe Geraghty. The last of the big spenders.'

Maria, the landlady stood over me, hands on her hips, but more importantly, a smile on her face. I stood up and hugged her. 'Good to see you.' It was the truth. A friendly face was just what I needed to see. 'How's business?' I asked, sitting back down and scooping up Okorie's business card in one movement.

She placed her handbag and iPad on the table, stacking up empty glasses on the neighbouring table before answering. 'Surviving.'

'Place is looking good.'

'It looks no different to the last time you was in.'

'That's what I mean.' I couldn't help but laugh.

She sat down opposite me. 'So what brings you back?'

I told her about Don. 'It was the funeral this afternoon.'

'Sorry to hear it. He was a nice bloke, even if you two did argue like cat and dog.' She looked over my shoulder in the direction of the bar, someone shouting her name. 'I've only been out for an hour,' she said, rolling her eyes.

I pointed to the iPad on the table. 'Can I borrow it for a minute?'

She hesitated for a moment before passing it over. 'Break it and I'll break you.'

'More than my life's worth.'

Going online, I headed to The Northern News Alliance website, reading it was about to launch later in the week. Clicking on the 'About Us' section, it was founded by Natalie Okorie and described itself as an independent news collective operated by and for journalists. The journalists would write the stories they wanted to write, explore the issues that were important to them and the North of England. It was based on a subscription model, with those supporting the website getting access to further stories and the chance to go behind the scenes by talking direct to the writers, both online and at face to face events. The Northern News Alliance promised high quality, independent reporting, something that came with a cost but also had great value. I couldn't disagree in theory.

Natalie Okorie had her own page on the website. It described her as an investigative reporter now based in Yorkshire. Her biography gave me a brief overview of her career. She'd started at the Hull Daily Mail, working her way to the regional press and then down to London with spells at The Independent and The Guardian working as a crime reporter and then on her own stories. It was an impressive CV. I didn't hear Maria approach.

She held her hand out, wanting her device back. 'If you've quite finished looking at Tinder?'

I smiled and handed it back. 'Have you got a minute?' Something made me want to tell her about the phone call Don had made to me. I waited for her to sit down before taking her through it. 'I didn't get back to him in time.'

'How come?'

I told her about my new life, how I'd been working outside of Amsterdam without my mobile on me.' I shrugged. 'I never take it with me. No one ever calls.'

'Until this time?'

'He wanted my help with something he was looking at.'

'An old case?'

'I think so.'

'What are you going to do?'

'I don't know.' I showed her Okorie's business card. 'She wants to meet me.'

Maria stood back up and collected more empty glasses. 'You might want to tell me to mind my own business, but it sounds like you know what you need to do.'

'It's not that simple.'

'It never is with you, Joe,' she said, walking away.

There was a reason for that, one fact I was struggling to get past. When my father needed help from the police, Don had let him down badly. I could maybe forgive, but I couldn't forget. I looked again at Natalie Okorie's business card, staring at the mobile number on it, weighing things up. Before I had chance to change to my mind, I punched her number into my handset. The call connected, a last hesitation before I started to speak, giving my name. 'We need to talk.'

FIVE

A steady tattoo of light rain forced my head down to the dirty pavements as I walked along Princes Avenue to Pearson Park. The green space was ringed with housing, substantial old buildings partially-hidden by trees and greenery. The 'To Let' boards told me the sizeable houses were now largely divided into small flats and bedsits. It was where Philip Larkin had made his home, writing the poetry that told of life in a cold, grey Northern city. I'd only read his poems after leaving. Maybe I'd always needed that distance to start understanding what made the place tick.

Finding the flat I needed, I pressed the buzzer and stepped back. Moments later a light in the hallway came on, a figure approaching the door.

'You came, Joe.' Natalie Okorie opened the door further. 'Nice to meet you at last.'

'You knew I'd come.' She invited me to go up, gesturing to the stairs behind her. I hesitated for a moment. 'You're very trusting.'

'A friend of Don's is a friend of mine.'

It was a comment designed to provoke a reaction, so I said nothing. Looking around her flat, the front room was small with a free-standing lamp in the corner next to a large bookcase. Gentle folk music played on the stereo, a lavender candle burning on the windowsill, arts prints on the walls. She was a similar age to me, maybe slightly older. Her flat said she had her shit together, though, that she knew herself.

'I've not got much in, I'm afraid,' she shouted from the kitchen. 'I can put the kettle on or pour you a juice. If you like, I can open a bottle of wine.'

'I'm good, thanks.' I walked over to the window and looked out. It was open far enough that I could hear shouting in the park now the rain was starting to ease, a mixture of languages from around the world. Okorie walked back to the room. I turned to face her. 'You went to some trouble to get a message to me.'

'I took my chances.' She headed over to a desk in the corner of the room, pushed the laptop lid down. 'I knew you'd be back today and wouldn't be able to leave things alone.'

'Even so.'

She gestured to a chair. 'You're not an easy man to track down.'

'I'm not based in the UK anymore.' I stayed on my feet.

'Where are you living?'

'I'm on the move.' I didn't want to tell her any more than that. 'No real roots placed down at the moment.'

'Must have been tough for you after what happened to your wife.'

I stared hard at her. 'My wife?'

'Don't pretend you didn't expect to be checked out.'

My wife had died in a house fire, something I'd largely managed to put behind me. If it was locked away at the back of my mind, it couldn't damage me any further. That was my theory, but it was always being tested. 'I know a bit about you,' I said to her, wanting to move the conversation away from where she'd taken it.

She picked up an e-cigarette and inhaled before releasing, ignoring what I'd said. 'You're off the grid.'

'Here I am, though, back in Hull.' I was uncomfortable with how much she knew about me. 'I didn't see you at Don's funeral?'

'I was in two minds about going, but wasn't sure if I'd be welcome, given my line of work.' She toyed with the e-cigarette. 'How did it go?'

'People keep asking me that.' I didn't really have an answer to the question, though. 'It was fine.'

'His daughter must be inconsolable.'

Okorie moved around the room. Maybe it was a throwaway comment. Maybe it was a loaded question. The later was my guest. I settled for nodding, letting her take my response however she wanted to.

She vaped again before speaking. 'Shall we cut the shit, Joe?'

'Why not?' We were sparring, both letting the subtext of the conversation work for us. I was tired of such bullshit. Okorie handed me a photocopied newspaper story dated thirty years previously inside.

'John Gove,' she said. 'You remember him? Unsolved murder thirty years ago.'

I had a vague memory of it, the name familiar. Glancing through the report, it came back to me; The Car Boot Murder. Gove had been in his early-twenties, his body found in the boot of an abandoned vehicle in a multi-storey car park. The city had been a tough place back then, battered and bruised like everywhere in the North, but it was still shocking. It was the kind of place where violence came via fists and boots, lessons dished out, rarely murder. It was a story that cast a long shadow. Glancing at the byline on the newspaper report, I wasn't surprised to see Okorie's name.

Okorie passed me a photograph of John Gove, hair flapping down across his forehead. It was the haircut of the time matched with a brightly coloured t-shirt and flared jeans. It had been a time of all-night raves, the second Summer of Love. It hadn't been to my taste, but it looked like Gove had fallen under its spell. I continued to flick through the reports, stopping to stare at the photograph buried in the last report. The image embedded showed Don standing outside of the crime scene, hands in his pockets, caught slightly surprised as his conversation with another detective was captured. There was something about seeing him as a younger man which stopped me in my tracks.

I handed the pieces back. 'You worked it, the classic young journo desperate for a break that would take you out of here and on to the real newspapers?' I took her business card out and held it up. 'The Northern News Alliance? Hardly the big time, is it?'

She took another drag on her e-cigarette, ignored my comment. 'You wanted to be a rugby player?'

'Turns out that wasn't within my control.' I thought back to the wet turf in St Helens, the pain in my knee as it twisted and popped, the darkness as I drifted in and out consciousness. I closed my eyes momentarily. The long road back to even walking again.

'That was crass of me,' she said. 'I apologise.'

I snapped back into the moment. 'It was a long time ago.'

Okorie paused for a moment. 'I think we can help each other here. We both want to know the truth.'

I thought about the message from Don, how he'd needed my help. I wasn't sure if I wanted to share that load, certainly not with someone I barely knew. 'The police are investigating what happened to Don. Why don't you let them do their job?'

She gave a throaty laugh. 'You're not prepared to walk away from this.'

'You don't know anything about me.'

'I know enough.'

'It's officially a hit and run, nothing more. There's no story, is there?'

She walked over to the window, standing next to me. 'You really believe that? You don't believe in coincidences any more than I do, Joe. You're like me. You always ask questions. It's in your blood, and believe me, there's plenty you don't know. I suspect we're both holding different pieces of the same puzzle here. Think about that.'

'Don came to you about this?'

She nodded. 'It wasn't something he could leave alone.' She picked up a set of car keys from the mantelpiece. 'Let's take a drive, Joe.'

SIX

Natalie Okorie nudged her car out of the tight parking space and headed for the park gates. Guessing where we were heading, I asked to turn towards Princes Avenue, wanting to see it again. I shuffled the piles of paper, empty chocolate wrappers and empty CD cases on the floor to one side.

'I do a lot of miles,' she said, noticing what I'd done.

'It's your car,' I said, turning to look at her. 'I've had to borrow my brother's.'

'So where are you living at the moment, then?'

'Amsterdam.'

'Seriously?'

'Seriously.'

'Do you like it?'

I stared out of the window, not answering the question. The stretch was still lined with bars and restaurants, though some had different names, different signage above their doors. They were largely deserted, all chasing the same limited pool of spending money. I could see it had changed since I called it home. Five years was both the blink of an eye and enough time for it all to appear out of focus. We skirted past the city centre, crossing the river which split things down the middle. I wasn't sure if the hotel on the corner of Ferensway, its neon lights beaming out across the traffic junction like an alien spacecraft, had been there when I'd left. The new buildings further along forming part of the college campus were definitely new to me, space being swallowed up by insatiable developers.

'I don't think I can come back,' I said.

'You can always come back.'

'Maybe you need a reason to do that?'

She took her time before answering. 'Sometimes it's enough in itself.' Eyes on the road, she continued to talk. 'I was the odd one out at school,' she said. 'Nigerian father, English mother. Wasn't many people like me around in a city like this in the Seventies or Eighties.'

Her hands stayed rigidly on the steering wheel, eyes on the road. Okorie had moved well-beyond the city, working on stories with much-wider implications, but the city hadn't quite released its grip on her.

'If I can come back to this city, anyone can.'

I stared out of the window, unsure if a response was required, no idea what I should say.

'Gove's parents wouldn't let it go,' she told me, changing the subject. 'Both dead now, though. His mother went a few years ago, his father a few months back.'

'Right.' It must have been tough for them, all that unconditional love and no resolution. I'd gone into bat for my brother and nephew in the past when they'd found themselves in trouble over a missing consignment of smuggled cigarettes, no second thoughts, despite the danger.

Okorie told me there was a story I should look at, passing me her mobile when I told her I didn't have Internet access on mine. Following her instructions, it was the last interview the local paper had carried out with Gove's father. It looked like the piece was a last chance to put the story back out in front of the public, appeal for justice before the story died with him. A photograph showed him sitting in his living room, staring straight at the camera, the strain of what had happened etched on his face. His words referred to unanswered questions, a lack of care and interest from the police during their investigation and subsequently through further reviews. Reading between the lines, he was suggesting it was because their son had a criminal record, a feeling that people were happy to have him gone and buried. Time wasn't necessarily a great healer. I knew that much.

'John Gove had a record for possession,' Okorie said. 'Sailed close to the wind in relation to more serious charges and word was he was in deeper than that. My feeling is that he was a small-time dealer in Ecstasy, even if no one wanted to say it on the record. In all likelihood, he was probably just supporting his own habit, the money he was making funding trips to various raves.'

I looked up, the car slowing down as Okorie pulled up outside of a city centre multi-storey car park. The night's rain showed up the damp patches on the walls, water trickling down from broken guttering. The car stopped, engine switched off, but the headlights stayed on to illuminate the area. I got out, the cold air hitting me, waiting for Natalie Okorie to follow.

Okorie pointed at the front entrance, a shutter in place across it. 'Back in the day it was a barrier, but it wasn't working around the time the car was abandoned. Back then, someone would take the money and issue a ticket. The car didn't have a ticket inside the window, so it never paid. The worker didn't recall seeing it when he knocked off his shift, so the theory is it in came over night.'

Okorie led the way over to an unlocked door down the side of the building, the way in for the last few remaining customers to collect their vehicles, the electronic shutter controlling cars leaving. Heading up the cold staircases, shoes echoing on the bare concrete, she held the door to the third floor open and pointed to a space in the far corner partially hidden by a pillar.

We walked across to it, only a handful of cars left on the floor. It was dark, many of the lights out of action. I doubted it had been much different thirty years ago.

'What happened?' I asked. 'How was it discovered?'

'A member of public on her way to work the following morning. She saw the boot was slightly up and that there was broken glass around the driver's door. Thinking local scumbags had been up to no good, she thought she was doing the right thing by taking a look.'

'Poor cow.'

'You're not kidding. She raised the alarm.'

I tried to put myself in the shoes of whoever abandoned the car. It felt like a gamble to me, that it would be noticed eventually. But abandoning it anywhere else would also be noticed. Someone would report it eventually. Maybe it wasn't a bad spot, somewhere people didn't linger, somewhere people didn't see things. 'What about the car? Was it traced?'

'Stolen from a manky second-hand yard on Beverley Road.'

'No witnesses to the theft?'

'None.'

'How about motive?'

'Nothing.'

I thought about that for a moment. 'Really?' I looked at Okorie. 'Bullshit.'

She followed my train of thought, but didn't bite. 'I covered it all back then, tried to find someone who'd talk. No one wanted to help and there wasn't really anything in the way of cameras back then to track the car. Plenty of theories, all drug-related, but nothing stuck.'

It was tempting to draw a line from John Gove's known habits to his death, but it wouldn't have figured in Don's thinking. A victim was a victim, a principle he'd instilled in me. It was the kind of case that would haunt Don, justice never served. Putting my hands into my pockets, I tried to put myself in the police's shoes, visualising how it all stacked up thirty years ago. Okorie was holding more back from me, I was sure, but it would keep for now. We both shivering, trying to fight the cold off. There was nothing more to see. We walked back down the stairs towards her car. 'What do you think happened out here?' I asked, the door closing behind us.

'I'm open-minded about that.'

'There must have been suspects? Maybe Gove owed money? Maybe he'd stepped on the wrong toes if he was dealing?'

Okorie shook her head. I watched her draw on the e-cigarette, wondering what she was really thinking.

'There are always reasons, Joe,' she said with a shrug. 'Nothing that happens exists in a vacuum.'

It wasn't really an answer to my question. 'Did you speak to Don at the time?'

'Briefly.' She took another hit on her e-cigarette, stared at me. 'We were on different sides, remember'

'It wasn't one of Don's cases, was it?' I would have known if it had been. We'd spoken endlessly about them over the years, particularly the ones that had left an impression on him. 'Who ran it?'

'DI Jagger,' she said. 'It was nothing to do with Don, not officially at least. He was on the scene, hence the photo, but he was reallocated to another investigation.'

I chewed it over. 'Why do I know that name?

'Jagger's an MP now,' I listened as she filled in the details for me. Jagger had left the police fifteen years ago after medical complications. I nodded, remembering. He'd taken a bullet in the leg stopping an armed robbery in a jewellery store. I remembered because it had been national news. He'd chased the culprits along a busy shopping street, only stopping when the shooter had turned and fired at him, putting him down.

'He was off duty at the time?'

'That's right.'

It was cynical of me, but the perception of being brave wouldn't have hurt him when it came to a move into politics. I wondered if I'd be able to talk to him about John Gove. Okorie unlocked the car, telling me it was getting too cold to be standing outside. I did as she said.

'This is a big story if the right people are asked the right questions,' Okorie said, switching the heater on.

'That's why it's important to you?'

'I'm here for the same reason as you.' The e-cigarette went back into her handbag. 'Some things require closure.'

'Sometimes it's better to leave things in the past,' I suggested. Going along with her thinking had implications, I knew that much. It was dangerous road to go down and left me with a decision to make. Don had called to ask for help. Maybe I had to do the same now. My instincts had led me to being a lone wolf, but that hadn't worked out all that well for me. 'Don called me the day before he died.'

The atmosphere between us changed, as she weighed up what I'd said. What it meant.

'What did he have to say?'

'Nothing.'

'This is a two-way street, remember?'

I took my mobile out and found the message I'd been left, held it out to her. 'Have a listen.'

Once the message had played through, she handed it back to me. 'That's it? What did he say when you called back?'

'I didn't pick the message up in time.'

'Shit.'

'You're telling me.'

She understood the implications. 'You need to pick a side, Joe.'

Trouble was a siren song to me, something I couldn't ignore. Hiding away from the world in Holland was all well and good, but asking questions and teasing the truth out of a situation was maybe the only thing I was good at. I looked out of the car window at the multi-storey car park, weighing things up. Don had effectively reopened the investigation and I owed it to him to finish it. I had no choice in the matter. 'I'm in.'

1989

The last of the drizzle falling from the newspaper print sky only added a layer of misery to the scene, the morning sun struggling to make a breakthrough. Don Ridley stared straight ahead at the queue of Monday morning rush hour vehicles being turned away from the multi-storey car park, knowing a worse storm was about to break. He glanced at DI Jagger. 'Fucking hell.'

'You're not wrong.' Jagger took a packet of cigarettes out, fumbled around in his pocket for a lighter. 'Want one?'

Don shook his head, watched as a driver argued with the uniformed officer telling him to reverse and pull away, listened as the timeline was explained to him. The job had taught him to expect the worst, but a body in the boot of a car was a new thing. He spared a thought for the woman who'd raised the alarm. It was his job to swallow down such things, but it would leave a bruise on her soul. She was in the small car park's attendant's office, drinking sweet tea in an attempt to calm her down.

'Go to the football on Saturday, Don?'

'Sarah didn't fancy it. Had to take her to McDonald's instead. You'd think the novelty of the place would have worn off by now, wouldn't you?' There was no chance of that happening any time soon. 'Decent game?'

'Another hat-trick for Grant Piercy. He's not long for City, mark my words. Liverpool are in for him. Deal's all but done.'

Don nodded, knowing the DI thought he was in the know. Looking up at the car park, he wanted to be in there, see things for himself, away from the DI.

'His wife isn't keen on moving away, but she'll come round,' Jagger said. 'Who wouldn't?' Don didn't care.

'Say cheese, gents.'

They both turned round to where the shout had come from, the photographer from the local paper holding a camera up towards them. He lowered it and smiled. 'Help out a grafter, lads?'

'Piss off.' The response delivered in stereo. Photographers were a staple presence at crime scenes, tolerated, as long as they did their job.

'Who's writing the story up?' Jagger asked.

'Natalie Okorie.'

'One of the keen ones, then.'

'She's certainly keen to make a name for herself.' The photographer winked and headed closer to the car park entrance, camera at the ready. 'Catch up with you later.'

'About time she fucked off,' Jagger said to no one in particular.

Don turned to look at the DI, wondered if he'd misheard. 'Fucked off?'

'Heard she'd been down to London for some job interviews. It's the best place for her.'

Don tuned the conversation out, watched as the photographer disappeared into the car park. It wasn't his problem, Jagger could deal with him. Instead, he asked the DI what was known so far.

Jagger took another drag on his cigarette, a small shrug. 'Fuck all so far. No one will miss Gove. 'Live by the sword, die by the sword. One less drug dealer for us to be bothering with.' He explained how the barrier had broken a couple of days ago, stuck in the up position. 'Council's fault.'

'Shouldn't someone have been checking the cars, make sure they've paid?'

Jagger raised an eyebrow. 'I'm pretty sure we'll find out that the attendant is a lazy bastard.'

Don put his hands in his pockets, squinting against the rain, thinking it took one to know one. 'Any witnesses see the car being dumped?'

'What do you think?' Jagger took another drag on his cigarette.

Car parks were transient, people always coming and going. It would be a struggle to find someone willing to talk, and that was if you could locate them. They had to be aware they'd seen something important first. As it stood, they didn't even know if the car had approached from the east or the west of the city, where Gove had last been seen. They had nothing. It was always fine margins, the possibility of walking into a situation you had no control over. Like sliding doors, maybe one car driven out as the one with Gove in the boot had driven in. It wasn't the kind of place you'd particularly notice other people in. You'd just want to park up and get on with your own business.

'We need to look at Gove's enemies,' Jagger said. 'People he's crossed, people he owes money to. You know the drill. Shake the tree and see what scumbags fall out. Go through the motions so everyone's happy.' Jagger took one last drag on the cigarette before throwing it to the floor, squashing it down with his foot. 'I've got to go back to the station and give an update.'

Don watched the DI head back to his car and drive away. Standing in the middle of the road, the rain starting to fall harder, he pulled his hood up and headed towards the barrier. He glanced through the office window at the woman who'd found Gove's body, hoping one of her family was on the way to comfort her.

Nodding to the uniform keeping the traffic at bay, he made his way up the ramps to the crime scene. The photographer was heading in the opposite direction, his work with the camera done. A handful of vehicles were still parked up suggesting they'd been left there the previous night, their owners most likely out drinking in the city centre. He made a note to ask the uniform by the barrier to take down details as these people returned.

Standing by the car Gove had been found in, the crime scene team had been and gone. They would have photographed and catalogued evidence, though it wasn't likely to produce anything quickly. Maybe they'd be lucky and find a rogue fingerprint. Looking again at the red Ford Escort, maybe the car dealer it had been stolen from might be the place to start.

Walking over to the edge to look out, a steady stream of buses and cars headed into the centre and the other car parks, their occupants probably talking about what happened here last night. Turning back to the car park, piles of rubbish had been blown into the corner by the wind. Taking out the torch he'd brought along, he walked around the perimeter of the floor, shining the light around, checking. Maybe no one really cared about John Gove, but a victim always needed someone to represent them, regardless of what they'd done or who they were. One corner had what looked to be several items of clothing thrown into a pile and largely out of sight. Without the beam of the torch, you wouldn't see them.

Edging closer, a dirty sleeping bag had been bundled together with the clothes. Nudging them apart with his foot, he could see a pair of trousers, a handful of shirts, all male items. Picking up the half-full milk bottle next to them, it didn't smell sour. A newspaper dated two days ago was next to it. Bending down, a collection of wood off-cuts and paper gave off a small amount of residual heat. Straightening back up, he had a clear sightline of the car and the crime scene. Maybe the DI was wrong. Maybe there was a witness to find after all.

SEVEN

I hadn't slept well, too much to think about. Staring out of the cheap hotel room window, the morning sky was streaked with grey and black, clouds bunched together like dirty pillows. The hotel was like countless others I'd stayed in, all corporate colours and discretely bolted down furniture. It was comfortable enough to entice you to stay a night or two, but not comfortable enough you'd want to do anything other than pass through.

I looked straight down at the block concrete and metal teeth of the Tidal Barrier, the water chocolate brown from decades of industrial use. It contrasted with the modern structures of the city's aquarium and digital enterprise centre I'd watched being built as I left the city. The offices on the Fruit Market would be starting to fill for the day up with the professionals who'd push the city forward if it was going to forge a new future; tech workers, digital start-ups and innovation companies. Further east along the waterfront, the overnight ferries from the continent were spitting out lorries and coaches heading for the road network out of the city. Finished wind turbine blades looked like cigarettes rising vertically out of the ground, green technology another growth industry for the region that was new to me. The city was changing.

I headed into the shower, leaning against the corner of the unit and letting the hot water rain down on me. I closed my eyes, thinking about the choices I'd already made. Natalie Okorie's words had been clear about picking a side. She might not have managed to get the inside track on the investigation in 1989, held back at a distance, but there were things she would know that I didn't. But help always came with a price tag, and I wasn't sure I was ready to pay it just yet.

Out of the shower, I towelled myself dry and dressed, already having second thoughts. Maybe I was a lone wolf and that was the way I needed to operate. My mind whirled with questions and possibilities I needed to think through, a growing sense I was wading into dangerous waters.

I hadn't heard the text message arriving from Marieke, asking what time I would land at Schipol. It was another message I wasn't going to reply to just yet. I couldn't leave without speaking to Sarah. Her words to me at the funeral had hurt, and they weren't unexpected, but it wasn't how it should end. It was another thing that needed putting right.

I didn't have online access on my mobile, but the hotel offered the facility of what was described as a 'business-centre'. Heading downstairs, I was directed to a desktop computer in the corner of the lounge. Entering the password I'd been given, no one paid me any attention as I went to work. A handful of business-people in suits eating breakfast in the near-by dining area, huddled together around a laptop.

I wanted to look again at the interview with John Gove's father that Okorie had pointed me towards last night. I'd skimmed it as she'd driven, but there was a video of the interview embedded into the article. Reading was one thing, but being able to listen to him tell the story in his own way was important. It was as close as I could get to looking him in the eye.

I clicked play on the video file and lowered the volume so only I could hear it. The footage slowly settled on an elderly man sitting on a chair, the date stamp putting it just over a year ago. Stan Gove stared intently back at the camera without speaking. He was well into his seventies, frail looking with waxy looking skin on his hollow face. He was wiry and lean, but alert. It was a look that said he'd been down this road several times before.

A journalist not visible on the film started to talk and set the scene, explaining that Mr Gove had wanted the interview to be recorded and released in full without editing, a condition of giving the interview.

Gove cut in, chin jutted out. 'I haven't got long left. I know that. It means I can be blunt because I'm not embarrassed, certainly not ashamed.'

I settled back, understanding what he really meant. The story essentially died when he did and that scared him. Once he was gone, no one would care. Looking behind the man, I could see a row of framed photographs on the wall. Pausing the footage to look more closely, I could see they essentially told his son's life story. The images started at school and ran through the Scouts and sports teams to the picture I'd seen online. It was a carefully constructed narrative, telling me the story he wanted to present. The house looked like it hadn't been updated since the 1980s, the mismatched furniture as threadbare as the carpet and curtains. A budgie shuffling around in a cage in the corner reminded me of my own grandparents' house.

I rolled the footage on. The interview started with some background on John Gove, the small details that made him human to the viewer. His father explained he was a Hull City fan, always scraping around to find the money to watch them play. He spoke about how his son had recently split up with what he thought might be a serious girlfriend, but it had been something he'd kept to himself, not wanting to talk about it.

'John was always scribbling away on something,' he said, talking about his son's love of art. Maybe I should have taken it more seriously, encouraged him to see it as a possible job, or something. Maybe things would have been different.' He looked away from the camera for a moment, collecting his thoughts. 'Wasn't my world, though.'

'What do you remember about that day?' the journalist asked him. Moving the conversation on.

Gove's face changed momentarily, pain briefly passing across it before he composed himself again. 'Worst day of my life,' he said quietly, clearing his throat.

I listened as he talked about the police knocking on the door, how he felt the investigation had been lazy, no real interest in catching whoever had murdered his son. 'We'd received the occasional progress update as the years passed, mainly through DI Jagger, but that's all.'

'Ian Jagger, the MP?' the journalist asked, wanting to make the point.

'That's right, but once they decided it was too difficult to deal with, my son's death was brushed under the carpet.'

The journalist let the comment settle before speaking again. 'What did you do about that?'

Gove's eyes narrowed, a flash of anger before the sadness of the reality of the situation visibly hit him again. 'We did our best, me and his mother, but no one listened.' The fire returned to him, a deep breath. 'Plenty of other people have knocked on our door, you know? We've had to listen to them as he was called a drug dealer who got what he deserved. It's even been suggested he didn't suffer enough as he died and all because he made mistakes as a young lad. Our son was starting to turn his life around, but his reputation went before him. We had journalists, book writers and people whose jobs I don't understand knocking on our door over the years. We've even had mediums wanting to talk to us, claiming they can unlock the truth for us.' He jabbed a finger out at the camera. 'The point is, plenty of people have wanted to prey on us for their own reasons and it's not easy working out who's genuine and who's not.'

'How do you feel now it's just you?'

The journalist was doing a transparent job of asking leading questions.

'I buried his mother without her ever knowing the truth,' he said. 'You can't even begin to imagine how that feels. No one should have to feel that way. Burying a child isn't normal, it's not the way it should be for anyone.' He stopped talking for a moment, chin jutted out towards the camera again, defiant. 'Chances are I'll die not knowing, too, and I've got to make my peace with that.'

The journalist changed direction, taking a harder line by asking if his son was a drug dealer. I leaned in, wondering if John Gove had crossed the wrong person, a situation gone too far. Maybe it was that simple. My gut though told me it was never that easy.

Gove's father remained static in his chair. 'It hurts me to say this, but I didn't know my son. Can you imagine how that feels?'

It was as if the man was staring straight at me in a way that suggested he knew far more about pain and loss than any human being should, something I recognised all too well. Okorie had brought up my wife's death when we'd spoken. As much as it was in the past, it was always in the present. It was everywhere and nowhere.

'Have you got a message for the person, or persons, who killed your son?'

'I just need to hear the truth, that's all. Doesn't even have to involve the police.' His voice faltered again, spent. 'I just need to know,' he repeated. 'People are full of conspiracy theories and I don't want to hear them anymore. I've had enough. Actions speak louder than words, don't they?' He took a moment to compose himself before continuing. 'No one cared enough, that's the bottom line. None of the police cared. They couldn't get away from us quickly enough.' He said the words with real venom. 'They made it clear they didn't care for our son, that his death was self-inflicted. Live by the sword, die by the sword, they said. Those were the words they used.'

The interview finished there, but I didn't move for a moment. Rubbing my face and drawing myself back into the moment, I explored some of the links at the bottom of the story on the website. One took me through to a report on Stan Gove's funeral, two months after the interview had been filmed. The poor bastard never stood a chance of getting the answers he'd needed. He was right though, actions did speak louder than words.

EIGHT

Don's cottage in Paull was too tempting, too much of an opportunity. He'd always been a planner and a thinker. It was ingrained in him. He was an excellent detective, but he understood the importance of order and leaving a trail. I was sure there'd be something to find.

Leaving my car at the waterfront, I pulled my cap down against the morning sun. I'd stopped on the drive east in a supermarket, picking it up as a makeshift disguise to obscure my face. Finding a shop selling mobile phones, I now had a handset with online access. Having little in the way of contact information when I was off the grid was fine, but circumstances had changed.

The village was quiet, with no one around the row of cottages down the side of the lighthouse. Satisfied I was alone, I walked to the rear of the properties. The fences were knee height, easy to step over. The empty cottage's garden was overgrown, a pile of rotten timber piled up against the wall, but it helped me to stay out of sight. Pulling my sleeves over my hands, I tried the back door to Don's cottage. It was wooden, a bit of give when I tried the handle.

Kicking it open would be easy, but Coleman wouldn't have my back if I found myself in trouble. I kicked at it regardless, the lock snapping instantly. I quickly moved inside and nudged the door closed, standing in the kitchen. It was neat and tidy, a small pile of mugs and plates stacked up on the draining board. I glanced at the calendar on the wall, no entries made on it. Nothing looked to be out of place, or obviously missing.

The front room was small, a chair and two-seater squashed into it. I recognised the furniture from his previous house. The far wall was lined with a large bookcase containing a number of well-thumbed paperbacks, the mantelpiece used to display framed photographs. The largest one in the middle had been taken on his wedding day, the rest charting Sarah's life. They showed her as a baby, her first day at school, enjoying being a young adult dressed to go out for the night and then with Lauren. I stood still, feeling a mixture of emotions; shame at breaking in and invading Don's space, shame that I hadn't been able to help, but also resolve and determination to repay the debt I owed him, finish what he'd started.

Moving upstairs to the bedrooms, the main one was small, little space to walk around the double bed. A wardrobe and chest of drawers with a mirror on top made it feel cramped, more paperbacks. The second bedroom had been converted into an office space. It was largely bare, an old desk and chair I recognised, more piles of books pushed up against the walls.

Flicking through the notepads on the desk, he'd developed his own form of shorthand, symbols and marks that didn't make sense to me. It was his way of operating, talking to people rather than communicating by text message or email. I turned to the pile of books, finding a small number of folders containing various items of paperwork. Flicking through, most of them related to household matters, some were bills, others solicitors letters in relation to ownership of the cottage.

I found the occasional reference to our partnership, some related to his time in the police. Don had been a good detective, but experience told me it was never that black and white. I knew he'd done things he hadn't been proud of, blurring the line between right and wrong, just like I had. Things had only started going to shit when I'd effectively rebelled and kicked back, working a case he cautioned me against touching. I hadn't listened. A large cardboard carton had been pushed into the corner. Lifting the lid, I flicked through the manila folder, quickly seeing each section contained documents relating to investigations he'd carried out during his years in the police. It was a mixture of his own notes and media reports, some photographs, too. What I couldn't find was a file on John Gove and his murder thirty years ago.

Heading back downstairs, I looked again at the photographs on the mantelpiece. I felt bad for doing it, but I took one of Don with Sarah out of its frame. It was as up to date as I was going to find and would be helpful when speaking to people. A visual aid always jogged memories more effectively.

I picked up the contacts book next to the telephone. Flicking through it, I noted down Gerard Branning's address before closing it, nothing else of obvious use. The flashing light on the base of the telephone handset indicated a bank of stored messages. Hitting play, I listened to a mixture of mechanical messages about mis-sold PPI and claiming damages for accidents Don probably hadn't had. I hit redial, a force of habit more than anything else.

'Hedon Cabs.' The voice at the other end of the line was female and harassed, probably busy trying to deal with more than one job. I paused for a moment before launching into an explanation, sticking as close to the truth as I dared to. 'It'd be useful to know when and where Don booked a car for, please.' It might be something, it might be nothing.

'Police?'

If I said no, it was unlikely any information would be forthcoming. There was a decision to make, but I was already in a place I shouldn't be and it was something that could come back to bite me. It would be another line crossed. I told the woman I was police.

I listened to the clatter of keys, the woman telling someone else she'd be with them in a moment, too harassed to show any further interest in the question I'd asked.

'Give me a minute.'

The line went dead. I waited, wanting to kill the conversation and get out of the cottage. The woman came back on the line, explaining that the driver who'd taken the call was in the office. The date she gave was the day before Don died. She read out an address, a block flats to the east of Hull. 'We take Don to an address in Hull every week, his daughter's by the sound of it, but it was the first time we'd taken him there.'

Driving back into the city, the floodlights marking out Hull KR's rugby league stadium dominated the skyline, its windswept terracing reminded me of my youth and a sporting career over before it really got started. It perpetually existed in black and white in my mind, the sport of the North. Parking up, the three tower blocks lined up like dominos, an anchor memorial outside signalling that they were named after lost trawler boats, all swallowed down by greedy arctic seas. I'd heard the stories about the hardship endured, a time when the city made its living from its hands and brawn.

Killing the engine, I watched and waited, figuring out the best way to approach things. I'd done it often enough over the years, often in far tougher scenarios, but this felt different. It was returning to work I thought I'd left behind. Numerous flats meant numerous people. Numerous potential witnesses.

My theory was that if you held something, it gave people something to remember other than your face. Not wanting to be remembered, I pulled my cap back on and walked to the rear of the flats, finding the large communal bins. The first recycling container contained a flattened Amazon box. Knocking it back into shape and heading back to the entrance, I slowed and pretended to check my mobile, waiting for someone to appear. It didn't take long. Grabbing at the door when the next person left the building. I headed inside, the communal entrance smelling of cheap bleach and fried food. Post boxes lined one wall, a pile of leaflets tucked into the opposite corner ready for disposal. The flat I needed was on the third floor, my shoes echoing off the harsh concrete stairs as I climbed.

Two rows of flats faced each other the length of the corridor. The one I needed was in the far corner. Knocking twice, there was no answer. Looking around, a television blared out from the neighbouring flat, canned laughter leaking out from behind the door. It took two attempts to receive a response, knocking louder to be heard. The sound muted, a man in his mid-sixties answered the door. He wobbled slightly, a can of cheap lager in his hand.

'What do you want?' he said, looking me over.

'I'm looking for your neighbour,' I said, pointing back at the right door. 'Amazon delivery.'

'A parcel?'

'That's right.'

'Are you sure?'

'I go where I'm told to go,' I made a show of looking at my mobile. 'It's for Steve?' It was the first name that came to mind, but I'd be unlucky if I was right.

The old man shook his head. 'You've got the wrong place, mate.' I pointed to the door again. 'What's your neighbour's name?'

'Dave.'

'Dave got a surname?'

'Bolder.' The old man focused, a throaty laugh. 'News to me that he's back, though. He did a runner about a week ago. Surprised me, as I've never seen him move so fast. Daft old fucker's probably older than me.'

'Can you remember exactly when that was?'

The night he gave me tied in with the hit and run. I had a bad feeling, not believing in coincidences. The man looked at me again, focusing and taking my face in, clarity to his thinking.

'You're taking it a bit personally for a delivery man, aren't you?'

NINE

Making slow progress along Hessle Road, I glanced out of the window at what had once been the city's proud fishing community, an area battered by the consequences of decisions made on their behalf by politicians and moneymen. I stared at an empty pub, once a vital community hub, but now standing silent and keeping its stories and secrets to itself. A handful of ghost signs on the side of walls told of long-gone businesses, other walls covered in colourful murals relating to the area's heritage, but it was clear the afterglow from the cultural spotlight the city had enjoyed wasn't being felt much outside of areas like the Fruit Market.

I needed some help if I was going to make sense of what Don had been doing. I knocked on the door and stepped back, waiting. The long, straight road was packed with identical terracing on both sides. It was narrow enough to be one-way only, a parcel delivery van creating a bottleneck as the driver waited for a door to be opened. I knocked again, louder this time.

I took the time to breathe in the air, surprised the fresh smell of damp in the air didn't carry a faint aroma of fish from the docks. It was something I remembered, like the scent of the cocoa mill on Stoneferry, but times changed.

I could see the outline of someone approaching the door, shouting they wouldn't be a minute followed by a hacking cough. The door opened. 'Morning, Gerard,' I said, holding up a carrier bag. 'I've brought breakfast.' It was the necessary currency to secure a conversation. Sometimes it was cigarettes, sometimes it was a drink. Sometimes it was cash or an information exchange. You had to judge your audience. My thinking was that after a day's drinking at Don's funeral, Branning would need something to soak it up with.

My foot was ready to prop the door open in case he tried to close it on me, but dressed in a tatty dressing gown, he was too surprised by my appearance to take control of the situation. He read the script and stepped away to let me enter.

'I should warn you, I'm not much of a cook these days.'

Following him through the house and into the kitchen, I got a quick glimpse at the front room. It was markedly different to Don's cottage, untidy and disorganised, dark and musty smelling. Don's place had order borne out of routine and habit. This was the opposite. Branning slouched at the kitchen table, staring at me sullenly.

Glancing around, I could see a number of used mugs on the kitchen top, more in the sink. The remains of a takeaway had been pushed to the corner of the unit top.

'Help yourself,' Branning said, gesturing towards the hob.

I found a clean frying pan in the cupboard he directed me to and placed the bacon I'd bought in it. I went to work, flicking the kettle on.

Branning poured himself a glass of water and searched for a packet of painkillers. 'I saw you at the funeral. The beard is fooling no one.'

'It's not meant to.'

'Surprised you came back, if I'm honest.'

'I wouldn't miss the funeral.'

Branning set the glass down. 'Been a while, hasn't it?'

'You're not wrong.'

'Looking after yourself, then?'

'Trying my best. How about you?'

'Just me now.' He paused. 'Don't worry, though. I've got no plans to move out to the middle of nowhere like Don.'

'Keeping busy?'

'Doing my best.'

His answer didn't sound very convincing. I knew enough from Don to know policing was a job that asked for everything and then took some more. That way of living had inevitable consequences.

'How's Sarah doing?' Branning asked, dragging me back into the conversation.

'I haven't spoken with her.'

Branning sniffed, focused on me again, ready to move on. 'You didn't come here to cook my breakfast and make small talk, Joe.'

'That's true.' I turned down the heat on the hob, the bacon starting to colour already. 'I need your help.' I flipped the meat over before turning to face Branning. 'Don called me just before he died,' I said, getting to the point. I told him about the message on my phone.

'Don't go there, Joe.'

'I need to ask you some questions.'

'Not now.'

I told him how the trail had led me to the murder of John Gove. How Don was looking into it before death. 'You must have your doubts over what happened to Don, too? A hit and run?'

'The best advice I can give you is to leave it to the police to investigate.'

I ignored the suggestion, both of us knowing it was going to happen. 'You were around back then. Did you work it?'

Branning swallowed a mouthful of water and pills, eyes narrowing as he looked at me. He set the glass back down. 'It wasn't one of mine.'

'But you must have followed it, talked about it around the station? Murder's always a story, right?'

'True.'

'It wasn't Don's investigation, was it?'

'No.'

'So why did he involve himself?'

'He was reassigned.' Branning shrugged. 'Sometimes you don't want to let go of something. Maybe he felt he'd been sidelined?'

It made sense to me. Don could be like a dog with a bone, the sort who'd work it off the books if he thought it was required.

'I'll tell you this much about Gove, though. He was a drug dealer who ruined lives.' Branning paused, looked me in the eye. 'It was one less piece of rubbish for us to be dealing with.'

I held his stare for a moment, Branning unrepentant for his words. 'It was still a murder,' I settled for saying. It didn't hit a nerve with him like I wanted it to. 'Tell me about the investigation?' I settled for asking. 'It wasn't one of Don's. Jagger led it.'

Branning snorted. 'You know he's a politician now?' The words were delivered with enough venom to make his distaste clear. 'He was lazy in my opinion. Wasn't particularly respected, but he's a hero these days.'

I zeroed in on what was important. 'He wasn't thorough with the investigation?'

'Only when it suited.'

It didn't directly answer my question, but it essentially did. I thought about the video interview with Gove's father. 'Was the girlfriend spoken to at the time, or the friends he went to the football with?'

'Don't think so.' Branning shook his head. 'It wasn't necessarily anyone's fault. From memory, the investigation closed down pretty quickly. Sometimes there's nothing more you can do. You follow the trail, you speak to the right people, but sometimes it's just a dead end. You know as well as I do, this isn't a television drama. There's no guarantee the bad guy will be caught.' He placed the glass back down and rubbed at his face. 'Smells like the bacon is ready.'

I took out the breadcakes I'd bought and made a sandwich for him. 'With compliments of the chef,' I said, placing it on a clean-looking plate and handing it over. I didn't doubt Branning knew more than he was saying, but I had to respect we were sitting on the opposite sides of the table. His loyalties lay with his people, not me.

He lifted the sandwich up and nodded. 'Not bad, Joe. You're a man of many talents.'

I poured the drinks, placed a cup of tea in front of him and tried a change of direction with the conversation. 'Ever run up against Natalie Okorie? She covered the story back in the day.'

Branning nodded, pushed his plate to one side. 'Now there's a name I remember. Went down to London to work for the nationals. Always was an ambitious sort.' The penny started to drop. 'Why?'

'She's reached out to me.'

'This is what you really came here for, isn't it?'

I nodded. 'I guess it is.'

'Rated herself. Always thought she was too good for a place like this. She wanted to embarrass us with a story, like a dog with a bone. You know what it's like in a place like this. You rub up against the same people repeatedly, don't you? Back with her tail between her legs now, I hear.'

I wasn't sure if I was expected to answer, but my experience was largely the same. Hull would always be the largest of villages.

Branning sat back and shrugged. 'Fuck her.'

My thoughts weren't required, but I was tempted to suggest she was on the side of justice. Just as he should be, so I laid it out for him. 'No one was arrested for Gove's murder, never mind charged and convicted.'

Branning cut across me. 'That's not always our fault. It's not an easy one for people close to it to accept and understand. Gove's family certainly lead a vocal campaign against us, as is their right. It kept the paper interested, too. Giving us a kicking always helped them shift copies of their rag.'

I held my hands up, signalling I understood. 'So why would Don be so concerned about this one if it was just a drug dealer no one particularly cared for?' I was thinking aloud. He'd taken part in countless investigation, leading many of them. He'd confronted terrible people and seen things that were best left unspoken. Why had this one stayed with him?

Branning lifted his mug again, another salute. 'Only one person who can answer that question.'

'Not necessarily.' Experience had taught me that wasn't always true. There was always another way of looking at a problem.

Branning smiled, shook his head. 'Okorie's been filling your head with shite, hasn't she?'

‘I can make my own judgment on that.’

‘I thought you were sharper than that, Joe, a better judge of character. Okorie is using you as part of her vendetta against the police, can’t you see that? That’s the bottom line here. She’s using you and you can’t see it.’

‘Strange nothing was shaken loose during the course of the investigation?’

‘Maybe no one cared enough?’

‘Maybe.’ I wasn’t going to argue with that conclusion. ‘But I’m doing it for Don.’

‘I need a piss,’ Branning mumbled to himself, standing up. ‘You should let sleeping dogs lie, Joe.’

TEN

I walked across the marina, head down with my hands buried in my pocket, the cold off the waterfront pinching at my face. I had plenty to think about. I figured I needed to be closer to the story. Jagger was now a Member of Parliament, but that made him all the more visible, his movements public. His Twitter feed told me where he'd be.

Approaching the digital enterprise centre, I hung back from the entrance, the repetitive thump of live music being sound checked inside signalling preparations were well under way. Security staff pitched in, helping haul gear inside, as well as clearing people for entering the event. I would have one shot at getting inside. A quick circuit of the building confirmed it was one way in, one way out.

Watching a team of sound engineers push a number of speakers towards the entrance, I moved closer with my mobile in my hand, so I didn't look like I was paying attention to what was going on. I stayed on the blindside of the two security guards helping to grapple with the equipment. Close enough to hear the sound of laughter and conversations drifting out of the door when the music stopped, I waited until both members of the security team were fully distracted.

Heading straight in, I made sure to lose myself immediately in the crowd of people going about their business. I pushed deeper into the room before allowing myself a backwards glance, but there was no hand on my shoulder, no one coming after me. Standing in front of the large window, I took in the view out over the River Hull, The Deep directly in front of me, it's fin-like structure pointing out to the water.

Turning back to the room, the band in the far corner continued to set up, catering work already underway. Plenty of the city's great and good would fill the room in a few hours time. The rest of the room would be made up of arts professionals, maybe those who'd worked on City of Culture if they were still around, and corporate sponsors.

I spotted Jagger deep in conversation with Grant Piercy. Recognising Piercy from the article I'd read in newspaper, he was a little older than me, his well-fitting jumper telling me he was in good shape. Age was wearing well on him, his neatly cut hair peppered with grey around the temples. I wondered how genuine Piercy's love of the Fruit Market was. Maybe it was a necessary change, or maybe it was opportunistic behaviour for business gain. Maybe it depended on how cynical I wanted to be about the man. Both of them stared back at me, realising I was watching them. I started to make my way across, a woman leading Jagger off to a news reporter and camera before I had chance to speak to him. Piercy stepped out in front of me. 'Let's have a talk, shall we?'

I was guided me away by my elbow and towards a quiet corner of the room. It was a practiced move, smooth and barely noticeable.

'I won't lie to you, Mr Geraghty. Your reputation precedes you.'

'Hope it's good?' He knew who I was. Word had reached Jagger that I was in town.

'I didn't say that.' He drew himself up a little higher before speaking, wanting to assert his height advantage. Intimidate me, as he introduced himself. 'We've got things in common. We're ex-sportsmen, aren't we?'

'You did better than me. I barely got on the pitch.'

'Doesn't make the passing of time any easier to accept, I can assure you of that.'

'We could have been contenders?'

'You speak for yourself.'

I smiled, knowing I'd already needled him. 'Was I interrupting something with the Member of Parliament? It looked like you were both talking about me?'

The mask slipped for a moment, maybe wondering how I'd gained access to the room. It was quickly pushed to one side, a smile painted back on his face.

'You should have a word with your security people,' I said.

'I will be doing.'

I smiled again, 'Smashing place you've built here. The area's certainly changed a lot since the old warehouses I remember.'

'I'm pleased to have played my part in it.'

'But modesty prevents you from telling me about it?'

It was Piercy's turn to smile. 'Not necessarily.'

'This area was a building site when I left five years ago.'

'Five years is a long time.'

'I recognise enough.' I knew all too well that you could change the appearance of something, but changing what was underneath was an altogether tougher proposition. Sometimes it remains dark and defiant, not listening. 'You can't always cover up bruises,' I settled for saying.

'That's the wrong type of thinking. It's old-fashioned.' Piercy turned and gestured around the room. 'You can always rewrite the story. Everyone laughed when I said I was going to change things, but they're not laughing now, are they? This place was the UK Crap Town champion when I decided to put my money where my mouth was. It would have been the easiest thing in the world to continue putting my time and effort into properties, shit cash from them. But where's the fun in that? No one remembers you for doing that. I got into bed with this area and the idea of culture as a driver for change because I believed in it.'

'Good for you.'

Piercy drew a breath in and a flash of anger crossed his face at my attitude. 'People say I took advantage in some way, moan that I've made a lot of money from what I've done. Do you know what I say to that?'

'Surprise me?'

'I say, fuck them. Every penny I've made, I've earned. This city needs more people who are prepared to stand up and be counted.'

'And that has to come down to money every time? It's always about profit?'

'You prefer plain talking?'

'Is there any other way?'

Piercy shook his head. 'Look at the state of you. You've got some balls, I'll give you that, crashing this place.' A small smile settled on his face. 'But I like your approach, if I'm being honest. Most people prefer to tell me what they think I want to hear.'

'Like Jagger?' It was a punt, but I wanted to see his reaction.

Piercy didn't bite, batting the question away. 'It's good to have people like him down here today. It sends a statement out.'

'Is that so?'

'Our MPs are ambitious for the city and we need more forward-thinkers, more modernisers. It's where the game's at.'

'Don Ridley,' I said, dropping the name, looking for a reaction. 'He was my partner and now he'd dead, a hit and run.'

'You have my sympathies.'

'Don was looking into an old case, the murder of John Gove. You might remember it as The Car Boot Murder. Jagger led the failed investigation.'

'He had a long and distinguished career as a detective.'

'Not this time.'

'No one's going to solve every crime. I'm sure he did his very best for the victim. What you have to understand is that policing now is a very different job to how it was back then.'

I zoned out, letting him talk around to the point he wanted to make, which I was sure would be to defend Jagger. I looked around the room, watching as more food was brought in, a lectern set up on the stage ready for speeches to be made from. The subtext of his words had hit home, though. Different times, different standards. If you lifted a stone up, you couldn't predict what you'd find underneath it.

'You don't fancy an old story resurfacing?' I said, feeling patronised. 'Not good for the image of the city? Not good for someone like Jagger in his new role?'

'I don't care either way. Why would I? The media aren't going to go into bat for a drug dealer. No one is bothered, but if an old case is closed, it's good news. It shows people still care. What I'm sure won't be tolerated is the good name of the police being dragged through the mud. Especially by someone like you.'

'Me?'

'Look around you. This is the new Hull. This is a city moving forward and building a future for itself. I'm already part of that and so are the local MPs, but you're peddling yesterday's news. No one cares.'

'Natalie Okorie hasn't given it up.'

Piercy laughed. 'I'm old enough to remember her when she was a proper journalist.'

'She's still a journalist.'

'Believe me, I know how she likes to play at it still. She's like a kid asking for sweets when it comes to Freedom of Information requests about my business affairs. She probably has my team on speed dial.' Piercy relaxed, hands in his pockets. 'You're working with her?'

'Maybe.'

'She's a fantasist who'll be using you for her own ends.'

'I can look after myself.'

'I'm sure you can.' Piercy's beckoned a member of the security team over. 'I think we're done here, but a word to the wise – don't fuck with people who are operating above your league. It won't end well for you.'

'I want to talk to Jagger about John Gove's murder.'

'He's going to be busy for the foreseeable future, but I hope I've answered your questions.' Piercy started to turn away, ready to talk to another guest. 'Don't go making a scene as you leave.'

ELEVEN

The murky water of the Humber in front of me was choppy, angrily butting up against the wooden boards of the Pierhead underneath my feet. It chimed with my mood after talking to Grant Piercy. If he thought I wouldn't be speaking to Jagger, he could think again. The Pierhead was where ferries docked prior to the Humber Bridge being built. Now it was somewhere to sit when you bought an ice cream from the nearby cafe when the weather was more suitable.

Waiting for Coleman to join me, I shuffled into a position on the wooden bench. The Minerva to my back, the pub had once been a place trawlermen would congregate, a place for some to get a last drink before jumping on the ferry across to the other side of the Humber. The pub had benefitted from a recent spit and polish, but if you looked more closely, the ingrained cigarette stains on the wall and the chipped paintwork told the story of days gone by.

My mobile buzzed with the arrival of another text message. It was Marieke again, asking if I was home yet and offering to cook a meal to celebrate my return. I didn't reply, knowing I was choosing to dodge the issue again. It sounded again, this time a text message from Natalie Okorie. She wanted to talk, the address of the restaurant she was eating at tonight attached as an open invite to join her there.

'You don't get to call the shots here, Joe.'

I looked up and gestured to the space opposite me on the bench, suggesting to Coleman that he should sit down.

He shook his head. 'You've got some nerve, but don't think we'll be making a habit of this. I'm not a fan of being told to drop everything at your say so.'

'Would you rather I came looking for you at the station?' For all his bluster, Coleman had done as I'd asked and headed straight here. He maybe didn't want to be seen with me, but he'd listen to what I had to say.

'Can we go inside?' he asked. 'I won't keep you long.'

'Pleased to hear it. I need to be at home.'

'You patched things up with your wife?'

'None of your business.'

'Fair enough.'

I glanced out along the water, watching a ferry prepare for its departure back out to the continent. I hadn't really thought about it, but the decision to live on a canal boat in Amsterdam had a subconscious undercurrent to it. The water was in my blood. 'I need your help.'

Coleman shook his head again. 'No.' He took his mobile out of his pocket, the ring tone unnecessarily loud and harsh, held it up to me. 'I need to take this.'

He edged away, standing next to a caravan the pub had turned into a mobile gin bar. I knew enough to recognise Coleman's ambition. It felt like a game of poker with neither of us wanting to reveal the cards we held. It was always about what the other person knew and if you could leverage it. I had to give him something, compel him to act. Regardless of how cold a case felt, there was always hope it could be closed. Forensics advanced, people's allegiances changed over time. It was never over.

Coleman walked back over, phone in his pocket, but agitated. 'Five minutes, Joe. That's all I've got now.'

'You remember John Gove?' I said. 'The Car Boot Murder thirty years back?' Coleman thought about it for a moment. 'He was a drug dealer?'

'Small time at best,' I said, 'but no one deserves to die like he did.' It didn't sit right with me. It didn't add up to a motive in my eyes.

Coleman interrupted, knowing where the conversation was heading. 'Don worked the case?'

'It stayed with him.' It was as vague and open-ended as I could be. 'He didn't run the investigation?' Coleman knew I was bullshitting him.

'What do you know about Ian Jagger?' I asked.

'The MP?' Coleman shrugged. 'Former cop. Not afraid to trade off his background when it suits.'

'He led the investigation.'

'No doubt he led lots of investigations.'

'You know he took a bullet for the cause?'

'Who doesn't?' Coleman smiled. 'The man's a politician. He needs to sell himself.'

'I need to know why Don died,' I said. 'I won't stop until I do.'

'Don't say it.' Coleman held a hand up to stop me from talking further. 'There's a procedure to follow.'

'Fuck your procedure.' I'd taken a step closer to the detective. Taking a breath, I stepped to the side. A smoker leaned against the door of the pub watching us, a smile on his face.

I took a piece of paper out of my pocket and held it out to him. 'Don went to this address the night before the hit and run. The guy there is called Dave Bolder.'

Coleman looked at it, no suggestion he recognised the man's name.

'He's missing.' Coleman tried to hand the piece of paper back, but I wasn't going to stop. 'A neighbour said he did a runner.'

'People do that all the time. He probably owes money and fancies his chances of outrunning the problem. It's bullshit.'

'I don't think so. It's not going to be a coincidence.'

Coleman stood up and paced in a small circle in front of me. 'Don't ask me to do it for you.'

'There's more,' I said. 'Don called me before he died,' I said, explaining about the message he'd left. How I hadn't got to it in time. I cued up the voicemail message Don had left, letting him listen to it. 'I'm not doing this on a whim.'

He listened and handed it back. 'It doesn't necessarily mean anything. Don't go seeing things that aren't there.'

I stood up, not wanting to feel like he was looking down on me, pushing on. 'Maybe Bolder's family have reported him missing?' I suggested. 'I just need to know a bit more about him, that's all. I'm not asking you to do anything more than that.' Coleman didn't offer any encouragement. 'Background stuff, so I can figure out why Don wanted to speak to him. How it all ties together?'

Coleman stopped pacing and started to listen to what I was saying. 'What's your theory on Bolder?'

He was on the hook, but I had little real information to reel him in with. It was something I'd thought about, though. I told Coleman that Dave Bolder had been described by his neighbour as being old. 'Maybe he's someone Don spoke to back in the day about Gove's murder?' It had to be connected. 'I know it was the first time the taxi firm had taken him to the address. It wasn't a social visit.'

Coleman's eyes narrowed. 'What's a taxi firm got to do with it?'

I'd said the wrong thing and he'd zeroed in on it immediately. 'It was on redial in Don's cottage.'

'And they just gave you that information?'

'There may have been a misunderstanding as to who I was.'

'Christ, Joe.' Coleman rubbed his face, ignored his mobile which was sounding again. 'You best hope they don't realise what happened and raise a complaint.'

'They've no need to.' I smiled, warming to the job I was doing, not really caring.

Coleman angled himself away from the smoker. 'You need to calm yourself down.'

'It's not a game.'

'Your life isn't here anymore.'

'That's not the point.'

'It's exactly the point, Joe.' He pocketed his mobile. 'Don't ask for my help on this. You think I haven't got enough on my plate as it is? It doesn't matter if I'm dealing with clever or stupid criminals, it's a never ending case of swimming against a tide of shite with the smallest paddle imaginable. I don't need more to do.'

'It's important,' I said, knowing the city would be constantly vomiting up more investigations and nightmares for him. 'Just ask around for me about Bolder?'

Coleman looked back at me. 'Ask around for you?' He stepped closer. 'You want me to upset people on your say so? No one cares about John Gove, why would they? What do you think my bosses would say if I started to involve myself in things that are none of my business?'

'They might thank you if you help shake something loose.' Natalie Okorie had said I needed to pick a side. I was starting to understand.

Coleman headed away, done with me. 'Like I said, you don't change, Joe.'

TWELVE

I stood outside of the Kurdish Restaurant on Spring Bank, weighing up whether to go inside or not. It stood on a corner, green tiles around the window, red and yellow lettering on the signage. It was colourful and fitted in with the area, a pocket of multiculturalism in the city. The restaurant window had steamed up, the rain outside having eased. I moved aside, a customer wanting to enter, the sound of laughter and chatter from inside as the door opened. I could see small groups of diners huddled together around tables, people who didn't appear to be carrying the weight of the world on their shoulders. I was brooding over what Coleman had said, how he wasn't prepared to help me. I thought back to the video interview of John Gove's father I'd watched, how deep his pain had been. I thought again about Don and debts owed before pushing at the door, knowing I was out of other options.

Natalie Okorie had taken a table for two towards the back of the room. She hadn't spotted me, hunched over her tablet device. I made my way over, grabbing her attention as I came to stop in front of the table.

She stood up to greet me. 'You came.'

I nodded, knowing I was always going to.

'Take a seat,' she told me, pointing to the empty chair. The clientele was mainly male, speaking in languages I didn't know, the nearest conversation was particularly animated with the names of footballers occasionally cutting through the language barrier. I pulled out the chair and sat down.

I waited for her to speak, unsure of how to play it. All I knew was that I needed to tread carefully. I was more used to trying to extract information from people. This time it felt like I was the one under the microscope.

'Water?' She lifted the bottle from the table. 'No alcohol in here.' She looked at the e-cigarette next to her. 'Best go outside when I want a go on that, too.'

'Water's fine, thanks.'

She pushed a menu across the table. 'Don't make me eat alone, then.'

I didn't look at it, sitting back in my chair, trying to work out if I could trust her. A waiter appeared, notepad in hand. I listened as she ordered a lamb kofte, telling me it was a kebab served with lentil soup, salad and naan. 'You'll have the same?' I wasn't given a chance to answer, as she told the waiter I would before handing the menus back. 'It's my favourite place to eat, but I haven't tried the lamb yet. We'll take the leap together.' We waited for the waiter to head over to the kitchen before speaking again, both of us happy to sit there for a moment in silence.

I folded my arms. 'I watched the video of John Gove's father talking to the local paper.'

Okorie nodded, moved her tablet to one side. 'What did you think?'

'He was obviously still hurting.'

'As you would be. He's a parent. It's unconditional love.'

'It must have been a lot of weight to carry.' I relaxed a touch, rubbed my face, knowing we all had that burden, but some had to carry more than others.

I changed the subject, saying I'd spoken to Gerard Branning. 'He thinks you're full of conspiracy theories.'

'Calling something a conspiracy theory is often easier than confronting the truth, wouldn't you say?' She leaned closer, her hand going to the e-cigarette on the table. 'You're not that different to me, you know?'

'Sounds like you're making assumptions to me.'

'If I had a file on you, what would it say?'

'Why would you have a file on me?'

'Humour me.'

'I wouldn't know.'

'It would tell me you're a competent investigator, more than that, actually, but one who chose to walk away from the job despite there not being many people around here with your skills. It would also tell me you're a prickly individual, prone to thinking he knows best when it's not necessarily the case. It would also tell me you're working out in Amsterdam, labouring on building sites, probably bored out of your head because it isn't really what you're cut out for.'

She'd hit the bullseye, but keeping my face neutral, she didn't need to know that. 'Maybe I've got a file on you?' I said.

'It's already a matter of record. I don't life my live in the shadows.'

The waiter arrived with our food, sizzling as it was placed down. It also saved me from immediately replying to her assessment of me. I ignored my plate, despite Okorie gesturing I should eat. 'Why did you check me out?' I asked.

She took a bite from the kebab, chewing and swallowing before answering. 'I like to know who I'm working with.' She gestured again at the plate in front of me. 'Eat up before it goes cold.'

We ate in silence for a few minutes before I washed my mouth out with water. 'It still sounds like you're making assumptions about me,' I said, cutting her off from saying more. 'Tell me about The Northern News Agency?'

She put her food down. 'I'd say we're not that different. You're curious, you ask questions.'

I let her have that one and encouraged her to continue.

'It's quite simple,' she said. 'I'm going to write the stories about the North that interest me and the ones readers will want. It's about making sure you understand where these two things intersect. I probably don't need to tell you that the print media is dying on its arse. It needs a new model fit for the new realities it faces.'

'And you're going to provide that?'

'It's part of the answer, but everything's changing. It's happening fast, but no one really trusts the old school people any more, do they? They broke their model and don't know how to make it right. They think all people want is clickbait and celebrity gossip. Maybe some do, but I know some still want stories that mean something.'

'And they're willing to pay for it?' She'd probably heard the same question a million times, but didn't take the bait.

'There are ways of managing the process,' Okorie said. She counted them off on her fingers. 'Subscriptions, pay-as-you-go access, fundraisers, targeted advertising. It's all about knowing your audience and treating them with respect. They get to go behind the scenes and learn more. That's what people really want.'

'What about your independence?'

'I'm the one who makes the decisions. If it's not right, it won't happen, but no one's going to influence what I write. It's my judgement call and I believe the North needs a voice. The London media doesn't give a shiny shit about us up here. I've worked for them, so I know. The local press is largely impotent because they either haven't got the resources, or they can't risk upsetting the wrong people. People need holding to account and it doesn't always happen as it should. I'm not going back to writing for an editor or a shareholder, or anyone with their own agenda. It's down to me and it's how I can make a difference.'

They were fine words and difficult to argue with. It all sounded very persuasive. I watched her hand go towards the e-cigarette again, recognising I was being pitched to. I sipped at my water. 'So why this story about John Gove?'

She took her time, too, before answering. 'Because there are things you don't know about the police and their involvement.'

THIRTEEN

'Are you going to enlighten me?' I asked.

She shook her head. 'We want the same thing here. It's unfinished business for both of us.'

'What are you proposing?'

'That depends on what you know.'

I sat back and puffed my cheeks out. 'You've had thirty years on this story, I've had a single day. It's hardly a fair exchange. Why would I have anything to share with you?' I was trying to needle her, but wasn't landing a punch.

She smiled and went back to her food, chewing on a piece of bread before speaking. 'You should be willing to share with me for those precise reasons. I suspect there's a lot more for you to learn than there is for me, but it's about what you can put on the table. It's all about what you can contribute.' She drank more water. 'That's The Northern News Alliance ethos.'

'I don't work for you.'

'Not for me, but you could work with me.' She went back to her food. 'Tell me about your relationship with DI Coleman.'

'You're well-informed.'

'It pays to be. From asking around, it sounds like he owes you.'

'It's not that simple.'

'Things are only complicated if you make them that way.'

I wasn't so sure about that. Some things just happened to be complex. 'He won't help me,' I settled for saying.

'You're not asking the right questions, then.'

It was blunt and to the point. I pushed my plate to one side, my appetite gone. It was decision time. I sat back knowing I was wading into what would be dangerous waters. If you did that, it was easy to end up out of your depth. But sometimes you discovered you could swim. I had to give her something that unlocked some reciprocal help, something that showed I was trying at least. Nothing came cheaply. 'I tried to speak to Ian Jagger earlier, see what he remembered about John Gove.'

'He's not an easy man to access.'

I told her how it had come about, effectively crashing the set-up for the *Hit The North* launch party on the Fruit Market. 'The area seems to have changed a lot recently, too.'

'Jury's still out on City of Culture, I'd say.'

'Maybe you should write a story about it?'

Okorie smiled. 'Now you're thinking like a journalist.'

'Fair to say I was warned off from making any waves around Jagger.'

'Who by?'

'Grant Piercy. Remember him? Ex-footballer turned businessman. Seemed somewhat protective of Jagger.'

'Why was that?'

With everything that was going on, I hadn't really stopped to think about it. Clearly, that was a mistake. 'Who wouldn't want to cosy up to someone with power if you're in Piercy's game?' I suggested.

'They're cousins,' Okorie said. 'Jagger's best part of ten years older, but they're tight.'

It put a different spin on things, an invitation to consider how legitimate their business connection appeared to be.

Okorie spoke again. 'Piercy is, shall we say, very much aware of his own image. People like that are the reason why The Northern News Alliance needs to exist. The man has a lot of power around here and it's largely unchecked. It no doubt suits him to keep the story and his cousin out of the headlines. Or the wrong kind, at least.'

'I'm sure.' Blood is thicker than water, but maybe I hadn't been direct enough, either. 'You must have a theory about John Gove's murder.'

'I live for theories.' She caught the waiter's attention and asked for the bill. 'But you need something to back them up.' She offered her credit card to him, going through the motions of thanking him. She pushed her chair out, ready to stand up and leave before stopping herself, instead going to her bag. Okorie placed a photograph face down on the table. My hand went towards it, but she stopped me.

'What's your theory, Joe? Why didn't the police get to the bottom of it and make an arrest?'

I let the photograph go, shrugged. 'If you've got something to say, you need to say it.' Her hand remained on top of the photograph. My eyes went back to it, wanting to see what secrets it held.

'Jagger didn't run the investigation, not really.'

If she was playing with me, I wasn't in the mood. 'So what?'

'Detective Constables Forrester and Mail did all the leg work for him. He was nowhere near as hands-on as he should have been.'

I listened as she described Forrester as the leader, the one with the brains to lead the pair, before filing the names away, glancing again at the face-down photograph.

'They were junior and inexperienced,' Okorie said. 'Maybe John Gove just wasn't a priority for them?'

'Stands to reason.'

'They weren't well thought of. Mail left within a few months of the investigation, Forrester went a couple of years later.'

'They walked away from their careers?'

'Mail never looked back.'

I wasn't sure what I was supposed to take from that, but it didn't sit right. Okorie's inference was clear.

'Word is Mail didn't fancy it as a career,' she said. 'Forrester moved away from the area, went totally off the map. Mail is still local.'

She let the photograph go, releasing it to me. I flipped it over. It showed a man in his mid-fifties standing in what looked to be a haulage yard, work overalls on and a mug in his hand. He wasn't aware he was being photographed. The lorries behind him were either partially obscured, or parked at such an angle that meant I couldn't read the company name in full. 'Which one is it?' I looked again at the photograph, sure the man was going to be either Forrester or Mail. I looked up at Okorie, aware my heart was beating a little faster. I knew I was heading out towards dangerous waters with her. 'Did you take this yourself?'

'Don did.'

FOURTEEN

I placed the carrier bag carefully down on the pavement, the cans clattering against the wet concrete, aware I was swaying slightly. I stared up at what had once been the home of Ridley & Son Private Investigators. The Old Town was tightly-packed with cobbled streets running alongside the river, its buildings leaning in close to each other. What had once been merchant warehouses were now apartments and offices for start-up businesses, numerous small pubs with names nodding to the area's maritime history. I didn't consider myself a sentimental person, but having thrown several drinks back after talking to Natalie Okrie, I felt the need to see the place.

Our office had been one of many small businesses within a shared building, but now it stood empty, a To Let sign hanging above the windows on the ground-floor. Staring at it, there was something powerful about the building and the old office, something I couldn't explain. I wasn't thinking rationally as I walked to the back of it, an unoccupied rubble car park. A tired-looking security sign told me the property was routinely patrolled, a 24 hour phone number at the bottom. I doubted it was true. Looking up, the alarm system appeared to be dead. I looked at the number pad on the door, its code engrained from years of use. Using my mobile as a torch, I slowly pressed the numbers in sequence with the flat of my thumb, wondering if it would open. It did. The alarm didn't sound.

I closed the door behind me, letting my eyes adjust as I listened, even though I knew I was alone. What had been the communal kitchen area was cold and smelled of damp. I walked slowly through the building, taking care in case the floor had fallen into disrepair. The door to what had been our office was closed, but unlocked. Heading inside, standing in the middle of it felt strange. To my left in the corner behind the door was where Sarah's desk had been. Opposite in the far corner had been my area. Don had taken the largest working space down the length of other wall.

I flopped down on the floor and took a can of lager out, Popping the ring pull, I offered up a silent toast to Don and Sarah. We'd done good work here, good things together. We'd also argued and fallen out. The whisky had taken the edge off, the lager helping me think things through more clearly. I'd wandered into numerous situations over the years, but Natalie Okorie's suggestion the police knew something about what had happened to John Gove was more dangerous than most. I'd always known Don's death would have implications and repercussions, but hadn't expected it to be so insidious and dark. But if I believed Don's death was murder, it would need a strong motive and evidence to make it stick. It was more than just an unsolved case, a lack of justice. It was potentially something that went to the very heart of society and institutions.

I focused the light from my mobile on the photograph Natalie Okorie had given me, calling it a gesture of goodwill. I'd asked who it was, but she'd said I'd figure it out. It was test. I slugged back almost half the can of lager and looked at it again, the rush from working with a purpose pushing aside the effects of drink. Forrester and Mail had been young detectives when investigating John Gove's murder. There was little to go at. If they were young men in 1989, it stood to reason they were in their mid-fifties now. Social media was a dead end, the men not the obvious demographic for it. There were other routes I could go down – electoral register, marriage records, possibly even death certificates – but dealing with bureaucracy took time.

Looking again at the photograph, I focused on the backdrop, putting the part of the company name I could see on the lorry parked in the yard into Google. I quickly got a match. Dunston Haulage was based between Hedon and the village of Preston, less than five miles away from where Don had been killed. Finding a website, it stated they were a family-run business, a fleet of light haulage vehicles running around the country and further afield from their base. Their contact details didn't come with any names. I could cold call in the morning and see if either name prompted a reaction, but it felt obvious that I had to be cuter than that.

Some of the training I'd received from Sarah in how to use public record information had lodged somewhere in my head. It was a limited company, its number displayed at the bottom of the website. Moving to Companies House, a smile on my face, I'd made a breakthrough. The company director was listed as Amanda Mail. Picking up the photograph, I was looking at Gary Mail. I drained the rest of the can, put the photograph away. There was nothing I could do until tomorrow.

My mobile buzzed with a text message, Marieke asking why I hadn't boarded my flight home. Shit. I hadn't replied to her earlier texts. She'd be waiting for me in Schipol Airport, a meal ready for me when we returned to her apartment.

I'd fucked up. Rubbing my face, the coward in me didn't want to speak to her at the moment. It would only make a bad situation worse. I tapped a quick text message, apologising, saying I'd missed the flight. It was a lie by omission at best. At worst, I knew it was cowardly. Ashamed, I turned the phone off, not wanting to read whatever reply she sent.

I stood up, pacing the empty room, the alcohol keeping me warm. I had to make the decision for myself. It had been left unsaid, but there were things I could do that Okorie couldn't. She had a reputation to protect, regulations and professional standards to adhere to. I didn't. Everything had changed and nothing had changed. It was examining the grey areas, looking at those who had fallen through the cracks where I thrived. The city looked like a slightly out of focus photograph; I knew it intimately, but it also held secrets. Sitting back down, I knew that however dangerous it was, I wasn't done with the place just yet.

FIFTEEN

Closing in on Paull, my car was the only one on the road leading to the village. A light drizzle started to fall onto my windscreen, the sky black and as on edge as I was. The lights on the infrastructure of the docks and its industry twinkled and flashed in the distance, like a message in Morse code. Or a warning maybe after my conversation with Okorie. I was thinking about the fact Jagger and Piercy were cousins, and what that meant. I was thinking about the two detectives leaving the police, going to ground, and how Don had found one of them. I was also thinking about what else Okorie undoubtedly knew and was holding back from me.

Parking up close to the pub, I walked the short distance to Don's cottage, head down against the weather. I knocked before entering, Sarah was sitting in the chair facing the door. She didn't look at me. I closed the door, apologised for being delayed.

'Something more pressing going on?'

'Not at all. Just something I had to finish.'

She straightened up in the chair. 'I've been here most of the afternoon, getting the lock on the back door fixed.'

I picked up a framed photograph from the mantelpiece, my back to her, playing for time.

'Funny thing is, Joe, I was given a description of the man seen breaking in, and guess what? It's you down to a tee, even the clothes you're wearing tally.'

I toyed with the photograph, but I knew I was in trouble.

'The police weren't fast enough to make an arrest,' she said, 'but they called me once it seemed nothing had been taken.'

I turned to face her. 'I can explain.' She cut me off, told me to save it, but I had to explain it as best I could. 'Your dad came to me for help,' I said, knowing there was no good way to explain it. 'He would leave a trail, or a file or something. He always did. It was the way he worked. There's a gap in his filing system.' Sarah held a hand up to my garbled explanation. It was a poor excuse for what I'd done.

'You broke in?' She stood up and paced the room. 'I can't believe you'd do that.'

'I was asked for help and I was trying to give it.'

She stopped and faced me. 'It shouldn't involve breaking the law, should it? The police don't see it the same way.'

'You called them on me?'

'It's what you deserve,' she said. 'Actions have consequences.'

'They won't find anything.'

'And that makes it ok? I'm struggling to believe a word you say, to be honest. It's typical of you, charging in without a thought for others or the consequences.'

Her words were unfair, but I had to accept them. I'd picked up the scent of something and immediately chased it instead of stopping to think it through. Story of my life. Sarah sat back down, head in her hands. She didn't speak for a moment. I leaned against the front door, unsure what I should do for the best.

'Don't even think about rationalising it.'

'I know.'

'You're way out of line here.'

'I had to do something.'

'You weighed up your options and made the wrong decision. It's the police's job to work out what happened, not yours.'

I pushed myself off the door and sat down opposite her. 'That's all the more reason to do it. I spoke to Coleman, he's not interested, not really.'

'There's a difference between not being interested and being professional.'

I told her about using redial on her dad's phone, laying it out for her. 'It took me through to a taxi firm and an address he'd been to in East Hull the day before he died. The guy who lives there is missing.' It was my turn to talk now. 'He was following something, Sarah, something that was important to him.' I told her about John Gove and what I knew about the night of his murder. It didn't amount to much yet, but it was enough to make the point. 'It doesn't feel right.'

'It doesn't feel right?' Sarah's voice was low and angry. 'Don't ask me what he was looking at because I have no interest in finding out. I refused to get involved, and I'll tell you why, shall I? It wasn't good for a man of his age to be getting involved, but he never listened to me, did he?'

'Of course he did.'

She looked around. 'I should never have let him move out here to the middle of nowhere. It gave him too much time to brood and think.' She went into the kitchen and poured herself a glass of water.

I followed her through. 'You couldn't stop him,' I said, knowing it was true. Don had always been his own man. 'It was his decision.'

'And you're reaching to justify your own behaviour.'

'I know what I'm looking at here.'

'You let my dad down.'

Sarah had her back to me, leaning over the sink. The words really hurt this time. I hadn't seen eye to eye with Don as things drew to a close between us, but I hadn't let him down. I'd never accept that.

'You more than crossed the line, Joe.' Sarah turned round, folded her arms. 'And then you went digging into my dad's past knowing no good would come of it.'

I walked over to her, stopping a few feet away. 'It's where things went. It wasn't deliberate.'

'You broke our family and then disappeared. What kind of person does that?'

'It wasn't like that.'

'It was exactly like that. You threw a bomb into the room and then you fucked off.'

I'd discovered things about Don, things he'd wanted to remain buried, things I'd dragged out into the light. The consequences for us all had been severe.

'You did it regardless, Joe.'

'The truth is the truth.' I wish I hadn't said it. It sounded sanctimonious at best, bullshit at worst.

'Ever thought not everyone wants to hear it? Why do you think my dad was getting involved with old cases again? It's because of you. It's as if he had to prove a point.'

'I didn't ask him to do this.' Her words stopped me in my tracks, unsure of what to say. 'This is tough for me, too.'

'Don't patronise me.'

'I'm not.'

'I see you, Joe. I really fucking see you.' She shook her head. 'And now you're back, throwing your weight around and causing trouble.'

'I'm not the only one looking at this,' I said, telling her about Natalie Okorie.

'I don't want my dad's name dragging through the mud.'

'It won't be.' If anything, Don was going up against the people he really shouldn't be; old colleagues and maybe old friends. His recent actions were brave. 'She's followed the story since the start.' I gave her a brief rundown of the journalist's career, how she'd headed for London and made a name for herself. 'She's back up here running her own show now, The Northern News Alliance website. She's driven and passionate and this story never left her.'

'She's not even a real journalist anymore?' Sarah laughed before shaking her head. 'What is she going to do?'

'Of course she's a real journalist.'

'You're working with her? Seriously?' She turned away from me, pushing her hair away from her face where the wind was blowing it.

'I'm not working with her.' I wasn't sure how true that statement was, but I didn't have to tell Sarah that sometimes you had to be pragmatic about things. It was how things got done. I told her that the two young detectives carrying out the investigation had done a poor job. I stopped myself suggesting there was something more sinister at play, where the finger of guilt pointed. 'It was important to your dad, whatever you think of me.'

'And my thoughts aren't important?'

It was a good question. I had a bad habit of steamrollering through what I thought was best, little consideration of other points of view. It was one of the reasons why things had gone so wrong with Don.

'This is as much about you as anything else, Joe.'

'Bullshit.'

'You can lie to yourself, but you can't lie to me. You don't like living out in Holland, it's written all over your face. It's not you, any more than living out here was what my dad should have been doing.'

'You're wrong.'

'Look at the state of you.' She pointed to my face. 'When did you last have a shave or a shower?'

I looked away, knowing she was right. I'd found trouble easily and knew I needed to clean-up. Sleeping overnight in the old office hadn't been a smart move.

'I hated my dad moving out here,' she said. 'There's nothing. It isolated him and I can't even begin to tell you how that made me feel.'

I stared at her as she continued to talk, wanting to say it was Don who had set things in motion, but forced the urge back. Turning it into an argument wouldn't help either of us. 'Your dad was fired up by the idea of justice and John Gove never got that.' That was the bottom line, the truth she couldn't escape from. Looking at her face, she knew that as well as I did. What I didn't have to say was that he'd died because of it and that demanded it wasn't ignored or walked away from. 'You sound like you don't want me back here?'

'I don't care either way. I've moved on. You should try it.'

'I need your help to do that.'

She pushed past me and back in to the living room. 'Don't even dare ask.'

'I'm trying to do the right thing here.'

'You're unbelievable.' Sarah looked out of the window. 'You keep saying you want to help, but you're not listening to the answer.'

'Not true.'

'You don't even hear yourself.'

'I need to see his notes about John Gove.'

'You don't need to, Joe. You just want to.'

'It's important. Maybe he put them elsewhere, but I need to know how far he'd got with things.'

She let the curtain go. 'I don't want your help and I don't want you anywhere near me. You need to move on and start again. Maybe you'll thank me for it one day.'

'Think about it. Please.'

Sarah shook her head. 'You best hope the police don't find any trace of you in here.'

I held her stare for a moment before leaving. There was nothing more to say.

SIXTEEN

I found a seat in the corner of the village pub like a moth to a flame, wanting to lose myself in the quiet buzz of conversation, a handful of drinkers winding down after a day's work. Night was starting to fall, meaning all I could see from the window was a black mass of nothingness out across the Humber. It suited my mood, a fog descending over me, as I pushed myself further into the corner, part of the scenery but a passive actor.

Sarah was hurting and she had every right to be. I'd lost someone who'd been a colleague and a mentor, but she'd lost more. Don should have enjoyed a quiet and lengthy retirement, but my disappearance had prompted the misguided urge to prove himself all over again.

Putting those thoughts to one side, I toyed with my mobile before finding Marieke's name and pressing call. Maybe isolating myself didn't suit me as much as I thought. Maybe I craved something, too. It took a moment for the call to connect. Marieke's greeting was guarded. 'It's me,' I said. This time there was no mistaking what the silence at the other end of the line meant. I pulled myself up right, angling myself away from the rest of the pub. 'I owe you an apology.'

'I came to the airport to collect you, Joe. You weren't there.'

'I missed the flight.' More silence at the other end of the line. I rubbed at my face, apologised again.

'If you missed your flight, you would have got the next one. You chose this.' She was more disappointed than angry, which only made it worse. I tried my best to explain things to her. 'I wasn't sure what I was going to find out here,' I said. 'Don was in trouble.' I hadn't told her the truth about the message he'd left for me, choosing to keep it to myself.

'What kind of trouble?'

'I don't know yet.'

'In that case, it's for the police to investigate, surely?'

'It's not that simple.'

'Of course it is.'

'Not for me.'

'If a crime has been committed, the police will do their job.'

'Maybe.' Given she worked as a lawyer, her attitude felt naive to me, idealistic as best. I put the mobile down on the table before picking it back up again. I was a man with a past, something she knew nothing about. It was a life she didn't need to be aware of. 'It's important to me that I pay my debts.'

'Debts? What does that even mean, Joe?'

'I have to do this for Don.' I struggled to articulate it beyond that without opening up a conversation I didn't want to have.

'You're like a closed book to me, Joe.'

'That's not true.'

'It's totally true. Talk to me, tell me what you're scared of?'

'I need to make sense of it myself first.'

'I should have come with you, supported you. I've never even been to Hull or met your family and friends.'

'I've not been home until now.' It was the truth, but it wasn't the point. She would be marking me down as petulant for such an answer. I glanced over to the bar, a new group of workmen walking in, fluorescent jackets and big boots on, most likely from the nearby chemical plant.

'I should have come with you,' Marieke repeated. 'It was a funeral.'

'I'm not on holiday.'

'That's unfair.'

She was right. I offered another apology. 'I just need a couple more days.'

'You'll do what you need to do.'

'What does that mean?'

'Whatever you want it to mean, Joe. I'm tired of this already.'

'I've got responsibilities here. I can't just ignore them.'

'You live in Amsterdam on a canal boat. You labour on your friend's building sites. That's your life.'

I stared up at the ceiling, looking at a large damp patch in the corner, wondering what the fuck I was thinking. 'I'm more than that.'

'I wouldn't know.'

I started to reply, but it was too late. The call had been cut short, Marieke ending it. I placed my mobile on the table and closed my eyes. It was another mess I'd made for myself. Maybe she was right. I should have asked for some help and support, but maybe I knew all along what was waiting out here for me. It was down to me to face up to it.

'You ok, son?'

I opened my eyes and looked at one of the workers I'd seen walk in a few minutes ago.

'You look like you've had a day of it.'

I stood up. 'You could say that.' Sarah had made her feelings clear to me, though she was the one person who would maybe understand. If I had a new life in Amsterdam that I liked, I should grasp it. But she could read me like a book and knew it wasn't going to satisfy me. I had to reconcile the two positions.

I picked my coat and returned my glass to the bar before heading outside. The door blew shut behind me, the wind forcing my head down to the pavement. It felt like a storm was on the way. I deliberately walked the long way round to the road Don had died on, not wanting to pass his cottage.

The road was quiet, no sign of any traffic on the road, pitch blackness once I was out of the range of streetlights. Using the torch on my mobile, I found the spot I wanted, the crime scene tape I'd seen previously still stuck to a nearby tree. Shivering, the temperature would have been even lower on the night Don had been hit by the vehicle, frost forming underfoot. Standing still and listening, the wind whistling around me, it was as bleak as it was isolated. It felt like the end of the world, a struggle to see Don walking a dog out in the area at night.

I was temporarily blinded by a vehicle's headlights as it appeared from around the bend, travelling at speed. It only took a matter of seconds for it to pass me, less than a few feet away. I'd taken an involuntary step backwards. My heart started to beat that bit faster from how quickly it had happened, but also from the realisation of what could have happened. The area had resettled immediately, pitch black and quiet.

Walking back towards the village, I hadn't expected to be so pleased to see house lights, street-lights, the occasional dog walker out and about. Walking back towards my car, Don's cottage was in darkness, locked up for the night, Sarah had gone home. I stood and stared at it for a moment, still struggling to make any sense of things.

1989

There was something different about the air around a crime scene, even when it was reset back to its proper purpose, something intangible and all too unsettling. It was a feeling Don Ridley knew all too well. The multi-storey was back open to the public, workers starting to arrive for the day ahead. He also knew he should leave it alone, but the recent signs of life in there couldn't be ignored. There was a potential witness to talk to. Walking towards it, the satisfying crunch of frost underfoot, it was another building with its own secrets. The space the car John Gove had been found in was unoccupied. Tyres screeched on concrete, a car pulling up close-by. The female driver quickly hurried to the stairs, probably running late, metal door thumping against the concrete wall. She hadn't even paused long enough to see him.

Walking over to the corner, the dirty sleeping bag and bundled up clothes he'd seen the previous day were still in place, as was the milk bottle and newspaper. The fire which had a residue of heat was now fully extinguished. It remained untouched since the previous night. It was a different car park attendant manning the barrier, but the same attitude.

The find hadn't been of interest to DI Jagger, the morning briefing nothing more than going through the motions. Jagger would be overseeing the investigation, but the leg work would be done by Forrester and Mail, two young detectives he didn't rate. Jagger had told him he was too valuable to tie up on it, that he was needed elsewhere. He'd listened before suggesting maybe there was a witness who'd seen what had happened. Jagger hadn't put a rocket up the people who'd shrugged and laughed, shown no interest in the suggestion. Some had even voiced it – Gove had got what he deserved - his known low-level activity had escalated and caught up with him.

Instead, here he was, poking through the remnants of a life, increasingly sure the owner had been spooked by something they'd seen. It was too cold to not return to a sleeping bag, to take some form of shelter. Carefully nudging the items apart, a pen fell out of the folded newspaper. Bending down to look closer, the crossword had been partially completed. Notes had been scribbled at the top of the page. Turning to the sleeping bag, he shook it down, a chocolate wrapper falling out.

The bag of clothes wasn't dissimilar. Tipping the contents out, he felt a pang of guilt at the thought people had to live like this. The damp and sweaty smell confirmed the clothes hadn't been washed for a while. Pushing the clothes back into the bag, something harder fell and hit the floor. Holding it up to the light, he looked at the cigarette lighter. It looked cheap, coated in green plastic, the kind you'd see on sale in every newsagent or corner shop.

Leaving the multi-storey behind, a nearby drop-in centre was only a short walk away. It felt like a good place to start. Pausing outside for a moment, Jagger had expressly warned against wasting time on Gove. Thirty minutes wouldn't hurt, not now he had something to share.

Inside, the floor was bare plywood, a selection of donated garden furniture in one corner. A group of three men huddled around it, mugs of tea on the table. In the other corner, a small kitchen area with a chalkboard above it detailing the food and drink on offer. Posters on the wall advertised various local council services.

The woman working behind the counter was busy, the smell of frying bacon in the air. She shouted she'd be with him as quickly as she could. The radio played a song he recognised, one from the Kylie Minogue album he'd recently bought for Sarah's birthday, his daughter insisting it had to be on cassette for her new Walkman. The thought was a reminder that everyone was the child of someone. John Gove had family expecting justice for him. Picking up the local newspaper from the counter, it was the early edition, news of Gove only appearing in the Stop Press column on the back page. Putting it back down, the next edition would carry more.

'Spare me five minutes?' Don said, showing his ID as she made her way across to him.

'That's all I've got, love.'

'You heard about what happened in the car park?'

'Who hasn't?'

'Looks like some of the homeless were dossing down there for some cover.'

'Stands to reason in this weather.' She nodded to the group of men. 'See what they've got to say.'

The men stared at him before all standing, ready to move off. He held his hand out to them, blocking off the door. 'Not so fast, lads. You haven't finished your food. Get you all another hot drink?' Turning to the woman behind the counter, he ordered more toast and drinks, gestured to the men to sit down. 'I won't take up much of your time.' Pulling out a chair, he sat down at the table, none of them prepared to look him in the eye. 'Know anything about last night, then?'

'No.'

'Sure?' He replied to the one who'd appointed himself spokesman for the group. They were all over forty, small bags of belongings on the floor next to them. It added to the suggestion that the belongings found in the multi-storey car park opposite the crime scene had been left behind in a panic.

'Definitely sure.'

'Know the guy who was murdered?'

'We mind our own business.'

'And you're wise to do so. Best way if you ask me.' Don leaned in. 'But what I want to know, though, is who was dossing down there when it happened? I've found some clothes and a sleeping bag.'

'Don't know.'

He put on a show of making himself comfortable. 'Take your time, have a think for me.'

'We weren't around there last night.'

'Where were you all?'

'It's none of your business.'

The reality was that there were numerous abandoned buildings around the city centre. It wouldn't be too difficult to find temporary shelter in an empty warehouse. It didn't really matter. It was a mechanism to keep them talking, hopefully gain some trust. The woman headed out from behind the counter with fresh mugs of tea for them. He placed the lighter on the table. 'Any idea who this might belong to?'

The men didn't look, but the woman did. 'That's your mate's, isn't it?' she said to them before turning her attention back to Don. 'Where did you get it?' She placed the mugs down. 'He's usually in here with this lot.'

Don looked around the table. 'It's time we had a chat about that, I reckon.'

SEVENTEEN

I leant against the wall of a shop, swallowed back two paracetamol with a mouthful of water. My head felt like it was being repeatedly hit with a hammer.

The pub on the other side of the road was the one my father had taken a tenancy on following the end of his own rugby league career. He'd been a club legend, a contrast to my own spell in the game. The pub trade was perfect for him, a place to hold court and tell stories about the glory days, take the punters through his best tries and games. I'd spent my childhood years living above the place, making it a home as well as a business. The brickwork needed some attention, the faded banner outside advertising live sport on the big screen need replacing, but I could remember every detail of the layout inside.

It was also a place that had been sullied in my mind. I thought back to what I'd learned just before leaving Hull. Don had visited the place as a young detective, watched as a corrupt detective, DI Holborn, beat my father as part of a shake down. Don had explained how it had been a show of power, a show put on that demanded he picked a side. Don had insisted he'd kept his distance from Holborn after that and I believed him. I'd spent angry nights, weighing it up, but I knew Don had been as straight as they come. What I couldn't move past was the fact he'd just stood there and watched my dad being beaten. Life always came down to choosing a side and he hadn't done enough.

I swallowed the last of the water and threw the empty bottle in the bin. Looking at the pub was like picking at a scab, something best left alone, but I'd still done it. However I felt, I owed Don for what he'd done for me. I had to find a bridge between the two opposing pieces of knowledge, find a way to live with it all, forgive but not forget.

Driving away, I had to figure out what I was going to ask Gary Mail about John Gove's murder, how I was going to phrase my questions and dig into the suggestion of a police cover-up. I had to look him in the eye, see what my gut reaction was. Looking again at the photograph Okorie had given me of Mail, he definitely hadn't been aware it was being taken. She'd always intended me to head for the haulage business where I'd find Mail.

I watched as a 4x4 pulled out of the haulage yard, turning towards Hedon, the tinted windows leaving me unable to see if the driver was male or female, never mind if it was Mail or not. I walked over to the yard, the ground underfoot uneven and cracked, marked with potholes full of rain water. Barbed wire sitting on top of the fencing marked out the perimeter, numerous cameras trained on the space. The repair centre at the back of the yard was busy, a lorry cab tilted forward to give access to the engine. In the corner, a rack of tyres and spare parts. In the other, a portacabin out of sight from the road, its door closed and lights off.

'Help you, pal?'

I turned to look at the man asking the question. It wasn't Gary Mail. This man was tall and muscular, not yet thirty years old, wearing oil-stained overalls. The family resemblance was clear, though. I was willing to bet money that I was looking at Mail's son. Regardless of who he was, he was holding a heavy wheel jack in his hand. I pointed back to the portacabin. 'The office looked empty.'

'The boss has nipped out.'

'Mrs Mail?'

'Have you got an appointment?' I didn't answer the question, angling myself slightly away from the man. 'Good people to work for?'

'They're pretty decent.'

There was an obvious hesitation, not wanting to say the wrong thing. I turned back and looked him in the eye. 'Must be weird working with your dad, though? Don't think I could have ever done that.'

'My uncle,' he corrected me. 'And I don't really think about it.'

I offered a smile. 'Suppose it's not too bad if you get along. Your uncle's ex-police isn't he?'

We both saw the 4x4 sweep back into the yard, stopping outside of the portacabin. The man walked off, saying he'd leave me to it. He wasn't going to entertain my questions any further. The woman who got out had to be Amanda Mail.

She was the right age. She ignored me as she juggled with the keys and unlocked the door. I headed over, knocking before heading in.

'Can I help you?' she said.

'I hope so.' I closed the door.

She bent over, switching the electric radiator in the corner on. 'It'll soon warm up.'

The office space was tidy. Metal shelving was full with ring binders, all neatly marked with the paperwork they contained, a computer in the middle of her desk with its screen angled away from me.

'I would have been ready for you if you'd made an appointment,' she said, sitting down and placing a sandwich on the windowsill.

'I was passing.'

'I doubt that very much.'

I put my hands in my pocket. 'Is that how you welcome all potential new clients?'

'You don't just pass a place like this, and forgive me for saying this, you don't look like the usual sales-people we get knocking on the door.'

'You've got me.'

A grim smile on her face. 'You're with the old man who's been watching the place, right? You think I didn't notice him?'

'Not exactly.' The news was a surprise to me, but not all that surprising when I thought about it.

'Who is he?'

'Don Ridley.' I was looking for a reaction, but she didn't give me anything, no indication she knew the name. 'He died in a hit and run last week out in Paull.'

She fiddled with the mouse next to her computer keyboard. 'I'm sorry to hear that.'

The news had definitely made an impression and rattled her. She wasn't able to look me in the eye. 'I don't think it was an accident.'

'The police will decide that, surely?'

'That's where I have a problem.'

She pushed her chair out and stood up, nearly as tall as me. 'Who are you?'

'It doesn't matter who I am. Don Ridley, though, was a police officer when he was younger, a detective. He was around the same time as your brother. They worked a case together, John Gove?'

'I don't know the name,' she was lying, her eyes looking anywhere but at me.

'The Car Boot Murder thirty years ago, what did your brother tell you?'

'Get out of my office.'

'Where is he?'

'He won't want to talk to you.'

'Sure about that?'

'Absolutely sure.'

I leaned across the table, aware both of us had raised our voices. 'Did Don speak to him recently?' I didn't receive an answer. Instead, she looked over my shoulder to the door. I turned to see her son standing there, staring at me. There was no question he could physically throw me off the premises given the necessary encouragement.

'Just leave,' she settled for saying.

I took a pen out of my pocket and picked up the pad of Post-it notes and wrote down my name and number before throwing it back down onto the desk. 'Get your brother to give me a call.'

I brushed past her son and stepped outside. If I smoked, now would be the time to have a cigarette and think. It was old-school, but if I waited outside, Gary Mail would have to return at some point. I could doorstep him, find the words necessary to make him talk about the 1989 investigation, figure out how it connected to Don and the hit and run. If I could do that, I could return to Amsterdam, back to Marieke, a weight off my shoulders. A debt repaid.

My arm went up my back, twisted into an unnatural position, pain shooting through it and forcing me to scream out. Another hand grabbed the back of my head and a handful of hair. I was spun around, my face forced against the side of the portacabin. I closed my eyes as it was forced further into the rough surface, my legs pinned apart so I couldn't move. A male voice in my ear. Gary Mail's nephew.

'Who are you?'

'Fuck you.' Belligerence seemed to be my default setting, even when it really wasn't appropriate. Pulled back again, my head was thrust forward, bouncing off the wall's rough surface.

'Who sent you?'

'No one.' I managed to spit out. I moved my tongue around, tasting blood in my mouth. My face was on fire, stinging. The pressure released on me, it was an effort not to collapse down to the floor.

'Don't come back,' Mail's nephew said, walking away.

EIGHTEEN

Heavy traffic slowed my progress across the city. Lengthy road works near the centre were in the process of adding a new flyover and bridge to ferry pedestrians from the shopping area to the Fruit Market. No doubt it was all part of Grant Piercy's vision for the area. I pulled off the main road and parked up, needing to get out and move my shoulder around. My body ached from the warning Mail's nephew had given me. Ten years ago, I would have walked away unscathed, but not now. Touching my forehead, it was covered in several small marks from being ground into the rough portacabin wall. Back into my car and the crawling traffic, there was more than one way to get the information I needed.

I had a lead on Mail, but I had nothing on Forrester, seemingly the brains of the operation. Waiting for Gerard Branning to respond to my knock on his door, he was the person to speak to. He'd been around the investigation in 1989, however peripherally. The trick was to convince him to help me. He clearly didn't have any time for Natalie Okorie, or John Gove, and might not be willing to help. Branning slowly approached the door, an assortment of locks and chains removed before opening up. This time he was fully dressed, no sign of a hangover.

'No bacon this time, Joe?' He looked me up and down. 'The state of you.'

'I ran into a spot of trouble earlier.' I edged forward. 'I figured it was your turn to supply the food.'

'You should have listened to what I told you yesterday.'

He moved to close the door, but I'd discretely made sure my foot was in place to stop him from doing that. 'This is for Don.' We eyeballed each other on his doorstep and I gave him a small nod. I wanted to know about the rumours that had circulated following Gove's murder. I could understand his loyalty towards the police, but to my mind, Don's death transcended that. It was about the truth now, closure for everyone. 'I need your help.'

Branning looked at me, clearly weighing up if I was being sincere, before relenting and allowing me inside. I closed the door and followed him into the living room. He sat down in an armchair. There was no offer of a drink, no suggestion I should take a seat. I walked over to the window and looked out for a moment, a postman a few doors away. I turned back to face him, leaned against the windowsill.

It was down to business. 'I know the name of the two detectives who did the donkey work in relation to John Gove.' He didn't offer anything. 'You didn't tell me about Mail and Forrester.'

'You've done your homework.' He glanced at me. 'Also, you didn't ask me.'

'I'm asking now.'

Branning chewed the question over for a moment before answering. 'They were young lads looking for an arrest,' he said. 'They were inexperienced and maybe shouldn't have been given it, but it's a sink or swim type of job. They were ambitious. You worked with Don, so you're not naive about the reality of it. We've always had cutbacks and budget pressures. Like it or not, Gove was a drug dealer. No one gets a thank you for pushing resources at something like that.'

'He was still a victim.'

'Never any shortage of them around these parts.'

'How does reality stack up knowing Mail left the police soon afterwards? Didn't take Forrester long to get out, either?'

Branning's gaze levelled back on me. 'You are well-informed, Joe. Don always said you were good.'

His face didn't give anything away, but a slight shuffle in his chair told me I was making him uncomfortable. He drank from his mug next to him, playing for time. 'Not everyone is cut out or suitable for the job.'

'You said they were ambitious?'

'That doesn't necessarily equate to ability.'

'They were incompetent?'

'I didn't say that.'

Quite, I thought. His comments were guarded, deliberately so.

Branning wasn't going to tell me anything easily. We both turned as we heard the letterbox creak, a small thud as the day's post hit the floor.

'More bills, no doubt,' he said, glancing towards the door.

'What do you remember about Forrester and Mail?' I asked, wanting to keep him on track.

Branning picked up the mug from next to his chair again. 'They were cocky, as you'd expect, thought they knew more about the job than they did. There was a small gang of them throwing their weight around.' He shrugged. 'Not a crime to be that way when you're young, is it?'

'That depends.'

'On what?'

'If you were serious about your responsibility.' I had to pick my words carefully. I knew Branning was testing me, not so much a game, but trying to get a feeling as to how much he was prepared to share with me. I had to unlock things. 'It feels like it was a sloppy investigation to me,' I said.

'Is that so?'

'The car Gove was found in was stolen from a yard, right?'

'That's right.'

'But no one was ever arrested for it?'

'The place wasn't locked up properly, wasn't all that difficult to find the keys in the office.'

I drummed my fingers on the windowsill, holding Branning's stare, before changing the subject. 'I spoke to Coleman.'

'Bet he was pleased to hear from you?'

'He managed to keep his pleasure under wraps.'

'Was he willing to help you?'

I folded my arms, not answering, but you can't kid a kidder. Silence could break many people, make them want to fill the space by talking, but not a former-copper who knew the ropes. I took out the photograph Natalie Okorie had given me, wanting to see his reaction. 'Recognise him?' Branning didn't answer. He'd only given it a cursory glance. 'It's Gary Mail.'

If Branning was curious as to how I knew that, he didn't show it. 'I tried to talk to him at the family business, but his nephew wasn't keen on my line of questioning.' I pointed to my face. 'I was told not to bother.'

Branning squinted, examined the damage. 'Doesn't look too bad to me.'

'It was a warning. I'll survive.'

He glanced again at the photograph. 'Where did you get this?'

'Natalie Okorie.'

Branning shook his head. 'You're seeing things that aren't there. People like her have stirred the pot plenty over the years because it suits their own agenda.'

'She won't let this go. It's unfinished business for her after covering it thirty years ago.'

'The pretend journalist?' Branning smirked. 'I've asked around and she's a joke. What good is it being a journalist if you don't write for a paper where people can read it? All this rubbish about it being online. Don't make me laugh.' I went to speak, but he cut me off. 'We'll see how long she can make her daydream last.'

'You don't think she's serious?'

'Don't tell me you're getting pulled into her cult of do-gooders?'

'She wants to see justice done, too.'

'She wants a story.'

'We all want something.'

'I wouldn't trust her as far as I could throw her.'

I asked the question I really wanted an answer to. 'What about Forrester? Is he still around?'

'I heard he left for Australia. I'm going back years now. You're a bright lad with a computer no doubt. I'm sure you'll find him.'

'Maybe I'll try that.' I tried to keep the look of disappointment off my face. I could track down a phone number for him, I was sure, but there was no guarantee he would talk to me. If I could get myself in front of him, it would be a different matter.

Branning looked again at the photograph of Gary Mail. 'Seems to me that you've got something you want to say, Joe?'

'How about if I said I thought the police didn't do their job properly when it came to Gove?' I paused for a moment to make sure I had his full attention.'

'I'd say you've been listening too closely to fantasists like Natalie Okorie.'

'She's asking questions people don't want answering.'

Branning weighed up my words carefully, watching me, before speaking. 'Have you any idea how offensive your words are to me, how much I gave to the job over the years? I might not think the people you've mentioned were particularly committed detectives, but they don't deserve their reputations being raked over like this on the say so of some two-bit journalist.'

I disagreed with him. Justice hadn't been served, but I knew Don would have been hurting, too, at what was being suggested.

'I'd also say you'd need some serious evidence to back up such an offensive claim.' Branning stood up and moved towards the door.

'I won't leave it alone,' I said, following him. He bent down to collect the post. We were done, our conversation over. 'I don't care about reputations.'

'I warned Don and I'm warning you. Know this, Joe. You play with fire, you get burned. Your choice to make.'

NINETEEN

If Branning couldn't or wouldn't help me, I had to find a different angle of attack. I found an empty terminal in The History Centre, the city's archive that held back editions of the local newspaper. Getting to grips with the system, I brought up scans of the press reports around the date of John Gove's murder.

I wanted to know more about the car his body had been found in. Scanning the reports, it had been stolen the night before from a second-hand dealership on Beverley Road. Turning to the Internet, thinking I might find some information on the business via a nostalgia page, maybe a photograph, it would generate some names to research and follow. I was in luck. The dealership was still trading, it's website proudly saying it was a family business, still operating from the same premises it had opened in fifty years ago. Reading on, the business had been founded by Gordon Till, the man retiring in the mid-1990s. His son, Pete, had worked for the family business for over thirty years and was now in charge. I grabbed my coat and headed there.

Heading north along Beverley Road and away from the city centre, I let my mind wander back to the conversation with Branning. I knew enough to know it wasn't necessary personal when it came to dealing with people like him and he knew more than he was saying to me, I was sure. It felt like a test, one I'd only pass if I said the right thing to him. He'd been outraged, but not surprised, at what I'd implied about the police investigation into Gove's murder. Maybe he'd heard it before, but there was something there for me to pick away at. Mail and Forrester felt like dead ends at the moment, but that could change. Sometimes you get a lucky break, sometimes you need to ask the right questions at the right time. It was the nature of things, something I felt coming back to me all too easily.

Parking up opposite the car dealership, I looked around the area. It was boxed in by a selection of shops, a newsagent on one side, a fishing tackle shop on the other. Thirty or so vehicles were dotted around, a couple of expensive cars to the front, but the overall prices were modest. It was the kind of place

I'd be shopping if I was in the market to buy. I headed towards the car being washed by a teenager, earplugs in, paying me no attention. Waiting, he eventually noticed me and took a single earplug out. Rap music leaked out.

'Help you, mate?' he asked.

'Pete in today?'

'Office, mate,' he said, pointing to a concrete hub in the far corner of the yard, putting the earplug straight back in. I thought about mentioning the exceptional service promised on the signage, but thought better of it. The door of the office opened, a man in his fifties shrugging a large overcoat on as he walked across to me, a smile on his face. His white hair was swept back, the wind making it look wilder than he wanted it to.

He held his hand out as he approached. 'Joe Geraghty,' I said, taking it.

'Pete Till.'

'Very nice to meet you.' I smiled, but my name didn't ring any bells with him. He wasn't expecting a visit from me.

'Can I offer you some assistance today?'

'I certainly hope so.'

'Let's get ourselves some ideas, then.' Till was a practiced mover, quickly looking me over to work out what I was likely to be spending. He guided me towards the far corner behind the lad at work washing the cars at the front. 'We've got some excellent bargains over here.'

He'd decided I had no real money to spend, but the main thing was being out of sight. We wouldn't be disturbed.

'Petrol of diesel, Joe.' Till was talking, but I wasn't particularly listening. 'Something for the family, or are you looking for yourself?'

I pointed to the signage behind us. 'You've been here for a long time?'

'Just over fifty years as a business and we're still standing. We believe in looking after people. It's what makes the difference.'

'So where do you fit in? Your father started the business?'

Till paused, a quick glance at me before continuing. 'That's right, God rest his soul. I joined straight from school after washing the cars for pocket money in my spare time. Never left and here we are more than thirty years later.'

'Must have some stories to tell?' I said.

'Good and bad.'

'Haven't we all?'

'Very true.' Till smiled, humouring me.

'How about the one concerning John Gove from thirty years ago?' I watched as he took a step back, colour draining from his face, as he processed the name.

'Who are you?'

'Why would I need to be anyone?'

'You're not police,' he said. 'And you don't look much like a journalist to me.' Till went to push past me, but I blocked his move. 'I only need five minutes of your time.'

Till tried again, this time hands going towards my chest as he tried to find a route past. 'I've got nothing to say.'

I mirrored the move, telling him to calm down.

'Get out of my way.'

This time I was more forceful, pushing him to the rear of the car, out of sight. The kid with the earplugs in hadn't noticed. 'Gove's body was found in a car stolen from here,' I said.

'So what?'

'I want to know what happened.'

'Nothing happened. It was stolen.'

'This place was left unsecured.'

Fear flashed across his face. 'How do you know that?'

'I'm well-informed.' I told him why I was asking questions. 'I used to work with Don Ridley.'

'I can't help you.' He knew what had happened to Don, it was written all over his face. I pressed on. 'Which detectives did you speak to when the car was linked back to here?'

'I don't remember. It was a long time ago.'

'I'll refresh your memory, shall I? DC Forrester or DC Mail? One or the other, maybe both?'

'Probably. Sounds about right from memory.'

'You just said you couldn't remember.' Till ran his hand through his hair, increasingly aggitated by the questions. I wanted to keep at him, push harder. 'It's not a trick question. Who was it?'

'I'm doing my best.'

'Sounds like you're saying what you think I want to hear?'

'Not at all,' Till said, shaking his head. 'I don't even know what you want me to say. If I could help you, I would.'

I took a step back, eased off a touch. 'I want the truth, that's all.' Till leaned back against the car, not speaking. I tried a different question. 'Are you surprised they never got any one for the theft?'

'Cars get stolen every day. Not everyone gets them back, do they?'

'Did the police do a thorough job?'

'From memory, I'd say so.'

I moved closer to Till, leaned in, letting him know I was turning things up again. 'I keep coming back to the same thought, though. Why was it stolen from here? Why this place? Why not another car dealer?'

Till shook his head, his voice lower. 'I don't know.'

The office phone sounded, amplified by a speaker close to us. We both looked up at it, the moment broken. The lad washing the cars paid it no attention. I took out a pen and paper, wrote my number down. 'Think about it and give me a call.'

Till hurried past me, didn't stop to look back. I stayed where I was, hands in my pocket, watching as the office door closed behind him. Sometimes you have to judge when to stop asking questions and let things play out of their own accord. We all make decisions that turn out to have unintended consequences. I couldn't prove anything, but I could feel it. I wondered if Pete Till had made such a decision thirty years ago. It was a gut reaction, but the degree to which I'd agitated him wasn't normal. He didn't re-emerge from the office, but I'd rattled his cage. Instinct told me he had something to hide and would do something about it. I was far from finished with the man.

TWENTY

The knock on the door was late. I pushed myself up and off the bed and headed over, pausing before opening up, unsure if it was a good idea or not to do it here. I stared back at Coleman who nodded, asked if he could come in, I stepped to one side and let him enter.

I kept my eye on him as he walked straight over to the window at the far end of the room. 'Some view you've got here, Joe. Always enjoy being able to see the bridge.' He turned and smiled. 'Almost worth paying for.'

'It's somewhere to sleep and shower.' I'd also spent time staring out of the window at the Humber Bridge, five or so miles east of us. Lots had changed in the city since John Gove had been murdered thirty years ago, lots had changed since I'd left five years ago, but some things offered certainty and continuity.

Coleman held out the laptop he'd brought with him. 'It's my daughter's, so don't break it.'

I placed it down the side of the bed and thanked him. When he'd called to set up the meeting, I'd asked him to supply me with one, partly-so I could read around things more easily, partly-so I could test him.

Coleman walked over to the table in the middle of the room and picked the travel kettle up. 'It's polite to offer guests a drink.'

I took it from him and walked through to the bathroom to fill it.

'I thought you might have taken my advice and gone home,' Coleman shouted out at me.

'Not my style.' I walked back into the room and set the kettle going. Coleman pointed to my face. 'You look rough.'

'I didn't sleep well.'

'Rough pillows you've got.'

I ignored the comment, pouring the drinks instead. My face was settling down, the stinging giving way to itching as the damage Mail's nephew inflicted started to heal.

'Like I said, you never change.'

'I owe Don.' It was more complex than that, but it was the bottom line. We both took our drinks back over to the window, looked out over the city once again.

Coleman cut in. 'Spare me it, Joe. I get it, I really do. I had a quick look at things last night, asked around a bit.'

I couldn't resist a smile. 'I knew you would.' Rightly or wrongly, an unsolved murder case was always going to be too much to ignore for a detective. Especially one who might want to progress up the career ladder.

'Don't push your luck.' Coleman sipped his coffee, wincing at the lack of taste from the complimentary sachets and dried milk. 'I haven't seen everything, but reading between the lines, it wasn't a brilliant investigation by any stretch of the imagination. It wasn't thorough and things weren't followed up as they should have been.'

'What about the stolen car Gove was found in?' I was thinking about my conversation with Pete Till, the dealer who owned the place it had been taken from, how he'd reacted to my questions.

'What about it?'

'It was an obvious lead, right? Why wasn't more effort put into finding out who stole it?' I didn't need to lay it out for Coleman. He understood my point. If the police got lucky, it was a direct line to the person who'd killed Gove and stuffed him into the car boot. Even if it didn't, it was someone to lean on, someone to press for more information. Things never happened in a vacuum. I sipped at my coffee, finding it as tasteless and bitter as he did. Speaking to me about a police investigation wasn't an easy decision for him to make, so he had to commit to a conversation about John Gove willingly. 'There must have been suspects back in the day?' I suggested. 'Someone who stood out?'

Coleman shook his head, said it wasn't really the case. 'The assumption was it was drugs-related, a turf war or whatever gone wrong. Known dealers were spoken to, but nothing came of it. The investigation just fizzled out. Way it goes sometimes.'

I knew how it went, but put the thought to one side. 'The two detectives who investigated Gove's murder left the police pretty quickly afterwards,' I said to him. 'Seems to me that it was a mistake to let two young detectives effectively run such a thing.'

'All a matter of opinion.'

He wasn't biting. 'Interesting that a current MP was the ranking officer, though.'

'He was probably under pressure, too. Maybe he was just let down by poor performance from others?'

It wasn't an unreasonable point. 'Handy, though.'

'Might be the truth?'

'No one seems to have a high opinion of Jagger.'

'You've spoken to Branning, then?' He glanced at me. 'Think I wouldn't find out?'

I nodded, letting him have that one.

'You don't need me to tell you about men like Branning. You're always going to get those old-school sorts who don't like ambitious, younger people taking the jobs they think are rightfully theirs. They never see them as proper coppers, all that bullshit. Jagger clawed his way up and has built a second career. Fair play to him.'

'Sometimes the old school knows best?'

'There's space for everyone. You need the plodders like Branning and you need those who want to climb the ladder. Sometimes you even need the dickheads. It's a broad church.'

I took his empty mug from him and placed it on the table next to the kettle. 'You didn't drop by for a shit cup of coffee.'

'Dave Bolder.'

He had my interest. I'd asked him to look into the man who Don had tried to talk to just before his death. I knew Bolder had disappeared from his flat immediately afterwards. It wasn't right, another thread to be pulled at. My mobile vibrated in my pocket. I ignored it, focusing on Coleman.

'You didn't get this from me, ok?'

I took the envelope off him, shook out a photograph and a Missing Person report, glanced at the details.

'There's some basic information,' Coleman said, giving me the background. 'Minor record when he was younger, and reading between the lines, problems with alcohol in the past. Doesn't look like he's bothered us for a while, though.'

'Probably just grew up,' I said, staring at the photograph. It showed him with a pink paper hat on, a smile on his face, sitting at the Christmas table. Age-wise, it fitted with what his neighbour had told me.

'Still working with Natalie Okorie?'

The question had been delivered casually, but it was anything but. He was keeping tabs on things and my movements. I put the envelope and contents down on the bed. 'I'm not working with her.' I wasn't sure what our relationship was, but I felt the need to hedge my bets. 'We've spoken, but that's it.' My card was being marked.

'Tread carefully around her.' Coleman passed over a scrap of paper, this time handwritten. Unofficial. 'You might want to talk to Bolder's sister. She reported him missing a couple of days ago.'

The wheels sometimes turned slowly, Bolder no doubt just one of many reported missing, not enough resources within the system to really care or help. I went to take the piece of paper, but Coleman's hand clamped mine on top of it.

'You report back to me on this, Joe. Is that clear?'

I nodded and he relaxed his grip. There was always a price to pay for information. Like with Natalie Okorie, I was being asked to pick a side, go to places where others couldn't necessarily go.

I pointed to my face. 'I got this from trying to talk to Gary Mail.' Coleman didn't say anything or make any move to warn me about harassing members of the public. He remained impassive. 'I'm told Forrester moved away, but I wouldn't mind having a chat with him myself.' If he was offering a deal, I had requirements, too. 'Can you look into him for me?'

'You're pushing your luck, Joe.'

'Was the investigation corrupt?' Coleman didn't respond. It was something on my mind, the direction the wind was blowing in. The fact Forrester and Mail had both left the police so soon afterwards didn't sit right. 'Which way will you jump if that's the case?'

'Don't labour under the apprehension here that we're colleagues,' he said. 'The extent of things is that if you have pertinent information, you give it to me. Is that clear? You mention my name anywhere, particularly to Okorie, and I'll personally run you out of town.'

TWENTY-ONE

I knew how I looked, appearing out of nowhere on her doorstep. I had one shot at convincing her, one card to play. 'I'm a private investigator,' I said, knowing it wasn't quite the truth, but close enough. 'I need to speak to you about your brother and why he's missing.' It didn't feel good to stand on her doorstep and tell her I was the only person likely to help her, her brother one of countless individual cases the police wouldn't be able to deal with. 'You can help me, too.'

She was wary, but desperate enough to let me into her house. It was a tidy mid-terrace, two-up two-down. Sitting down in the living room, it was too hot, the small room overheated by a gas fire and Sylvanian Families figures on every spare surface. Sheila Bolder sat down opposite me. I guessed she was pushing towards her late-sixties, slightly older than her brother.

'Are you looking for my brother?'

'Not directly,' I had to tell her. 'Does the name Don Ridley mean anything to you?'

She thought about it before shaking her head. 'I don't think so.'

'He was a detective. Retired now. We used to work together.' I took out the photograph I'd taken of Don from his cottage and held it up for her.

'My brother wasn't in any trouble. He'd put all that behind him.'

'I'm not suggesting that at all.' She glanced at the photograph, but I didn't detect she was lying to me.

'He found himself in trouble a bit when he was younger, mainly because of drinking and being homeless, but that's a long time ago.'

I looked at the photograph she'd passed me of her brother. It showed a man in his early-sixties, skin like leather and a pale complexion, missing teeth in the smile. Old before his time, but sitting in a pub I didn't recognise, he was clearly happy, a collection of empty glasses on the table. 'Can I keep this for now, please?' She nodded that I could. 'You reported Dave missing?' I asked, getting back to it.

'That's right.' She took her time, her decision to make as to how much she wanted to say. 'He hadn't returned my calls,' she said, 'so I went to his flat, see if I could set my mind at rest. I thought he might have just been out somewhere, or maybe his phone had no credit on it, something like that.'

'Did you speak to his neighbours?'

'Just an elderly gentleman who wasn't much help. He said Dave hadn't been around for a few days, but he wasn't really interested.'

It was probably the same man I'd spoken to. 'I'm sorry to be so blunt, but how about where he might have gone? Maybe he's with friends, or a girlfriend?'

She shook her head. 'There's nothing like that. Dave's a quiet man, keeps himself to himself.'

'Anywhere he might have headed for if he left the city? A favourite place, something like that?'

'Nothing springs to mind.'

I smiled, told her it was ok before changing direction with the questions. 'Has he been in the flat for long?'

'A couple of months, that's all. He'd been back in the homeless hostel in the city centre, but I was pleased he was getting straight again. I don't think he's happy about being so high up, but it's warm and dry, a fresh start for him.'

'Always lived in Hull, has he?'

'Never left, like me.'

I smiled, pleased she was on safer ground. I needed her to talk freely. I shuffled into a more comfortable position, leaned forward. 'Must have been tough for him being homeless?'

'I still feel guilty that I wasn't able to help him more.' She explained that her husband had served in the Army, his job taking them around Europe to various military bases

'Did he have any worries recently?'

She thought about it, starting to speak, before stopping herself. She glanced at the newspaper next to her, something about her changing. 'You mentioned a detective?'

'Don Ridley,' I repeated the name, looking her in the eye. She fell silent, the sound of a ticking of a clock coming from somewhere in the room.

She didn't look at me as she spoke, her voice low and hesitant. 'Dave said a detective had tried to speak to him.'

I sat up straight a tingle of excitement, knowing where this was heading. 'Did they manage to speak to each other?'

She nodded, her thought process catching up with mine, ignoring the question I'd asked. 'The old detective who died out at Paull?'

I glanced again at the newspaper on the arm of her chair. There was no doubt some coverage of the story inside it, maybe even of the funeral itself. 'We used to be partners, so I'm back for the funeral. I'm trying to finish things off for him.' She started to cry, shaking her head, joining the dots for herself. I stood up and found a box of tissues, handing it to her, giving her a moment before speaking again. 'It's why I want to find your brother. It's important.'

She blew her nose and dabbed at her eyes. 'Look at the state of me.'

'Perfectly understandable.'

She held out the tissue box for me to place back where I'd got them from. 'Do you know what they talked about?' I asked.

She shook he head. 'I could tell he was worried by it.'

'When did he tell you this?'

'He came here the day he went missing.'

She started to cry again. I quickly passed the tissues back to her, knowing there was more to come, knowing I had to keep going with the questions. I asked my next one quietly, prompting her. 'Did your brother mention John Gove to you, The Car Boot Murder, thirty years ago?'

There were more tears before she took in a deep breath, a slight nod of the head. 'He wanted to use my tablet, but he didn't know how to close it down properly. Call me nosy, but I had a look after he left.'

'You could see the stories he'd been reading?'

'I shouldn't have looked.'

'We all would if it was someone we cared about, if we thought we could help them.' She didn't respond. 'Where was Dave living thirty years ago?' I asked. 'Can you remember?'

The answer was almost a whisper. 'He was homeless.'

I let the answer wash over me, understanding the implications. Don had always known there'd been a witness to the murder of John Gove. He'd always known about Dave Bolder. I wondered what else had he had taken to his grave with him. It suggested several more questions I couldn't yet answer, but I was in no doubt his recent visit to Bolder's new flat had spooked the man enough that he'd decided to run. Maybe that had been a wise decision. Bolder might be in his sixties, but I suspected sleeping on the streets never left you. I wondered if he had it in him to sleep rough again. It would be one way of going off the grid. I had to find him.

'Dave told me he'd seen something he shouldn't have.'

I closed my eyes, knowing it was the confirmation I needed. Dave Bolder had witnessed John Gove's murder.

TWENTY-TWO

I pressed the buzzer on the hostel door and waited. Getting no answer, I tried again. Eventually, the intercom spluttered into life, a voice asking what I wanted. 'I'm looking for someone.'

There was a pause before the female voice responded. 'Aren't we all, love?'

'I think you can help me,' I said. 'Dave Bolder.' There was no reply. 'I'm worried he's in trouble. I only need five minutes of your time.' I stepped back to make sure the cameras above the door could see me clearly, that I wasn't a threat. It was a cold night. I shivered, thinking about the poor bastards sleeping on the streets. The door opened, a woman aged around forty staring out at me, Erin Riordan the name on her badge.

'I've just left his sister's house,' I said, taking the photograph I had of Dave Bolder out. I passed it over to her. 'I'm a friend of the family.' It wasn't quite the truth, not quite a lie.

She was wary, unsure if I was spinning her a line. I couldn't blame her for that, but she eventually relented, moving away from the door. 'You best come in.'

I followed her through the building and into the kitchen where she flicked the kettle on. 'Thanks for your time,' I said. 'It's appreciated.'

'I doubt I can help you.' She looked around for a clean mug. Not finding one, she picked a dirty mug out of the sink sand rinsed it out. 'Tea or coffee?'

'I'm fine, thanks.'

She threw a teabag into her mug. 'I can't give out personal information, you understand?'

'Of course.' The kitchen was basic, chipped paint on the wall, a staff rota pinned to it. I looked at the pile of dirty plates and cutlery. 'Want a hand washing up?'

She shook her head. 'That's very kind, but there's no need.'

I ran the hot water tap regardless and went to work. 'Dave's been reported missing and I know he was a regular here until recently before moving into his own flat.'

'That's right.' She looked me over. 'Why isn't he there?'

'He hasn't been seen for a while. I spoke to his neighbour.'

'We helped get him set-up,' she said, grabbing a tea towel. 'We made sure he had furniture, all the white goods he needed. Made sure he received the necessary support. Be a shame if it doesn't work out for him, as he was ready to move on and start over. Frankly, it's nice to feel like there's a success story from time to time. Good for all our morale. I'd hate to have that ripped away for all concerned.'

My card was being marked again and it wasn't subtle. 'I want to get him home,' I said. 'But I'm going to need some help.'

'Who are you, really?' she asked, looking straight at me. 'I know his family and there's nothing beyond a sister.'

'I'm a private investigator.'

'You don't look like one, if you don't mind me saying.'

'I've seen better days.' It felt pointless even trying to spin someone like Riordan a story. Her manner told me she didn't swallow any bullshit. It would have to be the truth. 'He hasn't done anything wrong, but I think he witnessed something serious a number of years ago.' I put the scourer down. 'Do you remember The Car Boot Murder thirty years ago?' It took her a moment to catch-up, a small nod. 'I think Dave was bedding down in the car park that night, maybe saw it happen.'

'Any proof of that?'

'He's gone to ground.'

'That's not proof.'

'It's not normal, either.'

Riordan stewed on that before speaking. 'Why should he trust you?'

It was a good question. 'Because this isn't going away.' I explained about Don and his death. I picked the scourer up and went back to work again on the pile of dishes next me. 'I'm the only who's going to help him.' She didn't respond, but I knew I'd made my point. 'Would he come back here if he was looking for a bed, just a one-off type of thing?'

'Doesn't really work like that,' she said. 'He can just turn up for a bed, but it comes with strings attached. He'd effectively have to talk to us, agree to a plan to get himself moving forward again. There are strings attached.'

I carried on washing up, understanding the point she was making to me. I didn't expect Dave Bolder to go back into the system. It felt more like he was lying low. 'How about informally?' I asked. 'Just a bit of help for a night or two.' I made sure I was looking at her as I asked the question. 'Off the books.'

'That would be against the rules.'

'I agree.'

'Are the police looking for him?'

'For what it's worth.'

She put her mug down on the counter, picked up a tea towel and started to dry the items I'd washed. 'We've got no money, they've got no money,' she said. 'It's a shit show if I'm being honest with you.'

'Doing more with less?' I said, echoing what Coleman had said to me about his job.

'That's about the size of it.'

'Must be tough out there with the bad weather coming?' We both looked to the door as an alarm went off, shouting from another part of the building. Another member of staff hurried past the door. 'All part of the job?'

'Constant fire-fighting.'

More noise from down the corridor snapped us out of the conversation. 'I should go and help,' she said. 'It's what they pay me for.'

I watched her go before picking up a piece of paper and scribbling my number down, just in case. I also took out what money I had on me, £30, and placed it next to the kettle. I hoped it would be seen for the gesture it was, not some kind of bribe in return for information. It was clear to me that the woman knew more about Dave Bolder and his whereabouts than she'd told me. It wouldn't be a surprise to learn he was staying in the hostel all along, rules or not, but I wanted him to speak to me willingly, even if the clock was ticking.

TWENTY-THREE

I stared at my face in the hotel room mirror, clumps of my beard sitting in the sink. I recognised the face staring back at me. Maybe it had been a disguise of sorts, but removing it was a sign of getting serious. Scrapping underneath my chin and around my face with the razor, careful not to catch the marks left by Mail's nephew at the haulage yard, I was making decisions that would have consequences and repercussions. I had Coleman's attention, but like with Natalie Okorie, his help had a price tag attached. Instinct told me I didn't want to be in his debt, but he could open doors I couldn't. Another mark in the debt ledger. Things were starting to weigh on me.

Finishing off, I walked over to the window and looked out across the River Hull, the Fruit Market a short hop away. The moon lit up patches of the water, dark black puddles reflecting back to me. It was where I'd find Ian Jagger tonight, his Twitter account giving me the details of a *Hit The North* event in a bar owned by Grant Piercy. I'd tried once to speak to him and failed, but this time I would be ready. I needed to rattle his cage, see what happened. The event was an invite-only reception for cultural dignitaries and VIPs and security would be even tighter after I'd slipped in previously. I didn't rate my chances of getting lucky twice, but scrolling through his Twitter feed, I noted Jagger was trying to give up smoking, multiple posts encouraging people to join him and signposting to help schemes in the region. A plan was forming.

I was tired, but momentum was important, the need to keep moving and asking questions. Grabbing my coat, I headed out. Walking past restaurants and bars, I glanced inside seeing they were largely empty, waiting staff standing around. A handful of people mingled about on Humber Street, no one paying me any attention.

Standing outside of Piercy's bar, I peered in, what sounded to be a great party under way. Music and the sound of laughter escaped when the security staff opened the doors for guests to come and go. I'd checked the place out online. The walls inside had been taken back to bare brick, a contrast with the shiny chrome of the bar, expensive bottles of spirits gleaming behind it. I knew there was a large black and white print above the bar showing the area in its pomp. It showed large stacks of sacks piled high in the street, workers with cigarettes in mouths loading them into numerous small industrial vans and onto open back trucks, the image dated in the 1960s. Looking around, that world had all but been erased. Piercy's vision was about the leisure spend, not the back-breaking warehouse work that once characterised the area.

I found a waiting spot at the mouth of a dark alleyway opposite the bar. With nothing else to do, I brooded, thinking about the implications of what I knew about the police investigation into John Gove's murder. Turning it over in my mind, the investigation had undoubtedly been sloppy, no credible suspects identified, let alone arrested and charged. Yet I'd already identified a witness. Maybe Gove had upset a bigger fish in the criminal world, maybe a more serious drug dealer than his criminal record suggested and he'd trod on the wrong toes. I wasn't sure if I believed that or not. In reality, I was struggling to form a clear answer, but murdering someone if they were strictly small time was far from a proportional response.

I watched as a man approached the door to the bar, immediately looking out of place. It took me a moment, darkness making it difficult to confirm, but I was watching Pete Till, the car dealer talking to the security team. He kept his head down as the one in charge moved away, hand to his ear as he spoke into his equipment. I wanted to head across, but held my ground. Eventually, the security team cleared him to go inside, the crowd swallowing him up. It raised more questions.

I stayed where I was for almost half an hour in the cold, starting to seize up before Jagger emerged from the bar. He looked both ways along the street, checking no one was watching, before taking a packet of cigarettes out of his pocket. I smiled, knowing I had him. Jagger walked across the street, staring into a shop window at a selection of upcycled furniture and vintage clothes. I headed across to him.

'Nice items,' I said, 'but a bit pricey for me.' His face remained neutral as he tried to place me. 'Joe Geraghty.' I offered my hand.

A small nod of the head. 'I assume you're in town for Don's funeral?'

'Just pleased I could make it back.'

'I was unable to get there, but I hear it went well.'

'Surprised you couldn't clear your diary for it.' I pulled the cigarette out of his mouth and let if fall to the floor before stamping it out. 'They'll be the death of you if you're not careful.'

'You sound like you've got something on your mind, Mr Geraghty?'

'Joe's fine.'

'We don't know each other.'

'Not yet.'

'With respect, and I'm sorry for your loss, but there's no real need for us to know each other.'

Jagger made a move to head away from me, but I blocked him off. 'We need to talk.' I guided him towards the alleyway opposite the venue he'd just left. Taking my mobile out, I accessed the voicemail I needed. 'I think you should hear this. It's a message Don left for me just before he died.'

Jagger listened, his face neutral before passing the handset back to me. 'I'm not sure what you expect me to say. I understand Don's death is being looked into and there's no evidence to say it was anything more than an accident.'

'I don't buy that.'

'It's not a case of whether you buy it or not. You're not investigating what happened.'

'I'm planning on sticking around for a while.'

'I can't imagine there's much for you here.'

'Don wanted to speak to me about John Gove.' I searched his face for a tell, recognition that the name had struck home. 'The Car Boot Murder. Never solved. Your investigation.'

'I remember.'

'I was too late to talk to Don, and that's my weight to bear, but I'm not letting it go.'

Jagger took a moment, looked at me. 'Don was obviously important to you. I understand that, but I say this genuinely to you, don't get involved. It's not how this works.'

'You let two inexperienced Detective Constables lead the investigation.'

'I followed the orders I was given.'

'Because no one cared about someone like John Gove?'

'Not at all.'

'Bullshit. There wasn't much pressure put on to get a result, was there?'

A smile spread across Jagger's face. 'I'd say you've watched one too many TV dramas.' He pointed at me. 'Tread very carefully here, both in what you say and what you do. You might think you're a detective, but you're nothing of the sort. You enjoy no special privileges in the eyes of the law.'

I smiled at the comment. 'I want to talk to Forrester and Mail.'

'They're no longer serving police officers, so I say very clearly that you shouldn't go bothering members of the public. There are ways of doing things and that would certainly be the wrong way. Am I being clear?'

'What's the right way? Maybe you should talk to your cousin, see what he has to say about things?'

'You think I haven't heard that one before? Next you'll be accusing me of underhand tactics and suggesting he benefits in some way from position? Everything's above board and you'll find he's extremely valued when it comes to this city and its future.'

'Maybe I should speak to Natalie Okorie who was around back then, see what she has to say about things, see what she knows and remembers?'

Jagger smiled. 'Don't worry about her. She's in regular touch with my office, asking questions. She's like a toothache you can't quite shake off, but one you learn to live with.'

'How about John Gove's girlfriend around that time? His father spoke about her, but she doesn't seem to feature?'

'There wasn't one.'

Gove's father had said he'd been dumped, so maybe Jagger was correct, if hardly thorough. 'Talking of things you can't quite shake,' I said. 'Where do you stand on coincidences?'

'I don't follow.'

'The actual car used in the Car Boot Murder. It was stolen from a local dealership, right?'

'That's right.'

'Why is Pete Till at the event tonight?' I asked, pointing to the bar. 'Hard to see what business he could have.'

'Evening, gentleman.'

We both turned to the alleyway entrance, looking at where the voice had come from. Grant Piercy stared back at us, two burly security personnel behind him, paying more attention to their ear-pieces than looking at me.

'Your wife is looking for you. Seems she wants a word about that charity event you're working on.' Piercy gestured to him. 'My lads will get you where you need to be.'

Jagger nodded his agreement before talking to me. 'Let the police do their work and I'll report back to you. If any new evidence in relation to John Gove comes to light, it'll be assessed, and if necessary, acted upon.'

I stared at Piercy, watching Jagger and the security team disappear back towards the event.

Piercy stepped forward. 'I thought I'd made myself clear.'

'Things change.'

'You think having a shave and smartening yourself up makes you legitimate in some way, that I'm going to tolerate your questions? Look around you. People are having a good time tonight because of people like me and Ian and the work we do. You don't get to walk in, smash things up and then simply disappear again. It doesn't work like that.'

'You don't think an unsolved murder is important?'

'I don't give a shit. It's the way it is and it's none of my business. The police will do their job, end of discussion. You leave it alone.' He pocketed his mobile, focused back on me. 'What I care about is this city, making sure it reaches its potential and being the best it can be for everyone.'

Fine words, but he was beginning to piss me off with his modern-day philanthropist routine. 'Helps if you turn a profit, though?'

'You take the risks, you reap the rewards.'

'A rather simplistic way of viewing things,' I said. Piercy made a show of looking me over, emphasising the fact he was physically bigger and stronger, a pantomime show of intimidation I wasn't buying. 'Must help when your cousin is the local MP?'

'I think you overestimate just how much power he holds when it comes to public money. Have you any idea how much oversight there is?' Piercy made a show of shaking his head for my benefit, wanting to make it clear I hadn't landed a blow on him. 'He's a decent man who doesn't deserve you hacking away at him alongside people like Natalie Okorie. It's disgraceful.'

'That's my decision to make.'

'Maybe so, but making a fuss over a deal drug dealer everyone has forgotten about is in no one's interest and will only cause you trouble.'

'Are you threatening me?'

Piercy leaned in closer to me. 'I don't need to threaten you.'

TWENTY-FOUR

I stayed where I was for a moment, watching Piercy walk back across the road to his bar, phone to his ear. The party inside the bar continued, guests coming and going. I'd rattled Jagger and was far from finished with him. Pushing myself off the wall, I buried my hands in my pocket and walked away, leaving the Fruit Market behind.

Crossing the dual carriageway, I dodged taxis ferrying drinkers back to the suburbs. The heart of the city centre was very different. Loud music leaked out of pub doors, adverts above doors promising cheap drinks and exciting entertainment. A small number of drunks staggered by, one or two trying and failing to make eye contact, others chanting, some eating takeaways. Spotlights illuminated the City Hall and Maritime Museum in Queen Victoria Square, grand buildings, but hidden away in the shadows an increasing number of the homeless huddled together in shop doors for warmth.

I thought again about Jagger and the fact he was a Member of Parliament. There was no way he'd want an old case in the news, especially if that investigation was far from sound. It wasn't difficult to make the leap and link things together. Piercy was essentially a property developer trying to cash in on the city's new direction. He could talk all he liked about building the city up, his commitment to culture, but it was about the bottom line. Follow the money.

Maybe it was a sixth-sense for danger, maybe it was just experience, but I tuned in to footsteps behind me. I'd been hearing them, but not processing the sound, since leaving the Fruit Market. Instinctively, I slowed, wanting the person to pass me, put me at my ease. The footsteps eased off, too. Looking into a shop window, I wanted to use the natural moonlight as a mirror, maybe see a silhouette of whoever was behind me, get an idea of how I was going to settle this. The angles weren't right, so I increased my pace. So did the person behind me. It put me on edge, but it also sharpened me up. Knowing the area on the corner of Jameson Street would be busy, youngsters hanging around outside of McDonald's. I made for it, steadily increasing my pace.

It was the right type of cover to allow me to stand still for a moment, pretend to be looking in and contemplating the length of the queue. I dragged the moment out, taking my time, even checking my mobile before deciding to set off again.

Nothing happened. Unsure of which way to head, I carried on in the same direction. The train station and a likely congregation of people meant I could lose whoever was following me. Listening, the footsteps were still there, but I had a choice. I could turn and face the person, bring about a confrontation. Anything could happen.

There was another possibility, taking back control and confirming the suspicions that were taking root in my head. My mind ticking over and running the calculations, I walked along Jameson Street, hoping my recollection of the area was sound. Reaching Chapel Street, I immediately veered left and hit a jog, needing a small window of opportunity. Twenty or so yards further on and an open arch way on my left opened up into a small parking area for the nearby businesses. Once the person following me realised I was out of sight, it would become obvious where I was, but that was the point. I wanted them to follow.

Large industrial bins had been pushed up against both sides of the walls in the archway. Quickly looking around, there was a small pile of timber on the floor next to the bin. Picking a piece up, I moved back into the shadows of a dark corner, controlling my breathing. Regardless of how cautious my follower might be, I wouldn't be seen until they were at least level with me. It gave me an advantage.

I heard footsteps approaching, growing louder, but slowing in pace. I was being hunted. My eyes adjusted to the darkness as I waited, staying still and silent. The figure walked past where I was. Tall and broad, definitely male with a cap pulled down to obscure his features, it meant I couldn't guess how old he was. My first instinct was that it was one of the men I'd seen at the Fruit Market providing security for Piercy.

I stepped out, and struck him on the side of the head with the piece of timber, quickly following through with another strike, this time to his stomach. He staggered down to the floor, crashing into a bin. I was down quickly too, bringing my weight onto his back so he couldn't move. Spreading my legs to pin his body down, one hand went to his head to keep it pressed down on the floor, the other went to his pockets. I pulled out a mobile phone, quickly transferring it to my own pocket as he struggled underneath me. I pushed his head further down towards the floor as he started to issue threats, telling me what he planned to do to me once he was free of my grip.

Light flooded into the area, blinding me. We both shouted out and I jumped up, hand covering my eyes. A voice shouted out. Disorientated, it took me a moment to realise it was a security guard, a dog barking alongside him. The man beneath me started to move, but I wasn't going to stick around. The situation in front of the guard would paint me as the aggressor. The man who'd followed me started to haul himself up, so I pushed him hard against the bins, sending him back to the floor. Turning away as the security guard closed in and shouted out, but I didn't stop as I headed for the exit and the street, running off quickly.

TWENTY-FIVE

Walking back to the hotel, the cold night air felt that little more brutal. I just wanted to lie down and think in my hotel room, let sleep take me for a few hours.

I'd talked myself into trouble, waded too far out to head back to the shore.

The receptionist stopped me as I headed for the lift, pointing to the chairs in the corner, a small waiting area. I tensed and turned around. Natalie Okorie was waiting for me.

'What are you doing here?'

Natalie Okorie stood up, shrugged. 'I thought it was time we had another chat, Joe.'

'I'm tired.' I wasn't in the mood.

She nodded towards the lift. 'You must have a kettle in your room?'

'Fine.' I rubbed my face, mumbled to myself before heading to where she'd suggested. I just wanted to get it over with. We stood next to each in silence, the lift making its way to my floor. The card opened my door. Fumbling for the light switch, I blocked off the doorway, not letting Okorie see inside. My bag of clothes had been emptied onto the bed, drawers in the room pulled out and thrown to the floor. She nudged her way past me regardless.

'You've been upsetting people, Joe?'

'Seems to be a lifestyle choice for me.'

I closed the door behind me, making sense of it. Someone had been inside and they hadn't been subtle about what they'd done. I quickly ran the calculation in my head. I'd asked questions around the city about an unsolved murder, something which was always going to attract attention and made a nuisance of myself. This was the result. Some people would always want such a thing to remain buried. The implicit threat from being followed and having my room turned-over was that I should mind my own business or there'd be further consequences. It was an assumption, but it felt like the right one. It wouldn't have been difficult to find me. Watching Okorie move around the room, she'd found me, too. The city wasn't that big.

Picking my clothes up, I put them back into the bag, starting to restore some order to the room. It didn't take long to put the furniture back to how it should be. There wasn't much to rake through, but a message had been sent.

'Someone went to some effort to get in here,' Okorie said. 'And they found you.'

'So did you.'

'That was the easy bit. Only took a few phone calls.'

'I'm back for a funeral. I didn't feel the need to hide.'

'You were naive.'

'Really?'

'Maybe you need some help?'

I looked at her. 'Is that right?'

'You know how it is.'

I checked the bathroom for any damage, telling her sometimes it's better to be a lone wolf. My toiletries bag had been tossed, toothbrush and deodorant can on the floor.

Okorie stood behind me, checking the bathroom for herself. 'You don't believe that about being a lone wolf, Joe. 'You were a sportsman for a start and then you worked with Don and Sarah. You've always been a team player.'

I shook my head. 'You don't know anything about me.'

'I know enough.' She headed for the door and opened it. 'I want to show you something.'

'Where?'

'Not far from here. It's important.'

I closed the door behind myself and followed her back to the lift, knowing I was being played but unable to resist. I could have just stayed in my room, locked myself away, but it was the last place I wanted to be at the moment. I stopped to ask the receptionist if anyone had enquired after me earlier in the day, any messages waiting for me, tried to make it sound as casual as possible. Telling me she'd only just come on shift, she checked, finding nothing. Thanking her, I followed Okorie out into the night.

We headed in the direction of The Deep, outdoor lighting illuminating it. The Tidal Barrier watched the estuary, making sure no harm would come to the city. Looking across to the Fruit Market, lights were on the apartments sold to those with deep enough pockets to live there. Okorie didn't speak as she led me to the waterfront, leaning against the barrier and staring out.

'I'm serious about The Northern News Alliance you know,' she said, turning to look at me. 'I'm not playing some sort of game here.'

'Good for you.' I put my head down against the cold wind, nodded to the lone dog walker as she headed past you. The path led to a large housing estate built on a former dock, prone to flooding. Okorie took out her e-cigarette, starting to vape with a plume of smoke circling above her and away into the night sky.

'I've come back to make a difference,' she said. 'It's a choice. I've got unfinished business here, too.'

'Very noble of you.'

Okorie laughed. 'You're full of shit, you know that?'

'Is that so?'

'You can't even say it.'

'Say what?'

'You can't even admit that you're still fired up by what you're doing. It's written all over your face, Joe. Investigating and resolving stories, it's what you're good at and what fires you up.' She paused for a moment before hammering out the words with her fist on the barrier. 'Justice and truth.'

Turning to look at the outline of the Humber Bridge in the distance, I knew she was right.

'Look at your face,' Okorie said. 'Look at the state of your hotel room. Yet you're still here, talking to me. You're fired up, but you've got to decide if you're stepping up to the plate or not.'

I turned back to her, a grim smile on my face, knowing she was trying to get under my skin. I couldn't resist taking the bait. 'You don't think I'm doing enough?'

'That's for you to decide, but if you want my honest opinion, you're not doing anywhere near enough.'

I folded my arms, weighing up her words carefully, not wanting to react emotionally. The attack on me and the way my hotel room had been turned over had put me on edge. I'd never been one to walk away, but I knew worse would follow.

Okorie pushed herself off the barrier and walked away from The Deep, telling me to follow. She pointed to a small complex of offices running parallel to the aquarium. 'One of them is mine from tomorrow, a proper base for The Northern News Alliance. It sorts out those who are committed to what I want to achieve. It's a base, but not somewhere you necessarily clock in Monday to Friday, nine-to-five. It's not that kind of work.'

'Offices bring back memories,' I settled for saying. Bricks and mortar, it implied a certain legitimacy, even if the world was changing. Okorie could work anywhere with her laptop, but there was a degree of sense in what she was doing.

Okorie looked at me. 'Good or bad?'

There was a question and one I didn't necessarily have an answer to. 'I slept on the floor of my old office the other night.'

'On High Street? I thought it was empty?'

'It is.' I shrugged, let her read between the lines. 'I wanted to see it again.'

'It's one way to put the past to bed, I suppose.' She turned to face me, shrugged. 'Question is, what are you going to do now?'

TWENTY-SIX

Natalie Okorie headed for the kitchen, promising drinks. I couldn't resist another look around her living room as I waited. I flicked on a lamp in the far corner of the room and set the record player going. A discordant Doo-wop number gave way to a country-tinged song, but I couldn't see the record sleeve to check who it was singing. Moving across the room, the bookcase on the opposite wall was tightly packed, paperbacks rammed into every available space. Glancing at the spines, it was mainly non-fiction, current affairs and titles that chimed with her work as an investigate reporter, but there was also a smattering of crime novels. Okorie walked back into the room, a bottle of wine and two glasses in her hands. She caught me red-handed inspecting the sleeve of the record on the turntable.

'Hurray For The Riff Raff,' she said. 'Do you know her?'

I shook my head. 'Can't say I do, but you can tell a lot about a person by what they listen to.'

She placed the items in her hands on the coffee table. 'Do I pass the test?' There was something about the music that grabbed me, something honest and earthy. By my own rules, I had to nod in agreement. Okorie passed me over a glass of red wine. I left it where it was, not wanting it.

'Want to talk about your day?'

I shook my head, unsure why I'd even agreed to be here. 'Not particularly.' I had little energy left in the tank for more confrontation.

'Must be weird being back, though?'

'It feels like I'm looking at the city through one of those funny fairground mirrors,' I said, running with it. 'Everything's there, but it doesn't look right.'

'Nothing stays the same. Rule number one in life.'

I asked for a glass of water, but acknowledged the point. 'You're going to make me drink alone, Joe?'

'I'm not in the mood.'

Okorie stood up and headed to the kitchen. I took out the mobile I'd taken from the man who'd tried to follow me. It was a basic handset, old and unlocked. Accessing the various menus, it was a phone to be used for work. The call list showed the vast majority of calls had been made to one person. It was a similar story with incoming calls and text messages. The contact list was limited to a handful of names, but it told me what I needed to know. There were numbers for both Grant Piercy and Ian Jagger. I considered that for a moment, only able to conclude it was a professional necessity if the man was security and needed to be in contact throughout public events. The handset lit up and vibrated in my hand, an incoming call from Piercy. I stared at it for a moment before pressing to reject the chance to speak to him. A text message arrived seconds later – Call me. It was tempting to return the call, let him hear my voice, but instead I placed the phone back in my pocket. I figured letting Piercy stew on things a little longer wouldn't hurt. Maybe there was a way to use it as leverage, maybe I wasn't as small time as he'd said I was. I quickly put it away as Okorie reappeared, placing the bottle down between us.

'I was treated like dirt when I started working for the paper here,' she said, refilling her glass. 'I was a kid and all I got was shit stories, no opportunities. Even then it was a rag for the benefit of advertisers and little else. Used to do my head in.' She took out her e-cigarette, drawing on it before continuing. 'I knew how people reacted to me. It's hard not to see it in when you're one of the few non-white faces in a place. Hard not to let it piss you off as well.' She shook her head. 'Stays with you.'

'That's why you left?' I refilled my glass.

Okorie made sure she was looking directly at me before answering, a look on her face I hadn't seen before. 'There was a tangible edge to my life here when I was young. I didn't really understand it back then, a sense of unease I could never shake. I had to get away, but this place has a strange pull, don't you think?'

She had a point. We were talking about an isolated city at the end of the motorway cul-de-sac. It marched to its own beat, seemingly with its back to the rest of the country, no place to hide. It made it different.

'It's why I struggle to see you living in Amsterdam.'

'It's a nice city.' I was learning Okorie had a habit of planting a seed, letting you think you had the upper hand in a conversation before turning the tables, striking out with a jab you don't see coming. The truth was living abroad was no picnic. I'd picked up enough of the language to communicate on a basic level, but still couldn't hold a proper conversation. I'd taken a liking to certain food, but pined for others I couldn't get. The bottom line, though, was knowing I'd run away. And that niggled at me.

'I wanted a career,' Okorie said, 'but I wanted to prove those fuckers wrong.

Leeds was better, a regional paper, but London was something else.' She smiled, drank more wine. 'Nobody looks at you funny down there, but it's easy to lose sight of the important things when you're writing for the big hitters.'

That was interesting. I asked what she meant by that.

'It becomes about the brand, left wing or right wing, whatever. You have to be careful about what you write and who you piss off. It's bullshit and why I had to get away in the end.'

'And the answer is to come home?' The annoyance in her voice was genuine, but so was my incredulity.

She stared at me, nodded and drawing on the e-cigarette, its flowery aroma filling the air. 'The Northern News Agency is going to work.'

'How are you going to pay for it?' I was no expert on the media, but I knew running an office was expensive. The puzzle to me was whether people would really pay for what she was offering. My thinking was undoubtedly old-school. I wanted the news print on my fingers.

Okorie leaned in across the coffee table, looking me in the eye. 'I've been left some money by an old friend.' She explained how a former-colleague had shared her vision for a new type of media, a plan they'd shared together, but when illness struck and with no immediate family, provision had been made to make the idea a reality. 'I can't tell you how motivated that makes me, Joe. It's the start I needed, but it's down to me to make it work now.'

I weighed her words up, trying to imagine what I'd do in that situation. I stood up and walked over to the window. Looking down on the street and the park, I could hear a game of football being played in the dark. 'I need to go home.' Things with Marieke needed sorting out.

'This is your home, Joe. Not Amsterdam.'

I moved away from the window. 'How do you figure that out?' My response was belligerent, but she could read me like a book.

'Some people just make sense in a particular place, don't they? It's where they belong.' She sat back, hands crossed in front of her. 'I won't lie as you're too long in the tooth for that. Sometimes you need a proxy for certain jobs and I've been waiting for the right person to become available to join my team. You know where this has been leading since I showed you the office. I need an investigator to work with me. I need you, Joe.'

TWENTY-SEVEN

It took me a moment to catch up with her thought process, now she'd finally said the words. There were places she wouldn't go, but would happily send me in her place. I shook my head. 'No.'

'That was a quick decision.'

'I'm not in the market for a job.'

'I think you are.'

I was tapping my foot on the floor, a visible sign I didn't like the direction the conversation was going. 'I don't want a boss.'

'Doesn't have to work like that.'

'Someone always has to make the decisions?'

'True, but I think we're on the same page here. I've got some really good freelancers writing for me and they've got excellent stories on the boil, but like I said, there are places I can't go. There are standards and rules, industry stuff.'

Like with Coleman, I understood. I would be a useful tool for her, a buffer from trouble. 'Work for a website?'

'You sound like an old man. The Northern News Alliance isn't just a website.' She sat back in her chair and folded her arms. 'Where do you read the news?'

'I try to avoid it.'

'And you're not wrong to do that.' She smiled again. 'Shall I tell you why? You don't read it because it's mainly a load of shite,' she said, launching into her reasons. She counted them off on her fingers. 'The BBC wouldn't know political balance if it hit them in the face, or if it was explained to them by an adult. Murdoch and his like? Total bullshit. Local media? May as well put it out of its misery now. People expect more, Joe. The future is finding people who want to engage with you and understand that the game is up for the old school. I'm not looking to report news, Joe. I'm not interested in piggybacking on other people's work. I'm going to be carrying out investigations, let others then report it as news. I'm going in deeper and setting the agenda. That's the difference.'

'Lots of these ventures have failed, though?'

'They haven't done it right. I'm going to take subscribers into the story. You don't just get the story here, you also get to go behind the scenes. You get web chats, forums and events. You get to ask questions and hold us accountable. There's no hiding place if you put your name to a piece. Subscribers want to feel involved. It's a two-way process when you do it right.' Okorie sat back in her chair. 'Real stories with real impact, Joe. Stories that resonate and change things, otherwise what's the point? That's what we're doing. Some will work, some won't. I know that, but it's time for me to step up to the plate.'

A knock on the door broke the moment. Okorie walked over to answer it. She took the pizza from the delivery guy, thanking him and closing the door again. 'Hungry?'

We both tore into the pizza in silence, neither of us at the stage of feeling comfortable enough to make small talk. Or share too much. The pizza was good, hitting the right spot. There were things I missed about the city, aspects of it I could happily live without, but it turned out I did miss takeaways. Thinking about Amsterdam made me think about Marieke and what I needed to do. It wasn't fair to leave her hanging. It was too easy, too tempting to think I could just slot back into Hull and my old life, but that didn't make it the right thing to do. I threw the last crust back into the pizza box, done, licking my fingers clean as best I could.

'There's always the link between Grant Piercy and Ian Jagger,' I said without looking at her. 'Stinks of corruption to me. Why not write about that? That's what you want, right? Why not write it and publish it, do it now?'

Okorie nodded, considered what I'd said before speaking. 'That's a fair point, but you don't go for the obvious. Piercy's a piece of work, make no mistake about that. He's got a reputation for shagging about, never been able to keep his cock in his pants. His first wife soon got rid of him because of it. It's surprising the current Mrs Piercy stands for it, but it's amazing what dazzles some people. It's also no secret he's skint. Look around the Fruit Market. His building work is slowing and footfall's disappearing. It's in danger of becoming a white elephant, but there's still a far bigger story than that.'

She wasn't wrong. I'd seen the area with my own eyes. I walked over to the record player, lifted up the needle, the room falling silent. Okorie was making all the right noises about the job and the website, batting away the easy option of a story. 'You said you've got the finance?'

'It was what my friend, Mo, wanted to happen,' Okorie said, though this time she wasn't meeting my eye. Her words weren't as forceful or as direct. It hurt her.

'She was important to you?'

'She took me under her wing when I needed it in London. I could write when I went down there, but she made me a writer. Does that make sense?'

I nodded, understanding, thinking about Don and how he'd made an investigator out of me.

'She taught me that the story wasn't always the story. It's what's going on underneath, that maybe the person you think is peripheral to it all turns out to be really fucking important. It's about finding the right angle.'

'Don taught me the same.'

'There you go.' Okorie found her stride again. 'I can't tell you how many bottles of wine I worked through with Mo in her kitchen talking about her stories and how she got them. It was an education I couldn't have got anywhere else.'

'What happened?'

'She died.'

'I'm sorry to hear that.'

'You have to move on. Maybe not overnight, but eventually.'

Maybe that's easier said than done, I thought. 'I spoke with Gerard Branning earlier. Remember him?'

She thought about it for a moment before saying she did. 'He wasn't directly involved, back in the day, though?'

'He helped fill in some gaps for me. He warned me off, like he'd warned Don off.'

'Stands to reason. It's dangerous.'

I thought back to the conversation we'd had in the pub on Anlaby Road. It felt like the retired detective was marking time, nothing to fill the empty hours stretching out in front of him. At least Don had tried to do something about it. 'Branning turned his back on me at the funeral, you know? Didn't want to know me in front of his mates. That's the way it is with those old-timers. They close ranks when they feel remotely threatened by someone. You're either with them or against them. There's never anything in-between.'

'Closure.' She shrugged. 'That's what you came back for, right?'

I didn't respond immediately, Okorie repeating the question. I eventually nodded, agreeing it was the bottom line. The mobile in my coat pocket sounded, distracting me. This time it was my own phone, not the one I'd taken from the man following me. The incoming call was from a number I didn't recognise. Accepting the call, the voice introduced himself as Gary Mail, I was told to listen and a place and time was given. I glanced across the room to Okorie, knowing she was listening in, despite trying to look as if she wasn't. The line went dead on me. I picked up my coat, running the calculation. I needed to be at Ferrybridge Services, forty miles west of Hull within the hour.

It was doable. I headed for the door, pausing only when Okorie said my name.

'Fuck Joe, whatever you think about me and what I do, do it for Don, do it for yourself.'

TWENTY-EIGHT

The service station bustled with people despite the late hour. I found a table giving me a view of the entire food court and waited. It always broke down into groups. Business people heading home after long-distance meetings were easy to pick off with their ties loosened, suit jackets unbuttoned. Some still hunched over their laptops, hot drinks in front of them as they continued to work. Lorry and coach drivers naturally navigated towards each other, killing time on the company clock. A handful of frazzled parents moved around, dragging tired looking children behind them. It was noisy, always busy, but I could be anonymous and fade into the background. It was how I liked it, observing but not being seen. I glanced down at my mobile, weighing up what to do. I called the number back, listening as it went straight to voicemail. I sent a text message saying I was ready to talk. No reply. There was nothing to do but wait.

I passed the time checking out Grant Piercy a little bit more thoroughly online. If he was coming for me, I needed to be prepared. His football career hadn't been quite as glorious as I'd assumed. He'd left Hull City in 1989, aged 23, heading for London and lowly-Charlton Athletic, despite reported interest from Liverpool at the top end of the league. I vaguely remembered it, but it hadn't properly registered with me. His career finished with an injury, just like mine had, but he'd invested in property and expanded from there. I read how he'd moved on from nightclubs to his current projects, now a voice within the city riding the rise in culture spending. He was a man with critics. Web links took me to stories objecting to his approach in the local media, how he'd shown little regard for planning regulations and normal business practices. Natalie Okorie had told me he was struggling financially, but he was a man used to winning and getting his own way. It made sense that he wanted his cousin to continue to hold power, help him bring his building schemes on the Fruit Market to a successful and lucrative conclusion.

I mulled over my conversation with Natalie Okorie, unsure of what to make of her. The job offer had come as a shock, but it wasn't right to make a kneejerk decision. Accepting would have obvious consequences about my life in Holland and my relationship with Marieke. I leaned back, on edge, the coffee in the cardboard packaging looking like sludge and tasting little better.

My mobile burst into life, a call from the same number as before. I listened as Gary Mail told me he was at the entrance. I looked up, spotted him and kicked out my chair. As I started to move, he turned away, disappearing from view. By the time I was at the door, he was gone. I looked around, swore under my breath. My screen lit up, a text message telling me to take the path to the rear of the service station and head for the motel.

I did as instructed. The motel was a small block, a budget option for those on the road. I looked around, trying to make sense of what was happening. A hand shot out, grabbed me by the shoulder and dragged me off the path. I was thrown against a row of industrial bins. My eyes adjusted. Mail had shaved his head since he'd been photographed by Don. He looked tired and pale, his clothes dirty. My working assumption was that he wasn't dangerous but that he would have something to say in relation to John Gove's murder. His eyes darted around before he was satisfied we were alone.

'We've got a lot to talk about,' I said to him. More than anything, I wanted to look him in the eye and weigh up whether he was telling the truth or not. 'I met your nephew yesterday,' I told him. 'Quite the brick shithouse.'

'He's young. Hits first, asks questions later.'

'Maybe that's not the best philosophy to have in life.'

'I know Ridley's dead,' Mail said, his voice flat, dismissing what I'd just said. 'I know you two had some sort of detective agency together.'

'And you two worked together, back in the day.'

'He was a decent enough bloke.'

'You want to talk about the unsolved murder of John Gove, get it off your chest?' There was no point in being coy. 'It's resurfacing.'

'What's it to you?'

'You're the one who asked me to come here. Maybe you want to talk about your old colleague, Lee Forrester, instead?' Mail still didn't respond, but he didn't need to. His face told me I'd scored a hit, that he was nervous and on edge. 'Is that why you asked me to make a forty mile journey to see you?' I took the mobile out with the voicemail of the call Don had made to me and played it to him. Mail didn't flinch as he listened. 'I don't believe his death was a coincidence, do you? He knew something about John Gove's murder that he wanted to share.'

'Don was always full of theories.'

'True.' I stepped closer. 'When was the last time you spoke to Forrester?'

'Not since I left the police.'

'You left pretty much after Gove's murder?'

Mail sniffed and wiped his nose on his sleeve. He lit up a cigarette, a small shake in his hand visible. 'The job wasn't for me. It wasn't what I thought it was.'

'I think you had the good sense to get out before it got worse, or before you got sucked into something worse.' I was wrestling him into a direction he didn't want to go. Maybe he'd thought he could control the conversation. Maybe he thought he could control me. We fell silent, nothing but the faint noise of the car park in the distance. 'You need to tell me what you know, Gary. You'll feel better for it.' No response. 'Tell me about the investigation, then? Tell me about your boss, Jagger.'

'I've got nothing to say.'

'Did you rate him?'

'Doesn't matter, does it? He's beyond people like us now.'

'Maybe he wants justice, too? It's an unsolved murder on his watch.'

Mail snorted, shaking his head again. 'Is that the best you've got? I thought you'd be better than that.'

'The truth is going to come out,' I said to him. 'But you've got to help me.'

'You have no idea what the truth is.'

'Go on the record and help me. It's cost you one career, don't let it take any more from you.' I eyed Mail, waiting it out, his life working as a lorry driver making more sense to me. Life on the road was anonymous, a mechanism for blending into the background. He was constantly running away. Maybe we weren't that different.

Mail stepped forward. 'You're looking at this from the wrong angle.'

'Put me right, then.'

He turned away, pacing. 'Maybe this is a mistake. You're not up to it.' Mail pivoted back, pointed at me. 'I thought I was dealing with a serious player, not a clown out of his depth.' He shook his head 'You know what happens to people who get out of their depth?' He didn't wait for an answer. 'They drown. That's what happens and it's never pretty.' He nodded to the path. 'Get in your car and head back to Hull, get on with your life. Pretend we never had this conversation.'

'I don't want to do that,' I said, growing angry at his words. Mail was visibly on edge, jigging from one foot to another, eyes darting around. 'There's a good detective interested in the story,' I said to him. 'He's looking at it again.'

'He won't find anything.'

Mail flew forward, pushing me in the chest and sending me tumbling against the bins. It took me a moment to pick myself back up, Mail already on the move.

He stopped, ten yards away, back on the path leading towards the main service station building. 'You stupid bastard, Geraghty. You've no idea what you're unleashing, have you?'

'Tell me then.'

He shook his head. 'I want to walk away if I talk. I want that written down in black and white. Tell that to your detective.'

'I can't promise you that.'

Mail quickly closed the gap between us. I was ready for him this time, but his strength was too much and he pinned me back against the wall. 'You leave me and my family alone, you hear me?'

I raised my knee and aimed between his legs. Mail was too fast, moving so my blow didn't land as intended. I was too slow to see his retaliation coming, a fist landing on the side of my head. It disorientated me, a struggle to stay on my feet. By the time the fog cleared, Mail was gone.

'What are you scared of?' I shouted, more in the hope he'd hear me. 'You need to talk to me.'

1989

Don Ridley stood up and walked over to the mantelpiece, listening to the noise coming from the kitchen. John Gove's parents were arguing, but lowered their voices, remembering there was a detective in their house. Don looked at the framed photographs, picking up the most recent one of their son. It showed Gove at the seaside, what looked like Bridlington, eating ice cream against the harbour wall. His clothes were the trendy choice for the summer, all bright splattered colours. Gove had a cheeky smile, a good looking boy.

'Had a good look at the photos of my son?' Stan Gove had moved back into the room, Don lost in thought. The man was in his mid-forties, powerfully built from his work on the docks. The industry wasn't what it had once been, but it still relied on the brawn of manual labour.

'I'm sorry for your loss,' Don settled for offering. It was never enough. 'You're working with the detectives we spoke to yesterday?'

'Yes.' It was a lie, but it was the easiest thing to say.

'They're barely out of nappies.'

Don grunted, knowing it wasn't a point to be argued. Gove had a broad Hull accent, all flat vowels. The imagery of the tattoos on his arms harked back the city's fishing days, already feeling long gone. He also wasn't wrong about Forrester and Mail.

'I wouldn't trust them to run a bath, never mind a murder investigation.' Gove lowered his voice, a glance at the door to make sure his wife wasn't listening. 'I'm warning you, don't take the piss out of me in my own home. They were going through the motions and didn't give a shit. I know what you all think of my son.'

'We don't think anything. He's the victim here.'

'Could have fooled me.' The man leaned in. 'My son was found in the boot of a car, treated like vermin. Can you imagine how terrified he must have felt as he died?'

'I can try.' Don held the man's stare, thinking he didn't need to explain what the job had taught him, or what he'd seen.

'Don't patronise me.'

Don stepped away from Gove's father. 'I'm a father, too.' Sarah wasn't old enough to be out drinking in the city's pubs and clubs yet, but the thought terrified him. Maybe it was the nature of the job breeding paranoia, maybe it was the realities of the world awaiting her. The sound of the telephone in the corner of the room broke the spell. Gove's father yelled out that he would answer it. Picking up the receiver, he told the person at the other end of the line that he'd call back. He told them, venom in his voice, that he was with the police.

Don moved back to the mantelpiece, looking again at the photographs. A handful of black and white ones showed old trawler boats, one showed a young man in a football strip, Stan Gove as a young man. Turning back to the room, Gove had his arms folded, watching him. 'What did the detectives ask you?'

'They went through the motions.' He thought about it before shrugging. 'They asked about my son's movements, if he had any enemies. Bullshit questions asked because they had no real clue what they were doing.'

'What did you tell them?' They might be bullshit questions that showed little imagination from Forrester and Mail, but they helped to paint a picture.

Gove's father faltered for the first time, not making eye contact. 'I wasn't able to help them much on that score. The lad treated this place like a hotel.' The man faltered, trying to find the right words. 'We'd argued about a few things, so he wasn't really living here with us at the moment. We're not sure of the details, but he was staying with some mates, sleeping on couches here and there. We let him bring a bag of stuff back last week, maybe a first step to sorting things out.' Gove's father's voice trailed off.

'Nature of kids at that age,' Don said, trying for an understanding smile, a bit of empathy. 'How about friends, or maybe a girlfriend?'

'He'd been dumped recently, so was moping around.'

'What about friends?'

'Couldn't really tell you about them. He certainly wouldn't bring them back here.'

'You were worried for him?'

Gove's father ran his hand through his hair, blew air out of his cheeks. 'I tried my best to keep him in check, but it's easier said than done at that age. I was wild enough myself. He wanted to move to London, start again with a job down there. He was pretty good at drawing, even if I say so myself. Maybe it was a pipe dream, but maybe he would have made something of himself by doing that, sink or swim. The idea tore his mother up, but it would have been the right thing to do.'

'You told the detectives this?'

'They didn't want to hear it, weren't interested. Neither did the one in charge who came round.'

'DI Jagger?'

'That's the one. Bone idle. You can smell it a mile off.'

Don nodded, not bothering to counter the point. It was the truth after all. 'How about the media? Are they bothering you?'

'Had the paper round, some black lass digging away, promising the world. Another one still in nappies, but the paper's more interested in painting our son as a bad apple, practically

gloating that he's dead.'

'That won't have been her decision.' Don knew Okorie was a decent enough journalist, one with her integrity still intact.

'Doesn't matter. Certainly doesn't matter to my wife. We're the ones who have to face the neighbours staring at us, all the people in the street talking about us behind our backs.' Gove's father cocked his head to one side. 'Why are you here? What's all this to you if there's already people supposedly working on it?'

They were interrupted by Gove's mother walking into the room, eyes red and puffy from crying. Don turned to her. 'Can I use your bathroom, please?'

She pointed to the stairs. 'First on the right.'

Pleased to be away from Gove's father and his questions, he walked up the stairs, stopping at the top of the landing. It had been a convenient excuse. Coming here had been a risk, something that could get him in trouble. But things didn't add up yet, too many questions that needed answering and there was the possibility of a witness to what had happened.

Looking at the slightly ajar doors, it was too tempting an opportunity. John Gove's bedroom was small, a single bed along the length of one wall, the curtains closed and a musty smell in the air. A hi-fi had been placed on a stand in one corner, a television in the other. Various records littered the floor, a poster of a band on the wall. Peering more closely at the name on it, The Stone Roses, it was familiar, but he didn't know their songs. On the opposite wall, various cuttings from the weekly rag Sports Mail were pinned up, celebrating Hull City wins. Don leaned in, looking at a match report from the end of the previous season, a brace of goals from Grant Piercy, the accompanying photograph showing him scoring with a diving header in front of the South Stand.

The bag his father had mentioned was on top of the bed. Looking inside, it mainly contained clothes, a couple of paperbacks at the bottom, a notepad on top of them. Flicking through it, it contained a number of notes that didn't make a lot of sense at first glance, numerous doodles confirming Gove was a talented artist. Maybe it would have been his calling in life. One doodle at the front of the pad caught his eye. It showed a young woman, smiling, a slight caricature element to it. Underneath, Gove had written her name, Angela, and drawn hearts around it to create a border. It was dated three months earlier.

Hearing a noise from downstairs, it was decision time. Breaking the rules would have consequences, short term and long term, but someone had to do something and hold Forrester and Mail to account. Placing the notepad in his pocket and quietly backing out of the room, he flushed the toilet to cover his tracks before heading back down the stairs.

TWENTY-NINE

The cafe sat in an ornate shopping arcade on the edge of the city centre. It had changed since I'd last been here, gentrified with gin makers and an independent book shop, the renovated indoor market next door. The cafe, though, remained resolutely old-school with its Formica tables and inescapable smell of frying food, a small queue forming at the counter.

I stirred more sugar into my coffee before slumping back into the seat I'd taken in the corner. I hadn't slept well, too much to think about to settle properly. I was sure Okorie hadn't told me everything she knew, but equally, I was holding back information, too. It was the nature of the game. Staring at the steam circling upwards from my mug, she was offering me more than that, though. She was offering me a new life, a new opportunity. I had to decide what I wanted my future to be.

I glanced up as the bell over the cafe door sounded. Coleman walked in, looking around for me. Spotting me, he made his way over.

'You look like you've got the weight of the world on your shoulders,' Coleman said, pulling out a chair, placing a rucksack on the floor.

'Maybe it's you dragging me out here at this hour?'

'You've got somewhere else to be?'

I sipped at my coffee. 'You'd be surprised.'

'I hope to be.' Coleman swivelled round to look at the menu behind the counter before looking back at me. 'Not eating?'

'It's too early.' In truth, DI Coleman's text message telling me where and when had come as something of a relief, a reason to quietly dress and leave the hotel. Coleman shrugged, said it was my loss, and ordered himself a sausage sandwich.

'Got to start the day right,' he said. 'Speaking of which, have you got good news for me? You must have found Dave Bolder by now?'

'Not yet.'

'I thought that was your job?'

I grunted a reply, saying it was needle in a haystack stuff. It was too early for his bullshit. If he wanted me to dance to his tune, he was in for a shock. 'I spoke to his sister,' I settled for saying.

'I hope that decision isn't going to come back and bite you?'

'You suggested I talk to her.'

'I shouldn't think so.'

I gave him a grim nod, understanding. He was covering his own position after going out on a limb. He could smell something, too and there was something in it for him. 'I tried a homeless shelter,' I said, explaining that Bolder had slept rough previously. 'They're not easy places to get information out of.'

'Surprised he's doing it at his age.'

'Turns out he was doing it as a young man, definitely thirty years ago.' I watched Coleman's face change as he made sense of what I was saying, and more importantly, what I was implying. We both sat back, mirroring each other. A worker placed his sandwich down in front of him. The grease leaking out of it turned my stomach. It didn't bother Coleman as he attacked it. He didn't take his eyes off me as he chewed. Eventually he placed his sandwich down, pushed the plate away.

'Sounds like you've got something on your mind, Joe?'

'Maybe there was a witness to Gove's murder?'

'And that witness was Dave Bolder?'

'Maybe.' It fitted with Don trying to speak to him with a sense of urgency.

'Sounds to me like you might want to find him quite urgently.'

He wasn't subtle. It was down to me to do it. 'How about a girlfriend?' I asked. 'Gove had been dumped just before his death. Any mention in the files? I'd like to talk to her.'

Coleman shook his head. 'Nothing like that.' He took out a sheet of paper, passed it over to me. 'This might be something. Might be nothing of course, but you know how important it is to be thorough.'

I glanced at it, reading over the notes taken by DC Forrester after talking to Gordon Till, the car yard owner whose vehicle had been stolen and used to dump Gove's body in. It was brief and to the point, nothing to read between the lines.

'He takes responsibility for the place being unsecured that night,' Coleman said, 'but it doesn't sound like he was a careless man to me.' He shrugged. 'Like I said, might be something, might be nothing.'

His son's reaction when I'd spoken to him had been defensive and agitated. My instinct had told me it didn't feel right, that I'd rattled him. Maybe I'd been heavy-handed, but either way, he certainly hadn't wanted to talk to me. And that was before I factored in the fact I'd seen him heading to where I knew Jagger was last night. 'Why that place?' I asked him. 'Why not one of the other countless car dealerships in the city?'

'Good question.'

There was always a weak point you could attack in any chain. The trick was to identify it and then press on it. I looked back up at Coleman. 'I need more help.'

'The police isn't a resource you can just tap into.'

'Even when it suits you?'

'Don't be naive about how things work, Joe.'

That was the second time I'd been called naive recently. I was strictly off the books, all the hassle and none of the glory. I had to work with it as best I could. I outlined to Coleman the fight I'd found myself in the previous night and how my hotel room had been turned over. 'I'd say I've made some new friends there.'

'Did you report it?'

'Don't you be naive.'

'Natalie Okorie's offered me a job,' I said, changing the subject.

Coleman laughed. 'Seriously?'

'The Northern News Agency is financed. It's real.'

'What does she want you for? You're not a journalist?'

I sat back in the chair, letting Coleman figure it out for himself. 'Support staff,' I eventually said.

'She's not a good friend to have.'

'I could use a friend.'

Coleman stuffed the last of the sandwich into his mouth. 'You can never have too many, I suppose, but run a mile. She's trouble.'

'Maybe I'm not inclined to do that?' Coleman remained impassive, like it was no big deal to him either way. 'I want the truth about why Don died, but I've still got some dignity. I make my own decisions.'

Coleman shrugged and sat back in his chair. 'You think Forrester and Mail were somehow involved in Gove's death, right?'

It was dangerous to agree, but I did, knowing it was the truth I was beginning to feel. I told him about speaking to Mail in the service station. 'I think there's something there.'

'You have been busy. How's he keeping?'

'He's on edge.'

'Something he wants to get off his chest?'

'He wants to talk to someone about what happened in 1989.' I made sure I was staring at Coleman, had his full attention. 'Once he's done that, he wants to walk away again.'

Coleman looked down at the ground, removing a scuff mark on the polished floor, decoding what I'd just said. 'That's a big ask, Joe.'

'Depends if you want the leg up the career ladder?'

'It's well-above my pay grade.'

'Whose pay grade is it?'

'I'd need to think about that.'

'Maybe you should do that.'

Coleman checked around making sure no one close to use was paying attention. 'I've done some digging into Forrester.'

'Right.' Unanswered questions niggled at people like us, regardless of whether we wanted to pretend otherwise. It was in our blood.

'Don't be thinking it's good news.'

I matched his move, sitting back, arm over the back of my chair. Coleman always found a way to burst my balloon. He took an envelope out of his rucksack and placed it down on the table.

'This is your last chance to walk away from this, Joe.' His hand lingered on top of it. 'You're not going to like this.'

'I thought the police wasn't a resource I could just tap into?' I was being manipulated, though Coleman wasn't as good as he thought he was. That said, I was always going to take the bait. We both knew as much. 'What have you got?'

'You sure?'

'I'm sure.' I stared at him, wanting him to know that I understood what he was doing. Coleman took a photocopy of a photograph out of the envelope and passed it to me.

'Recognise him?'

'Reg Holborn.' It was a struggle to keep my face neutral. 'Shit.'

'I'm the bearer of bad news.'

Looking at the photograph, I dated it around the mid-1980's. It showed Holborn walking up the steps of the court building, a raincoat on, not looking at the camera. His bulk was imposing, his reputation doing the rest of the work. But I knew better. The detective had been corrupt, a man Don had made an enemy of. I pushed the photograph back towards Coleman, not wanting to look at the image of the man.

'Holborn had his fingers into all sorts of things, including organised crime, before he retired, we know that,' Coleman said. 'I asked around. His retirement wasn't entirely a mutual decision. You know as well as I do that you always get a few bad apples, but it seems that period in time was a bumper harvest, if you follow me?'

I did follow, knowing how things were beginning to stack up. I took a moment, thinking it through. Coleman was waiting for me to say it. That was the deal. 'Forrester,' I eventually said, receiving a small nod in return. 'He left the police around the same time.'

'He was properly under Holborn's thumb.'

'Why did he leave?'

'Health reasons.'

'There's a thing.'

'Indeed.' Coleman leaned in. 'Here's a theory for you. Forrester was definitely corrupt, maybe Mail was, too, maybe he just went along with it, but Holborn was pulling the strings meaning Gove's murder was drugs related. Maybe Jagger always knew it, maybe his investigation was shit and lazy. Maybe he turned a blind eye to certain things, but it could damage him if it came out now. It's not a good look for a Member of Parliament.'

'It's a theory.'

Coleman took another envelope out. This time it contained a colour photograph, and if I was being asked to guess again, this one more recently taken. It showed a man closing in on sixty years of age, sitting on a boat, rods dangling over the side. He smiled at the camera, at ease with where he was.

'Forrester?'

'Runs his own business, so he's easy to find if someone was so inclined.' He pointed to the wooden board behind the man in the photograph. 'Look at that.'

It advertised fishing trips for tourists and experienced anglers alike. '01262?' I said, reading the telephone number out.

'Bridlington.' Coleman leaned in and pointed to the details on the board. 'Forrester's got himself a new name and identity.'

'Why would he do that?'

'Good question, but he might be a man with answers.' He stood up and slowly buttoned his coat. 'I wouldn't go repeating this in decent company, if I was you, or with someone like Natalie Okorie.'

'What's that supposed to mean?'

'Have you stopped to ask her, or even ask yourself, why she's back up here in Hull. Her own media company in Hull?' Coleman shook his head. 'It's a London game, Joe. Always will be.'

'Game's changing.'

THIRTY

Coleman left the cafe, the bell over the door sounding as it closed behind him. He didn't look back as he disappeared down the shopping arcade and out of sight. Glancing down at the envelope he'd left on the table, he'd been sure to deliver a message to me.

I put it to one side, not able to shake the thought of how things linked to Reg Holborn. It made it personal. Holborn's corruption had touched on my father's life, it was the reason I'd fallen out with Don. Maybe I was just tired of playing games. Coleman was positioning himself, chasing an easy result to boost his own promotion ambitions, and I was his battering ram. I had to figure out how far I would bend, how I felt about it.

I drummed my fingers on top of the envelope, not wanting to open it. Maybe Coleman wanted to help, to let me know who I was siding with or maybe he was manipulating me. The woman behind the till asked if I wanted a refill on my coffee. I nodded and waited for it to arrive before ripping open the envelope. Natalie Okorie had told me how important Mo Arnott had been to her, much like Don had been to me, a role model and inspiration. I also knew she was dead. It felt like I was snooping.

The first thing I removed from the envelope was a photograph. I was looking at the face of a woman in her sixties, sitting outside a cafe, smoking with a pint of lager in front of her. Looking again, she'd been caught off guard, totally unaware she was being snapped. The first question that came to mind was who'd taken it, quickly followed by wondering why they had. Arnott was laughing at something the man next to her had said, but he was looking away from the camera. They were leaning in towards each other, paperwork between them on the table. Looking more closely at the details, the business next to the cafe, a printing firm, had a London dialling code and number splashed across a banner. Going online, I checked it out. The bar was in Camden, North London.

I pulled out a collection of printouts, all paper-clipped together, all seemingly in some sort of order. The first print was a summary of Arnott's impressive career via Wikipedia. Her work had given her profile and standing, proper old school Fleet Street. She'd broken stories, brought down politicians and public figures, exposed stories to the light that people would have wanted to remain in the shadows. It was the kind of work that newspapers used to invest in and pay for, giving writers like Arnott the ability to produce stories without looking at the clock. A different world. Considering the information, I was sure she would have been a person with plenty of enemies.

The remaining prints concerned her death almost a year ago. I scanned the details before putting them to one side, thinking about Okorie's words. Maybe I'd jumped to conclusions, but the impression I had was that Mo Arnott had died from illness. Reading them again, she'd been murdered. Taking the media reports at face value, she'd been the victim of a burglary gone wrong in her home. Further reports appealed for witnesses to come forward, but no one had been charged.

My mobile vibrated on the table, breaking my concentration. Glancing down, the screen displayed Natalie Okorie's number. I stared at it, but didn't move. She was the last person I wanted to speak to at the moment. Coleman's words had implied there was more to Mo Arnott's death, something that might change how I viewed Okorie. Turning my mobile off, I went back to the print outs.

Coleman had spoken to the detective leading the investigation into Arnott's death, a summary of their conversation included, informal and off the record. I sat forward in my chair, knowing this was important. It was clear the detective was sceptical about what had happened that night. I knew burglary was a desperate crime, largely committed by desperate people. They were chaotic and highly likely to leave a trail behind them. It was the nature of them. This crime had been tidy, no obvious threads. The police had cracked heads together, spoken to likely suspects, but turned up nothing. The notes also observed that Arnott was security-conscious, her alarm bypassed, cameras revealing little. There was also the suggestion that easy wins had been left behind by the burglar; jewellery, even some cash, but her mobile, tablet and laptop had all been taken. It didn't stack up.

It wasn't hard to read between the lines. The DI leading the investigation hinted there was more to it than he'd been allowed to uncover. It came down to the usual reasons; lack of time, money and resources. The notes said that Arnott was semi-retired, but had been working on a story at the time of her death. It had proved to be a dead end. None of her media contacts, including Okorie, had anything to say, and she had no family to speak of.

I tidied the print outs up and placed them back in the envelope, knowing I would have to speak to Okorie. She hadn't been straight with me, certainly hadn't told me the full story. She was running away, too. It was a reminder I was ultimately on my own. We all had our burdens to carry.

I stretched out, flexed my hands, aware the cafe worker was watching me. I was on edge, but needed to find a way to channel my energy. I had the lead on Forrester to follow, knowing that prodding the hornet's nest was sometimes the only way. The decision was made on instinct. Going online with my mobile, I found Forrester's website easily. Coleman was right about Forrester having a new name, a new life. Maybe there were genuine reasons for it, but I couldn't think of any off the top of my head. The website advertised fishing trips out of Bridlington harbour, a seaside town thirty or so miles outside of Hull, and promised the chance of experiencing the thrills of deep sea fishing.

I had to do something. It felt like things long buried were slowly being dragged out into the light, piece by piece, and I wasn't controlling events. I made the call to the number advertised on the website. It went straight to voicemail, Forrester giving today's date followed by a message that he wasn't available, but would be at the boat tomorrow morning. I asked him to call back, deciding to leave my name, sure it would provoke a reaction.

THIRTY-ONE

I waited, brooding in my car, watching as the pub opened up for the day, the door unceremoniously bolted into place against the wall. The landlord nodded a greeting to the lone punter sitting down on the bench outside, waiting. The near-by stadium was supposed to kick start the area's regeneration, but looking around, it wasn't hard to conclude things had gone sour. It didn't take long for Gerard Branning to come into view, head down as he headed into the pub. I needed a second opinion on what Coleman had told me.

Heading into the pub and out of the cold, Johnny Cash competed on the stereo behind the bar with the sound of a vacuum cleaner in the main room next door. The back room was empty, a Post-it-note cellotaped to the television telling me it was broken. A series of framed black and white photographs lined the walls showing Hull in its fishing industry heyday, trawler boats looking heroic as they crashed through deep and dangerous waters, waves crashing up against them. I could imagine Cash's deep baritone crackling through the long-distance transmitters on board like a ghost, his voice breaking up as the radio signal came and went. The door in the far corner squeaked as Branning made his way back in from the toilets. He stopped dead for a moment, staring at me.

'You look like you've got the weight of the world on your shoulders, Joe.'

'You're not far wrong.' I managed a smile, looking around. 'Been a while since we had a drink in here, isn't it?'

'How did you know to find me here?'

'I hear you run like clockwork.' I'd knocked on his door, his neighbour only too keen to tell me where he'd be, how he was drinking too much. It was what seemed to happen to retired detectives. Branning was drinking himself into oblivion because he had nothing better to do, a life given to working around the clock, obsessing, before it's taken away leaving an empty husk behind.

A grim smile on his face. 'Bit of routine doesn't hurt anyone.'

He held my stare for a moment before letting it go. I nodded to the bar. 'What are you drinking?

'Cheap lager. What else is there?'

I turned to the bar and ordered, Branning taking a seat in the corner. Branning looked at my water as I followed him over.

'Not drinking?'

'No.'

He sipped at the froth on top. 'Not much of a life, is it, sitting in here most days, killing time?' Branning pointed to the crossword puzzle he was working on in the newspaper and the tatty paperback on the table. 'Never retire, that's the best advice I can give you.'

'I can't see myself ever having the luxury.'

'World's changed.' He put his drink back down. 'My lad can't even get a job and he's got his degree and everything. Won't be long before he's got nothing better to do than join me in here.'

'Tough out there for everyone.'

'I probably didn't help him by voting for Brexit like a daft sod, did I?'

'We all make decisions in good faith,' I told him. 'Can't always control the outcome, though.'

'Fathers and sons.'

I held Branning's stare, knowing exactly what he was driving at. 'It's why I'm back,' I eventually offered. 'You said you warned Don that he was playing with fire?'

'I did.'

'Reg Holborn.' The name immediately registered, as I'd assumed it would. 'He links to the John Gove murder.' I sipped at my water. 'But you already knew that.'

Branning stared at his pint before looking up. 'I knew you'd get there eventually, Joe.' He swallowed a long, slow mouthful of lager before speaking. 'Holborn was a rum one and no mistake.' He stopped me from talking with a wave of his hand. 'I don't think anyone appreciated just how far gone he was back then, though.'

'Don certainly knew,' I told him, keeping my voice level. Don had been there when Holborn had beaten my father in his pub for protection money.

'He was ashamed of that,' Holborn said, his voice low.

'He didn't do enough.'

'You're not going to thank me for this, but yours is an emotional response. If we weren't talking about your dad's place, you'd see that someone like Don back then had no way of stopping it. It wasn't an option for him.'

I wanted to think I was better than that, that I could move past it, but I wasn't sure I could. 'I can't forgive Don for turning a blind eye.'

'But you can understand it because you're not naive. You maybe have to turn it on its head. If you can't forgive, but maybe you can forget and put it to one side for now. Don was a good copper, an example to the rest of us. It would have been a poorer police force at the time without him. If he'd spoken up against Holborn, his career would have been over. You might not like it, but that's how it was.'

I wondered just how much blood Branning had on his own hands. What he knew and had buried. I toyed with my glass, thinking about the nature of complicity. Don had been a man with his own secrets, ones he'd been hording for decades. Maybe if I'd turned a blind eye, it wouldn't have driven a wedge between myself and Sarah. But I hadn't been able to. It wasn't in me. Turning back to Branning, he would have constructed a narrative in his head that made sense to him, excused himself and others in the name of a greater good, but it didn't feel like something I could buy into easily. Branning picked up his drink again. Leaning in, I noticed a slight shake in his hand. 'Forrester was one of Holborn's men, wasn't he?'

My question marked a shift in the conversation with Branning knowing exactly where I was heading. It was written all over his face. 'Was the investigation corrupt?' I asked, thinking about the theory Coleman had laid out for me.

'Don always said you were sharper than you looked. Maybe you've had to warm up a bit, but you've got there.'

Maybe that was true, but there was one question I had in mind for Branning. 'How dangerous is Forrester?'

'Danger is always directly proportional to what you know about someone.' Branning swallowed more of his drink, the pint glass nearly empty. 'It's quite a question, though. Sounds like the kind of thing Natalie Okorie might be interested in asking?'

We stared at each other, knowing it was dangerous territory. I took a step back. 'Why did you turn your back on me at the funeral?'

The question took him by surprise. Branning took a moment to compose himself. 'That day wasn't about you.'

'You think I shouldn't have been there?'

'Not my place to say.'

Branning went to stand up, but I told him to stay where he was. 'Whose place was it?'

'Don't do this, Joe.'

'Do what?'

'There's a time and place for things and that wasn't it.'

'You weren't keen when I turned up at your door, either?'

'We've all had some time to think about what's important.'

He sat back in his chair and folded his arms, a move I mirrored. What he meant was that I'd needed to prove myself all over again. He was part of a tight group of now-old men, all with their own secrets and reputations to protect. Maybe Don had broken free of that pact, or maybe didn't care for it any longer. Holborn's legacy as a corrupt detective didn't reflect well on any of them in the final analysis. It was something best left in the past for all concerned.

'How deep is Jagger in all this?' I asked.

'Jagger's a weak man,' Branning said. 'Always has been.'

'He's got his position to think about.'

'A rather cynical point of view.'

'But not the wrong one?'

'Not at all.' Branning drained his glass. 'Question is, what price are you prepared to pay?'

I laid it out for him, who I'd spoken to and what had happened to me. I wasn't sure how much it amounted to, but things were happening. 'I should be back home in Amsterdam now, but here I am in Hull, pissing people off as I try to get them to speak.'

'Seems to be a habit of yours.'

'I'm good at it.' I was beating the words out as my hand hit the table.

'I'm the only one capable of helping you.'

We were eyeballing each other, but I wasn't backing down.

'You've certainly been busy.' Branning picked up his coat.

'What did Don say to you when you spoke?' That was what I really wanted to know.

'Sounds like you already know.'

THIRTY-TWO

I left Branning to his drinking, knowing now there were some cages I could rattle, a plan starting to form. I parked up outside of Pete Till's car yard and killed the engine, needing to be sure he was at work. The radio played quietly in the background, a local phone-in show about the effects of Brexit on the local economy. Even the presenter sounded tired of it.

Looking out of the window, rain had started to fall again, a single customer walking forlornly around the yard checking out the cars for sale. Till's nephew appeared and initiated a conversation. I punched the business's number into my mobile and waited. Till answered, so I cut the call knowing he was on the premises. You attacked the weakest link in the chain. I hurried across the road, ignoring the blaring of car horns. Head down, I kept to the perimeter of the yard, Till's nephew too busy talking to the potential customer. I didn't knock on the office door before entering.

'Nice to see you again, Pete,' I said, closing the door behind me. 'Horrible weather.' I looked around. The portakabin was hot, an electric heater plugged in behind his desk. The space was designed to look appealing, but it felt like he was trying too hard. A pot of coffee percolated in the far corner, a table with motoring magazines in a neat pile, a vase of flowers in the middle, comfortable chairs around it. I paced around the room.

Till looked at me, confused, but started to speak. 'You can't just barge your way into here.'

'Looks like I just have.' I took my mobile out and offered it to him. 'Call the police if you like?' Till didn't take it, so I put it away and pulled up a chair opposite him. 'Let's talk about 1989 and John Gove again, shall we?'

'I've got nothing to say.'

'John Gove,' I repeated.

'It was nothing to do with us.'

'The gates here were left unlocked.'

'Accidently.'

'Your father took responsibility for that, but it doesn't really ring true with his reputation for being a careful man. I think it was someone else.'

'You don't know anything.'

I sat back, happy for him to have that perception of me before asking another question. 'Did you speak to Don Ridley back in 1989?'

'I can't remember.'

'He called me just before his death last week.' I stood up and walked behind him, leaned over his shoulder. 'Police still haven't made an arrest over his death. How hard can it be these days when it's a hit and run?' I let the implication of my words linger, something for him to think about. I wanted him to make the connection for himself. I wanted to put him on edge. 'Only a matter of time, though.'

'I can't help you.'

'How about the detectives who did the leg work, Forrester and Mail?' I said. 'Both young detectives. Remember them?'

'No.'

'You can do better than this, Pete.' I took a step back. 'It's not going away. You might not get another chance to put your side of the story across.' Thinking about Okorie, I told him a journalist was chipping away at things. 'Neither of us can control that. She's going to publish soon and then who knows what shit it'll stir up.' I wasn't sure how true that statement was, but the suggestion made Till visibly uncomfortable.

'She needs to be careful what she says.'

'Or what?'

'I've got a business to protect.'

I sat back and smiled. 'I thought you were implying something more than that.'

'What do you think I am?'

I let a silence grow between us, wanting him to feel uncomfortable. I still had my ace card to play.

'There's really nothing I can help you with.' Till stood up and gestured to the door. 'And I've got a lot of work to be getting on with.'

I told him to sit back down. 'Why was the car stolen from your yard, Pete? That's what I can't figure out. It doesn't make sense to me. It might have been bad luck, just one of those things, but I'm struggling with that. I was a private investigator for a number of years working with Don Ridley, self-taught to a degree, but there was one thing he did teach me. Do you know what that was?'

Till shook his head.

'If you feel something in your gut, you're probably right and you have a duty to pursue it. My gut tells me you're scared, Pete.'

He shook his head again.

'What did the police say to you?'

'I don't remember.'

'Did you speak to DI Jagger? He's an MP these days, an important man who doesn't want something like this resurfacing.'

'I don't remember.'

Till had looked away as he answered. I brought my hand down fast next to him on the table, watching him flinch. 'Try harder.'

'It's thirty years ago.'

'It wasn't a run of the mill day, though, was it? You expect me to believe you can't remember?'

'It's the truth.'

'Did you know Mail left the police shortly after the investigation?' I said to him. 'It fucked him up. Forrester is a different kettle of fish, though. There are all sorts of stories about him, the classic good cop, bad cop pairing. Interesting to learn he left the police under a cloud a few years after Mail. Seems to have been a bad stench around the place at that time.' Still Till didn't say a word, just stared forward over my shoulder. 'Who approached you? Who told you what to do?'

Till stood up and walked over to the window, looked out. 'I don't know what you're talking about.'

I followed and grabbed him by the shoulder, forcing him to turn around. 'You were what, in your mid-twenties? Surely that was old enough to take some responsibility for your actions? You shouldn't have been falling back on your father at that age.'

'You have no idea.' He shook himself free of my grip.

'Tell me, then.'

'Fuck you.'

Till lashed out, anger on his face. I saw the move coming and grabbed his arm, forcing it back down. 'Why were you talking to Jagger last night?' The power drained from the man. 'I saw you.' Till's face fell, unable to speak. I eased off. I'd rattled his cage and knew he was scared of something, or more accurately, someone. I took a breath, brushed myself down and backed away. I returned to my car and waited. It was his move to make.

THIRTY-THREE

Till slammed the office door behind, shrugging his coat on as he moved. He held a mobile phone to his ear, agitated as he headed to a car parked close-by. I watched as he stopped to talk his nephew, throwing the office keys in his direction.

Till pulled out of the road, heading towards the city centre. I allowed another car to go ahead of me before following. Progress was slow as we approached the junction with Spring Bank and Freetown Way. Closing my eyes as the lights turned red, I ignored the blare of horns and crossed onto Ferensway. Several more sets of lights made progress slow, but I kept Till in sight. The more difficult Mytongate roundabout meant I switched lanes, diagonally behind him, as we inched forward.

I drummed on my steering wheel, muttering to myself. Who are you going to see? I knew where I'd place my bet. Branning had remained coy about answering my questions directly, but there was no doubt the investigation into John Gove's murder had been dark and malignant. It wasn't right. Floating above that, the stench of Holborn and the suggestion he was controlling Forrester. Truth was, it was hard to disagree with Branning's explanation of Don's behaviour in relation to my father, even if swallowing it down was no easier.

Snapping back into the job at hand, I headed right at the roundabout, the dual carriageway leading west out of the city. Hanging back, Till stayed within the speed limit, steady and without doing anything erratic. I followed him off the road at the junction for the Humber Bridge. Till headed towards the large car park in its shadow. Assuming it was largely used by commuters, I made sure to park a safe distance away. The only other signs of life were a rundown tourist information office housed in a portakabin and a burger van.

Till got out of his car, didn't look around. I watched him walk to the end of the row and then stop before getting in the passenger seat of another vehicle. I couldn't see any more than that without getting out. Pulling my cap on and heading in the direction of the van, I walked down the row of cars, careful to keep my distance and my head down. I had my mobile by my side ready to take a quick photograph of the registration plate of the car Till was sitting in. Maybe Coleman could be persuaded to trace the owner's details for me. Glancing in, Till was arguing with another man.

Walking past, I didn't need to do that. It was a private registration plate – IJ 4386. Till was talking to Ian Jagger.

I lingered at the burger van, taking my time stirring sugar into my coffee. I was willing to bet Till and Jagger were arguing about my appearance at the car dealership, but I couldn't get any closer. I waited it out, ready to move. I let him return to his own car before throwing my drink into the bin, ignoring the shout of the worker in the van asking what I thought I was doing. Till didn't hang around, pulling straight out of the car park. He'd keep.

I increased my step, opening the passenger door of Jagger's car and seeing he was using his mobile, jumped in. Leaning across him, I removed the keys from the ignition and grabbed his phone. A glance at the screen told me he was talking to Grant Piercy, I cut the call before tossing the handset back to him. 'Fancy bumping into you out here?'

'You can't do this.'

'Looks like I just have.' I shuffled round on my seat to face him. 'Strange place to find your MP?' Jagger took a moment to respond, no doubt weighing up his options. 'Strange company to be keeping, too?' He stayed silent and I relaxed a little, straightening myself back up in the car seat. 'We never got to finish our chat last night, did we?' The car park was quiet, a council worker emptying a rubbish bin. A lone car pulled up, the driver letting a dog out. We watched as they headed over to the woods that ringed the car park. 'Did you know I was a victim of crime last night?' I asked him.

'No.'

'I was attacked in the city centre after talking to you and Grant Piercy in the Fruit Market.'

'Did you notify the police?'

'What do you think?' I looked at Jagger. 'It wasn't someone after my wallet or my mobile. I was followed.'

'I wouldn't know about that.'

I turned to face him and leaned in, making sure to invade his personal space, wanting him to feel uncomfortable. 'I didn't expect you to.' Jagger looked away from, playing for time as he got his thoughts together. 'The truth is going to come out about John Gove's death and it's going to happen soon.'

Jagger considered my words and returned my stare. 'The truth is we failed. We failed John and his family. That's all there is to it.'

'There's more it to.' I wasn't buying his words and could list a growing number of issues, not least Don's death. I settled for the target I hoped would needle him most. 'Grant Piercy is very invested in the situation.'

Jagger smiled, a slight shake of the head. 'He's very protective.'

'Blood is thicker than water? Sounds like it's about banking favours and judging when to make a withdrawal? He's a man with big plans.'

Jagger pursed his lips and sat back as best he could. 'If you're suggesting I can smooth the path for anyone, then you're more naive than I thought.'

I wasn't buying it. It was how the world turned; a back scratched, a blind eye turned.

'If you don't change and adapt, you get squashed,' Jagger said quietly. 'Sounds like you're trying to give me a warning?' I wasn't sure if he was talking about the Fruit Market and Piercy, or myself. Maybe he was even talking about himself. Jagger didn't respond.

'I know all about Forrester and Mail,' I said to him. 'Someone will talk even if it isn't you. Once they do, cracks will appear and the truth will surface.' I felt like I was close to making that happen.

'Time sometimes does that.'

'The investigation was a disgrace.' I was in the mood to lay it out for him. 'No suspects, no motive established, and that's before you even think about an arrest.'

'Not every murder is solved. That's the reality of the job.'

'You were lazy.'

Jagger shook his head. 'Not true.'

'You didn't unearth a single thing.'

'You're not privy to the details.'

'Let's talk about Forrester, shall we?

'Why?' Jagger angled himself towards me. 'He's long gone.'

'Happy with the work he did for you on the investigation? He was the leader, wasn't he, Mail the junior partner?'

'It's been raked over countless times. It still gets reviewed from time to time and probably will in the near future. There's nothing to find.'

Jagger turned away, watching a small group of dog walkers standing around in a small group for a chat. I grabbed him by the arm, forcing him to pay me attention again. 'Was Forrester corrupt?'

'That's a bold thing to ask a Member of Parliament.' Jagger weighed up what I'd said with a small smile on his face. 'He retired on medical grounds, regardless of what you say, and that's a tough thing to have to do.'

'Not quite as heroic as taking a bullet for the cause?'

He tapped the side of his head. 'The real battle's always in here. Was for me, would have been for him.'

'Forrester was one of Reg Holborn's foot soldiers,' I said, knowing I was jumping to conclusions, but it felt like the truth. 'I'm sure you remember Reg? You must have rubbed up against him, back in the day?'

'That's one way of putting. I preferred to keep my distance.'

'Why's that?'

'I wanted a career.'

'Sounds to me that his behaviour was an open secret?'

'It's what fires me up to do my job now.'

I told him to knock it off. 'I'm not the media looking for a sound bite from you here. Forrester went as part of the cleaning-up process post-Holborn. Good housekeeping or spineless management, I don't care. He went before he was pushed, that's what matters.' It raised questions. I looked to Jagger, wanting him to say something, but he remained silent. 'Drugs,' I said. 'How was John Gove involved.'

'That's your theory? Gove was killed because he was a threat to other dealers?'

'It's a theory I've heard.'

Jagger leaned forward, inspecting the windscreen for a moment before sitting back again in his seat. 'Don't think I don't have regrets.' I went to cut him off, but he stopped me dead. 'Don't forget this, either. If you're judging me by this standard, you're choosing to judge Don in the same way. Think about that. He wasn't the man you thought he was.'

My fists had curled into balls, my anger rising. 'Why were you talking to Till last night?'

'I'm pretty sure you can't prove that. If he turns up at the same party as I do, that's hardly news.'

'Why would a man like Till be there? He's small time, selling clapped out pieces of shit to people desperate enough to buy them.'

'It's honest work.'

I let him score that point. 'Still doesn't answer the question.'

'I think it does.'

'He's complicit in John Gove's murder,' I said. 'I keep coming back to Forrester, but I haven't figured out the parts everyone played in making the situation go away. The investigation was sabotaged, never taken seriously. I look around now and I see a lot of scared people and people with a lot to lose.' Done with the man, I had one last card to play. 'I've found a witness to Gove's murder.' He tried to hide the look of fear on his face, but wasn't fast enough in hiding it. I threw his mobile phone back into his lap and got out of the car, leaning back in to speak to him. 'Don't forget that, either.'

THIRTY-FOUR

This time I didn't have to figure out a way into Grant Piercy's bar, the only thing stopping me were the barriers outside with the Fruit Market being slowly transformed ahead of the *Hit The North* parade. Access was being slowly restricted, security points installed to control the large crowd expected to turn out.

The barman said I was expected and pointed to a door in the corner, saying I should go up. Behind the scenes, the place wasn't as glamorous. Boxes of cleaning materials piled together in the corner, a bare light bulb at the top of the metal staircase. Pausing at the top of the stairs, one door was slightly ajar. Jagger was on the phone, appeasing whoever was on the other end of the line. I heard my name, Piercy agreeing that I was an irritation, a problem that needed sorting out. With that, the conversation became a muffled exchange I couldn't make sense of.

I smiled to myself, willing to bet he was talking to Jagger about what had just happened down by the Humber Bridge. I headed straight in without knocking. Piercy had reclined in his chair, mobile phone to his ear, gestured that I should sit down. The office was in pristine condition. The laptop and tablet on the glass topped table expensive and new. My attention turned to the large print running the length of one wall. It showed Piercy scoring a goal for Hull City in the 1980s, a full-length diving header captured just before he landed on the muddy pitch, the ball flying beyond the despairing goalkeeper. I recognised the backdrop, Boothferry Park, the football club's former ground. It was another part of the city I'd grown up with long gone, replaced by a bland housing development. A large framed photograph on the wall directly opposite his desk showed him on his wedding day. It looked like a recent marriage.

'Can't beat the feeling, can you?' Piercy had finished his call and was pointing to the football print. 'Not joking when I say it's better than sex.' He laughed. 'But you'll know that, right? You must have scored a try or two in your time on the rugby pitch?'

'Not really.'

'You missed out, then.'

I glanced again at the print, noting it didn't show playing at the highest level he'd achieved. 'You signed for Charlton when Liverpool were after you?'

Piercy smiled. 'You've been checking me out?'

'Always.'

'Don't believe everything you read.'

'Liverpool were top dogs, though.' I sat down. 'Would have been quite something for your career.'

'If, buts and maybes. Charlton were down at the bottom, but they wanted me. Shit happens in sport. You know that as well as I do. Things worked out okay in the end, so I can't complain.' He opened a drawer and placed a bottle of whisky and two glasses on the table, poured two generous measures. 'The good stuff.'

I threw the mobile I'd taken from his employee the previous night onto the table. 'You might want to return that to your man.'

'Forgive me my sins.' Piercy nudged a glass in my direction before pocketing the handset. 'I appreciate your discretion.'

'You called me a risk last night.' I watched Piercy slug back half of his drink.

'A man starts to stick his nose in my business, I want to know why. That's all.' Piercy threw back the rest of his drink. 'I should apologise. Maybe that wasn't the right way to go about things.' He refilled his glass, a smile on his face. 'That said, you started the trouble. There was never any intention to attack you. You physically hurt my man as well as wounded his pride.'

'My heart bleeds.'

'He'll get over it.'

'What about my hotel room?'

'What about it?'

I picked up the glass, sniffed the alcohol. There was no doubt it was the good stuff. I placed it down without drinking it. 'It was broken into last night and turned over.'

'That was nothing to do with me," he pointed at my untouched whisky, 'drink up, Joe, or I might be offended.'

'I'm not really a day-time drinker.'

'You just need the chance to give it a go.'

I ignored the glass, despite the temptation.

Piercy glanced at his mobile phone screen before turning his eyes back to me. 'What do you want, Joe, once we strip all this bullshit away?'

'I want the truth about Don Ridley's death. I don't believe it was an accident'

'Ian told me the police are investigating. You have to let them do their job.

You can chase around pretending you're some sort of superhero, if you like, but at the end of the day, you're only one man.'

'I thought you were more of a self-starter than that? A man who got things done?'

Piercy sat forward, his fingers steepled, weighing things up. 'Ian told me you think you've got a witness to Gove's murder?'

I smiled. He had spoken to the man already. 'That's right.'

'You should work with Ian on it, then. You obviously know things he doesn't. Equally, he can open doors you can't. No man is an island, as someone far wiser than me once said. Ian deserves some closure on this, too.'

'What you think your cousin deserves isn't too high on my list.' I took a deep breath. Getting on board with such a suggestion was a struggle. 'He had his shot at closing the case thirty years ago.'

'We don't have to be enemies here, Joe. I know all about you and how you operate.'

'You said that before.'

'I've spoken to people you've worked for and they seem to like how you get results. Maybe it's time you stepped things up?' Piercy pushed his chair back and stood up. 'I've got something to show you.'

He led me back down to the bar and through another door I hadn't seen in the corner. It connected to the next building, essentially a building site. The walls had been knocked through, new plasterboard marking out the space's parameters. I listened as Piercy told me he was expanding the bar space and adding a performance space. He led me up the stairs and out on to the rooftop. I didn't want him to know, but it was an impressive panorama, spectacular even though it was a largely flat city. The marina was full of yachts lined up neatly, the last few grand old buildings in the city centre next to the dock covered by a shopping centre on stilts. Water mingled with buildings everywhere.

'An exclusive cocktail bar,' Piercy said, 'or will be soon enough. Plan is to have gigs and all that stuff going on up here, too. Look around, Joe, it's a fucking backdrop, isn't?'

I looked over the edge, the brick wall low. 'You'll need to do something about safety up here.'

Piercy laughed. 'That's what the suits will no doubt say. I'm laughing, but that's the kind of attitude I regularly have to kick back against. I know you're joking, but not everyone is the same.' He stood next to me and looked out. 'I want to see more bars and restaurants, more apartment blocks rising out of the ground. I want more hi-tech offices around here, a proper place to work and live.'

I looked down at the empty streets. 'Doesn't look that busy to me.'

Piercy ignored my criticism. 'This is just the beginning,' Piercy said, refilling his glass. 'I want to see the cruise terminal happen around here. I want to see the Humber Bridge turned into a tourist attraction with lifts offering the best panoramic views in the North of England. I want to buy the football club and get them back into the Premier League. You've got to dream big, Joe. It's the only way to live.'

'Good for you.' I was unsure if he was a genius or a bullshitter. Ultimately, it made no difference. Okorie's words that he was skint came to mind, though it was often no barrier. It would all be on credit of some form, a finely balanced set of arrangements. 'I'd be happy with a quiet life,' I said.

Piercy laughed again. 'I don't believe that for a minute. People told me you're tenacious and difficult, and I've seen that for myself.' He toasted me with his glass. 'You're Hull to the core and that means you're belligerent. It's not a bad thing. It certainly makes you too good to be pissing away your time working with someone like Natalie Okorie.'

'You know her?'

Piercy ignored the question. 'I've got a vision for this city and I need people with a variety of talents around me. I could use you.'

'Sure you can afford me?' He didn't bite to the comment. 'I need more help.'

'You want me to be your gofer?'

'We're all someone's gofer, aren't we?' Piercy shook his head. 'Come on, Joe. I wouldn't waste a man of your talents on pissy little jobs. What do you think I am?'

'Who are you a gofer for? Ian Jagger?'

Piercy paused, looked at me as if he was disappointed by my conclusion. 'Ian's an important part of the picture for sure. I want him to enjoy a long and fruitful career as a Member of Parliament for this area, driving change in the area forward.'

'I'm sure you do.'

'Be a team player, Joe. Help Ian put the story about John Gove to bed and then let's talk about you working for me.'

'The only thing I'm interested in is knowing why Don Ridley died. If that means things that some would like to remain buried in relation to John Gove's murder leak out, so be it. If you think you can scare me off by attacking my hotel room, or by sending your men after me, you don't know me.'

'I thought we were friends here?'

'You're all running scared because you know the truth is going to emerge.' I headed for the door and the stairs, done with Piercy. 'Fuck you.'

THIRTY-FIVE

It was an old habit, but walking and thinking was the best way I knew to clear my head. I walked west along the waterfront, closing in on St Andrews Quay. The car park was emptying for the day, the last few shoppers looking in the large retail units. Once the beating heart of the dock, the Lord Line office building stood abandoned, windows and doors boarded over up with sheet metal. Looking more closely, I could see graffiti visible on the lower levels. It was fenced off, crumbling brickwork and the dangerous overgrown dock in front of it. It was a mess that had gone too far to save, a blister on the city's skin that needed lancing. I was surprised a man like Grant Piercy didn't have plans for it, make the area's answer to the Baltic arts centre in the North East, trade off its industrial heritage.

Sitting down on a bench, my aim when I'd spoken to Coleman earlier in the day had been to stir things up to see what the fallout was. Mail and Forrester were slightly out of reach, but Jagger was here and I'd prodded him. He could hide it all he liked, but he was scared. He was certainly scared enough to involve Piercy. I thought back to the way I'd spoken to him, knowing I'd certainly unsettled things.

Standing back up, I kicked a stone out from underneath my feet. It felt like I was beginning to close in on the truth about John Gove's murder and the whole web around it. There was still one person I needed to speak to. Walking back, spots of rain started to fall, forming puddles on the broken path underfoot. The night was drawing in, darkness starting to descend to match my mood.

I couldn't leave it any longer. I headed to the offices by the side of The Deep. Catching the main entrance door as someone left, the entrance board displayed the names of the building's various tenants. The Northern News Alliance was already listed. I found Okorie sitting on an old office chair, hunched over a laptop carefully balanced on her knees. The room was an empty shell, its walls with faint traces of where the previous occupant had tacked things up, indentations in the carpet mapping where furniture had once been positioned.

She looked up. 'Wasn't expecting you to drop in.'

'I was in the area,' I said, pulling up a chair and placing it close to her. 'You didn't tell me the truth about Mo Arnott.'

Okorie stopped what she was doing and closed her laptop. She didn't answer immediately. 'You've been talking about me?' It was clear from the tone of her voice that she'd considered it a line crossed, that I was a wanker. 'You know fuck all, Joe. You think you know my grubby secrets, like I should be ashamed?'

'I didn't say that.' It wasn't what I meant. 'I always check people out.'

'What do you think you've found out?'

'I found I'd made a false assumption. I thought your friend died from an illness, but I was wrong. It wasn't the case at all.'

'You've got no right to go digging into my private life.'

I had every right, but I kept the thought to myself. I held my tongue, not pointing out the hypocrisy of her words. 'The police said it was a burglary gone wrong?'

'That's right.'

'Doesn't feel that way to me.' I laid out what I thought I knew from Coleman's file. 'You don't take laptops and phones, but leave cash and jewellery.' Okorie had her back to me. 'That's not how thieves operate, is it?'

'Thieves aren't necessarily rational thinkers.'

I moved around in my chair so I could see her. 'What was Mo working on when she died?'

Okorie turned around. 'That's an interesting question, Joe. You've spoken to the detective leading the investigation?' She paused for a moment, the truth dawning on her. 'You haven't, but you know someone who has? How warm am I getting?'

'Warm enough.'

'You and Coleman are proper buddies now?'

I didn't dignify that with a response. 'He thought I should have all the facts.'

'The facts are a good woman and the most fearless journalist I knew lost her life over a story. How do you think that makes me feel?'

'You tell me.'

'It makes me feel like shit, Joe.' Okorie headed over to the table in the corner, picked up her e-cigarette, drawing a deep hit in. 'I lost someone who meant the world to me.'

'You were working on a story together?' I offered it more as a statement than a question.

'How do you know that?'

'Call it an educated guess.'

Okorie took another drag, slowing the conversation down. 'She was helping me with something. It was what she did and there was no telling her.'

'The story was dangerous?'

'The people involved were.' She put her vaping equipment down. 'I never wanted her to get involved.'

'She sounds a lot like Don to me.' I stopped talking, letting her see the connection.

Okorie nodded her agreement. 'Peas in a pod.'

'I had to walk away from him in the end, let things go.'

She looked me in the eye. 'I'm not at that stage yet.'

'Sometimes it's the only way.'

'Bullshit.' She shook her head. 'You understand how this feels and how it works. You understand that some things can't be allowed to stand.'

'You don't know me.'

'And you don't know me.'

Okorie reached for her mobile, placing it between us. 'You should have a listen to this.'

A recording started to play back, Don's voice instantly recognisable by the way he flattened his vowels, his words slow and measured. Okorie's voice sounded on the recording, confirming I was listening to had been a conversation. 'You recorded this?'

'I thought it best.'

'Don didn't know?' It was more a statement than a question, thinking aloud. I zoned into the conversation, listening as Don talked about the 1989 investigation, how it fell short in his opinion. How John Gove's murder had always stayed with him. How he was taking a chance by talking to her.

'Don knew I was recording it. He was nobody's fool.'

'Why didn't you tell me you had this recording earlier?'

'Because he chose to speak to me, not you. What does that tell you?'

I didn't answer, listening in as Don continued to talk about the investigation, how he'd been sidelined from it. He wasn't pulling any punches, saying Jagger hadn't done his job properly. Okorie asked him why that was the case, the conversation dropping, the music in the background audible as Don thought about the question. Don explained how he'd worked the investigation without permission, trying to force the truth out into the light. Okorie then asked him directly what Forrester and Mail knew about John Gove's murder, what the truth was. There was a lengthy pause, but I knew how Don had operated. He'd have been running the calculation, weighing up what to tell Okorie, how much he trusted her with it. It was a question I was also asking myself. Don's voice sounded again, saying he knew exactly who killed John Gove. Another pause before Okorie asked him to say the name of the guilty party. Don took a moment, the silence weighing heavily on the recording before saying it. 'It's all in my file. Forrester and Mail did it.'

I wanted to be sick. My head started to spin, forcing me to breathe deeply focus again. There was a record of Don's investigation, something I'd suspected all along. The conversation ended, but all I could think of was how Don hadn't come to me. He'd gone to Okorie. I took my mobile out, starting at the screen. I'd zoned Okorie out for the moment. I knew who I needed to talk to. I sent a text message, wanting an immediate reply. It didn't come.

'I'm going to make this crystal clear for you,' Okorie said, snapping me back into our conversation.

I put my mobile back in my pocket, looked up.

'You're either with me, or you're against me. That's the way it has to be and it's your choice to make. I want it to be the first option, but I'm not begging here. The job offer still stands.'

'You didn't tell me the truth.'

'I didn't lie, either.' She picked up her laptop, going back to work. 'We've all got secrets. Think on it, Joe.'

THIRTY-SIX

The lights were off in the cottage, no answer to my knock on the door. I stepped back, almost blown off-balance by a gust of wind buffeting into me from the waterfront. It was where Sarah was supposed to be, where she said she'd be when replying to my text message. Looking around, the village pub was locked down for the night, lights off. Walking away, I knew where I'd find her.

I was still thinking about what I'd heard Don say on Okorie's recording of the conversation. I replayed it in my head, looking for the nuance, but there was no way of putting the fact he went to her to one side. The fact he'd turned to her, not me, was going to sting for a long time. I instinctively knew he would have turned a blind eye to being recorded, knowing he would have wanted it to happen. It was how he'd worked. He'd want a trail of evidence that could be followed. The more I thought about it, the more I was sure he'd been in control of what he was doing.

Head down, I approached the point on the road where Don had died. I stopped at what I thought was the right spot, shouted out Sarah's name into the darkness, receiving no answer. I tried again, ready to accept I'd guessed wrongly until Sarah stepped out from the trees at the side of the road, wobbling slightly. She didn't look like she was sleeping well, her face pale, hair tangled and unwashed.

'Have you been drinking?' I asked.

'Fuck off, Joe. If I want a drink, I'll have one.' She stared at my face for a moment. 'You're not looking much better.'

We both stepped back as a car passed, blinding us with its headlights. I put my arm out toward her, tried to encourage her to walk back to the village and cottage. 'This isn't what your dad would want.'

'Why do you always think you know what's best for everyone?'

'I don't.'

Sarah stood her ground.

'It's complicated,' I said, the best I could offer.

'Simplify it for me, then.'

'You want the truth?' I looked around, wanting to be away from the area. 'This isn't the place to find it.'

'Don't patronise me, Joe. Don't ever do that.'

I wanted to talk, but this really wasn't the place for it. Sarah started to walk down the middle of the road back towards the village, not stopping to check if I was following. I caught her up and tried to guide her to the safety of the side of the road. We walked in silence, the occasional sound of a ship out on the water and indistinct rumble of a car engine in the distance, the near-by chemical plant lit up like an alien space station in the distance.

Closing the door to the cottage behind us, I headed straight for the kitchen and filled the kettle. Sarah had balled herself up on the settee, staring at the wall. Staying in the kitchen until the water boiled, I poured the drinks, letting the steam rising out of the mugs warm my hands. Heading back into the living room, Sarah was bent over at the bottom of a bookcase, piling books into a large cardboard box. I placed the mugs down. 'What are you doing?' I looked around, the cottage had already been half packed away.

'What does it look like?'

A pile of boxes had been stacked up in the corner. 'It's not the time, surely?'

Sarah looked up at me. 'You don't get to tell me what to do.'

'I know.'

She dropped a framed photograph, the casing cracking on the floor. I found a small dustpan and brush in the kitchen, returned and started to nudge the broken glass into a pile. I worked the photograph loose, one of Don with his granddaughter, and handed it over for safe keeping. 'No harm done.'

I joined her on the settee and looked around, trying to imagine Don living here. If I'd been asked, I might have believed he'd retire to the seaside. Living in a village cut off from the city of Hull and without a car to drive told me he it was a deliberate decision to be alone. He'd sat in these four walls brooding, thinking about John Gove's murder, feeling a personal responsibility towards the man.

'I didn't mention your name to the police,' Sarah said, talking about the break-in.

'Thanks.'

'I didn't do it for you, Joe.'

'I went back to visit the old office.'

'It's stood empty since we left it.'

'It wasn't hard to get inside.'

'Looking back is becoming a habit for you.'

'I don't know why I did it.' There was no need to mention I'd been drinking.

'You always were too sentimental for your own good.'

'I needed to see it one last time.'

'Did you get the answers you wanted?'

I shook my head. 'I don't even know what the questions are.' In truth, it had been unsettling, too many ghosts in the room. I wouldn't be taking another look.

'It's just a building,' she said.

I stared at her, but was saved from answering by a clattering of paws on the stairs, Don's dog trotting into the room, immediately heading for me, aggressively sniffing around my legs. I leaned down and fussed it behind the ears.

'Dad got him after you left,' she said.

I couldn't resist a smile. 'I was always easy to replace.'

'Maybe not for him.'

Sarah always had a knack for taking the wind out of me with a handful of words. She knew just where to land them. 'That's why I'm doing this. There's a debt to repay.'

'You're doing it for yourself.'

The suggestion hurt, implied I was essentially selfish. Did she really see me like that? Had she always seen me in that light? I tried to form some words, find the right ones, but nothing came out. Maybe she was right and I was too close to things to see the truth.

She shuffled round to face me properly. 'Still working with that journalist?'

I nodded and said I was. 'She's offered me a job.' Sarah laughed. 'What's so funny about that?'

'I've looked Okorie up. You're a fool if you want to get involved with her GCSE media project.'

'You really think that?' I respected her opinion, and on some level, I craved her acceptance. Sarah was one of the few people who understood me, or so I thought. I flexed my hands and took a deep breath, refocused. 'Your father rated Okorie enough to speak to her about things. She recorded a conversation they had.' I felt bad for laying it out, but I needed her to understand. 'I've heard the recording. He trusted her with what he knew.'

Sarah stood up and walked over to the window, leaned against the frame of it. 'And what did my father know?'

'He was leaving a trail in relation to John Gove's murder.' I laid it out for her, how Forrester and Mail had investigated as young detectives, how her father was pointing the finger in their direction. Police corruption. At best, Ian Jagger hadn't done his job properly and now had plenty to lose by the truth surfacing, as did his cousin, Grant Piercy. I was still sifting through the pieces of the puzzle, but it was starting to tie together. I thought again about the trail Don had left, seeing his conversation with Okorie in a different light. He knew she would come looking for me. It was his way of making sure I didn't walk away. 'Your dad kept a file on John Gove,' I said to Sarah. 'He said as much on the recording. I couldn't find it when I was here the other day.'

'He needed an insurance policy?'

'I think he did.'

'The silly old bastard.'

There was a mixture of anger and dismay at her father's actions. Unsure of what to do, I put out an arm towards her. Tears were falling freely down her face. She turned towards me and slapped me hard across the face.

'This is your fault, Joe.'

My hand went to my cheek, looking away from her.

'This should have stayed in the past. Where it belongs.'

'It's way too late for that.' She understood all too well that actions had consequences, that you couldn't just walk away. I rubbed at my face, the initial hit of pain subsiding. 'Your dad was a good man who couldn't turn a blind eye to an injustice.'

'Don't take me for a fool. Not now, and certainly not here.'

It felt like I was sugar coating things, but it also felt like there was an essential truth in there. Don had made decisions that were sometimes complex, the morality dubious, but he had been a good man.

'You've no idea what this feels like,' she said to me.

'I don't understand what it feels like to have my world turned upside down by your father?' I let out a bitter laugh. 'It might not be the same, but I understand it all too well. Your father stood alongside a corrupt detective in my father's pub,' I said, outlining that he hadn't stopped Reg Holborn turning the screw, wanting a slice of my father's small pie because he could. 'I was probably in the pub at the time, just a kid.' I wasn't sure how she expected me to deal with that knowledge. Holborn was still in the background of events. He was the reason things between myself and Don had crashed. It was the reason I'd run away. Don had a score to settle with Holborn, and by connection, so did I. Maybe I was supposed to see this as a gift, a revenge we could both share. Maybe it was Don trying to make amends.

I rubbed my face, trying to focus on the bottom line of Don's death and what he was owed. The rest had to stay in the background for now. Ian Jagger had told me that Don's actions needed judging, just like anyone else's. The inference was clear, but I believed Don was a good man. I had to.

Sarah spoke again. 'My dad wasn't corrupt, so don't even think about laying that one on him.'

'That's not the point.'

'I'm the one who's lost here. Not you. Not really.'

I bit my tongue, but it felt like we were getting somewhere, laying our cards on the table for the moment of truth. 'I need that file,' I said.

'You should go back to Holland and your girlfriend. That's your life now.' I felt my mobile vibrate in my pocket. I took it out, glanced at the screen, surprised to see it was Pete Till calling. I paused, wondering if I'd finally got through to the man and he was prepared to talk to me about the car stolen from his yard the night of John Gove's murder. Sarah walked over to a box in the corner of the room, taking out a folder and placing it between us on the coffee table. I could see John Gove's name scribbled on the corner of it. I rejected the call, knowing he'd wait now. I stared at Don's file, wanting to know the secrets it held.

'If you take it, I'm going to assume you're working with that journalist and we're done, Joe. No going back. If you leave it here, I'll take it to the police in the morning.' She drummed her fingers on top of the file, not wanting to let it go. 'I've been doing a lot of thinking and I know how I want this handling. I won't have my father's reputation raked over and dragged through the gutter by you. Are we clear on that?'

Her eyes burned into me, but I didn't move. I didn't recognise the woman standing in front of me. The fact she'd argued with Don just before his death wouldn't be easy for her to process or accept. It added a layer of guilt I knew she'd struggle to come to terms with. Seeing her packing away her father's belongings in the cottage so soon after the funeral felt wrong. It felt cold to me, the wrong way to go about things.

'How badly do you want to continue playing at being a detective, Joe?' She headed for the kitchen. 'It's your call.'

I hesitated for a moment before picking the file up and walking over to the door. I took a last look behind me, but Sarah was out of sight, already done with me.

1989

The cafe started to empty, workers in dirty overalls leaving for a day of graft in the near-by factories, the last few dregs of industry on the docks. Don Ridley looked at Dave Bolder on the other side of the table, the man dragging nervously on a cigarette, the remains of egg yolk and bacon fat congealing on the plate in front of him. Bolder burped, a crash of plates from the kitchen behind the till area, laughter rippling through. The place had been chosen for privacy away from the city centre. He was taking a chance, Don knew he was somewhere he shouldn't be. He should have taken Sarah to school ahead of her exam later today, not just wished her good luck over the breakfast table before leaving. The nature of the job meant missing out. It was why it had to be made to count.

Don pointed to Bolder's plate. 'Enjoy that?' The man was in his early-thirties, but looked older, life taking its toll. He was painfully thin, hair matted to the side of the head in need of a good wash.

Bolder mumbled his thanks and looked away, eyes to the floor, working his tongue between his teeth.

'Full English always helps to mop up a hangover, right?' Bolder had been picked up by a uniformed officer, drunk outside of a pub in the city centre, bothering people for money. His punishment had been a night in the cells at Queens Gardens before being kicked loose. Don had waited outside the station, ushering the man towards the cafe hidden away on the waterfront amongst the numerous broken buildings and warehouses.

Bolder looked up, finished working the chunk of fat free from between his teeth, nodded. 'What do you want from me?'

'The truth, Dave, that's all.'

'What about?'

'Let's start with where you've been sleeping recently?'

Bolder looked away again, the shrill sound of the pay phone attached to the wall diverting his attention. He inspected his hands for a moment before answering the question. 'Here and there. You know how it is.'

'Wherever you can find some shelter, right?'

'Not a crime, is it?'

Don took out a packet of cigarettes, offered one to Bolder. 'I'm just interested.'

Bolder lit up, inhaled deeply and enjoying the hit of nicotine, closed his eyes.

'Ever sleep in the multi-storey car park on George Street?'

Bolder didn't answer immediately, levelling his gaze before slowly tapping the tip of the cigarette into the table's ashtray. He shook his head. 'Can't say I have.'

'Sure about that?' Bolder didn't speak. 'I buy you breakfast in here, all you can eat, fill you up with hot drinks and give you cigarettes, but you're going to lie to me?'

'I'm not lying to you.'

It was written all over the man's face. Placing the plastic lighter he'd found in the car park on the table, he waited for Bolder to run the calculation again. 'This isn't going away, Dave. I found it on the floor in the car park along with a bag of clothes.' Picking it up, Don held to the light. 'I know this is yours.'

Bolder went to take it, but it was pulled away out of his reach. 'I move around a lot,' he said. 'I forget.'

Don put the lighter back in his pocket. 'You've heard about the Car Boot Murder that happened in there the other night?' It was what the local paper had dubbed it already. Natalie Okorie and her employers, inflaming the situation unnecessarily. Bolder didn't respond, so he took him through it, wanting the details to hit home. 'John Gove was just a young lad, wasn't he? Maybe he was into something over his head, maybe he wasn't, but that's no way to die, is it?' A customer walked in, stared at them for a moment before heading to the till and asking for a bacon sandwich to take out. Don leaned in closer to Bolder. 'You just want a quiet life, right?' Bolder nodded his agreement. It was time to turn the screw. 'If you don't talk to me, you'll have to talk to Forrester. He's the one carrying out the investigation. Don't be thinking Jagger will give a shit, or swoop in to save you.' Bolder didn't look convinced. 'I know you've had a run-in before with Forrester.' It was a matter of record, a pressure point to be exploited. 'Let's be honest here, he's a proper bastard. He won't think twice about trampling over a man like yourself, maybe even find something to charge you with because he can. On the other hand, maybe he doesn't need to know I've got the lighter you left behind in the car park. Maybe he doesn't need to know that you were there at all.'

Bolder rubbed his hands through his hair, visibly agitated by the line of questioning, picked at his nails. 'I want this to go away.'

'And I'm the only friend you're going to have.'

Bolder thumped his elbows onto the table, head in his hands. He shook it vigorously before sitting back up. 'You don't understand.'

'Enlighten me.'

'I saw it happen.'

Bolder nodded his confirmation making it Don's turn to feel the world close in and tighten its grip, the sense of things moving out of his direct control. He took one of the cigarettes himself and lit it up, throwing the carton onto the table. 'We might be needing these.'

Bolder took another cigarette out and lit up again. 'Gove was alive when they got there.'

'Who got there?'

'No names.'

Don took a long drag on his cigarette, pleased that silence was giving him time to think, time to slow his brain down. 'What happened?' Bolder shook his head, but didn't speak. 'You need to get this out, Dave. It's the only way to make it better.'

'They'll come for me.'

'I won't let them.' It was a promise he knew he couldn't necessarily keep, but one made all the same.

'I'm not making a statement.'

The cafe worker appeared from the kitchen and cleared their plates away, a brief nod of thanks passing between them. Don dragged on the cigarette, thinking. Gove was a small time drug dealer. There was every chance he'd trodden on the wrong toes in the city and paid the price.

'You said Gove was alive when you saw him?'

'Two men dragged him out of the boot.'

'Did you recognise them?' No answer. 'Hear any names?'

'Gove was fucked, that much was obvious,' Bolder said, rubbing his face, eyes closed. 'They really laid into him.' His voice trailed off. 'It was horrible. They didn't stop. Once Gove was on the floor, he was booted in the body and the head. I could hear bits cracking and breaking.' He opened his eyes. 'Gove sounded like an animal in distress. I can't tell you how horrible that noise was. It wasn't human.'

Don shuffled forward, aware his leg was twitching. The question needed to be asked. 'Forrester and Mail murdered him?'

Bolder shook his head. 'That wasn't how it happened.'

THIRTY-SEVEN

Standing at the window, the morning still too dark to see outside properly. The train station on the other side of the road hadn't yet cranked into life for the day. I'd moved hotels on a whim, a safety precaution more than anything. It was another of Don's rules; you stayed safe. It wasn't a rule I'd particularly learned to pay attention to, but the hotel on the corner of Anlaby Road was as low-profile as I could find.

I sat down on the edge of the bed, not quite five o'clock yet, and stared at the floor. I'd arranged the material in Don's file into piles, skimming through it before trying to get some sleep that wouldn't come. Filling a glass with water, I was ready to start over the information knowing I'd paid a high price to obtain it. Don was dead and Sarah had made her position clear to me. It was over. It was down to me to finish things, draw a line under our partnership. After that, I didn't know yet.

Picking up the photocopies of contemporary newspaper reports relating to John Gove's murder, I ordered them, knowing I'd read most of them already. They didn't tell me anything new. Most were written by Natalie Okorie, nearly all the police quotes from Jagger. I tried to read between the lines, figure out what they both knew about events as they unfolded thirty years ago. I was guessing, wanting to see things that made sense of what I already knew, or what I wanted them to say.

Putting them to one side, I looked at the faded drawing pad Don had in his possession. It had once belonged to John Gove, which raised questions as to how Don had come by it. Flicking through it again, I was more interested in the contents. His father had said on the video footage with the paper that his son was a talented artist and I found myself agreeing with the assessment. John Gove had obvious talent, something that might have steered his life in a different direction. Circumstances and times would always constrain in a city like this. I doubted there was much in the way of an outlet for his skills in the Hull of the 1980's. The reality was, he probably never stood a chance.

The sketches at the front related to football, something his father had mentioned during the interview. John Gove was a Hull City fan, several drawings in different styles. I looked at the straight lines of the Boothferry Park stadium and contrasted them with over the top sketches of players. I paused at the ones of Grant Piercy. They showed him looking like a pumped-up Roy of the Rovers figure, every inch the star striker. The second image showed him connecting with a header, but had been crudely scribbled over, the sketch ruined in anger. Piercy's transfer from Hull City had maybe surprised fans. It had obviously angered John Gove, but as much as I disliked Piercy on a personal level, nothing ever stayed the same in sport. Players moved on for any number of reasons.

Turning the pages, I looked again at the series of sketches showing a young woman. Angela Howe was the girlfriend his father had referenced during the video interview. Her eyes and hair had been slightly exaggerated for effect, but it was still a face that looked like it would bear some resemblance to the actual subject. The first sketch was dated three months before Gove's death and showed her smiling, a beach and sun in the background. Flicking through the pages, further ones were darker in tone. They showed her face drawn using angry strokes, deliberately laid down on the page to make her look ugly and damaged. The backdrop was severe shading with the pencil, dark and brooding. It was unpleasant, but spoke about the state of John Gove's mind and his attitude to his ex-girlfriend.

Looking at the next pile of print outs, I knew she was dead. I picked up a notepad, wanting to make sure I understood it properly myself. Turning to the photocopy of a contemporary news report in the daily Sheffield paper, Angela Howe's face staring back at me. The headline and first paragraph told me all I needed to know. Local student dies from drugs overdose. Glancing through the details, she was a native of Sheffield, studied in Hull and had died at a warehouse rave in Manchester three months before Gove's murder. Don had noted the police had never made an arrest in relation to her death. It opened up a lot of questions in my mind and possible theories.

I looked over the handwritten notes Don had made. He'd visited Angela Howe's parents in Sheffield, a move I thought had been risky and dangerous. I sat back on the bed, weighing it up. He wouldn't have gone there to rake over something so personal to them without good reason. Looking at Don's report, he hadn't mentioned John Gove to them. My suspicion was that he'd lied about looking over the case of their daughter's death. They might have reported it, but he would have run the calculation and concluded that potentially uncovering the truth trumped giving them false hope. Knocking on a stranger's door, wanting answers to questions they maybe didn't want to think about, was the absolute worst part of the job. It was the act of digging up something bad, something long buried, and picking over the remains. It was a part of the job I hadn't missed. I wasn't sure I could go back to it.

I swallowed several mouthfuls of the water next to me before picking up my mobile. I clicked on Google Maps and looked at the address written down for Howe's parents. It looked to be a pleasant semi-detached house in Eccllesall, an affluent part of Sheffield populated with cafe bars and restaurants, leafy parks and boutique shops. It struck me as solid suburbia, far from cheap, but a pleasant place for a child to grow up. There were no rules when it came to drugs. They caused indiscriminate misery, but it wasn't hard to understand why Angela Howe would take the risk. She'd been young enough to see life staring ahead of, waiting to be grabbed. Nothing stopped you at that age.

Her parents had told Don they were sure she had a boyfriend in Hull, but that she'd refused to talk to them about the situation. A relationship with John Gove would fit the bill. It stood to reason she wouldn't want to introduce a low-level drug dealer to them. Howe's parents had been candid with Don about their daughter. They'd told him she'd enjoyed the finer things in life, always wanted to spend money she didn't have. It seemed she enjoyed eating out, new clothes and holidays. Her parents were worried about how she was financing her lifestyle. Maybe the passing of time meant they were more open about things. Like Gove's father, they just wanted answers.

I removed the plastic cigarette lighter Don had attached to the inside cover. There was nothing special about it, but the commentary Don provided said it had been left behind by Dave Bolder at the car park as he witnessed Gove's murder. It was potential evidence, something Don had decided not to pass along. I turned it over in my hand, thinking. It confirmed things, but didn't prove them. Raking through the paperwork, I wanted to know what Don had said to Bolder when he'd visited him in the tower block. There was nothing. It struck me that the file was incomplete because Don never had the chance to finish it.

Standing up, I walked back over to the window. The sun was starting to rise, the street slowly coming to life. The first trains would be running from the end of the line station. I needed to know more about Angela Howe's death and why no official link had been made to John Gove. Maybe it was just distance and a lack of joined-up work. Maybe it was more something more sinister. I had to use Don's file to my advantage, exert more pressure on people so they talked.

I walked back over to the stacks of paperwork and took photographs of various pieces from it on my mobile. I then sent them over to the number Mail had contacted me on, saying I wanted to talk. I couldn't promise him the immunity he wanted, but I suggested he was in a position to help himself. The next port of call would be Forrester at his boat. Looking down again at the bits of paper, it had to amount to something. The price tag attached to the file necessitated it.

THIRTY-EIGHT

I sipped at my takeaway coffee, watching a seagull flying in low around the harbour. Bridlington was still waking up for the day ahead, a strong wind making it a day for dog walkers on the beach rather than sunbathing. A street cleaning vehicle skirted past me, hoovering up yesterday's takeaway cartons.

Like the town, Forrester's boat had seen better days. From a distance it gently bobbed on the water, tyres tied to the side to buffer it against the harbour wall. It wasn't quite so picturesque close-up, the miles on the clock all too visible. The blue and white timber of its body curved up to a sharp tip, a small wheelhouse at the front for the captain. The main deck was a large, open space ringed by wooden benching. There was no sign of Forrester, though. Maybe I'd miscalculated by leaving my name on the message. Maybe he'd make the connection to Don. I sat down on a bench, waiting.

I pulled up Coleman's number, thought about calling him before deciding not to. Instead, I sent him a text message with Angela Howe's name and a brief outline of her death. I decided not to mention her link to John Gove, banking on him being curious enough to start digging a little. If he wanted some glory, he was going to get his hands dirty, too.

My thinking was interrupted by a text message arriving from Gary Mail's number. I read it twice, swearing to myself. He reiterated what he'd said at the service station. I wasn't seeing things from the right angle and that he wouldn't talk without guarantees. I replied quickly, wanting to know what he meant about what I was doing. Truth was, there was something I couldn't quite my put my finger on. He didn't reply. I stood up and threw the coffee cup into the bin and headed back to Forrester's boat, still no sign of the man. I still wasn't sure how to approach him, pretty sure he wouldn't want to talk about John Gove or Don. He was hiding out here under a false name for a reason. I glanced again at the wheelhouse. Maybe he was waiting for me, prepared.

I carefully used the railings around the decking area to jump onboard, taking a moment to make sure I had my balance. The decking area was empty, a bin liner in one corner with discarded sandwich wrappers and empty crisp packets, an empty tin of bait in the other. Trying the wheelhouse door, it was locked. I turned hearing the thud of someone landing on the deck behind me. It was instinct, but I balled my hands into fists, ready, as I turned around. It wasn't Forrester.

'Can I help you, boss?' the man said.

I relaxed, let the tension leave my body. The man was in his sixties, dirty jeans and a jumper which was slightly too big for his frame. I told him who I was looking for.

'Doesn't look like he's here, does it?'

There was a quiet steel to the man that suggested it wouldn't be wise to cause a scene. I grabbed a railing and jumped back out of the boat and waited for him to follow me on to the jetty. I held my hand out. 'Joe Geraghty.' My name meant nothing to him, not even a flicker crossing his face. 'He's expecting me.'

'Have you tried calling him?'

'Not yet. That'll be my next move, I reckon.'

'To be fair, he's usually here by now.'

Unless he's been spooked, I thought. I looked around, no sign of life of the other boats yet, either. 'He's a mate of yours?' I asked, focusing back on the man.

'We all are around here. Both been at it a while now, it has to be said.'

'How long?'

He considered the question before answering. 'Pretty much twenty years now. Time flies, I suppose.'

'He's a good guy?'

'You've booked with him.'

My phone vibrated in my pocket. I quickly checked the display, ignoring the call from Okorie. I'd call her back.

'He keeps himself to himself,' the man said, 'but that's fine with me. You won't get any trouble from him when he shows up, even if he's not a native of these parts.' The man started to move, heading back to the pavement running along the harbour.

I caught him up. 'I thought he was local? That was why I booked him.'

He laughed. 'Your man's an interloper, not the real McCoy like I am.'

'What does that mean?'

'Some of us have been doing this man and boy.'

I stepped forward, sensing it was an opening. 'What did he do before this?' The man looked at me, like it was a question he hadn't expected.

He shrugged. 'I'm not his keeper, am I?'

'Of course.'

He turned back to me. 'Tell you what, though. If you find out, maybe you can tell me?' He laughed and moved closer again. 'Your man's a bit touchy about his past.'

I matched his smile, knowing Forrester had good reason to want his past to stay exactly where it was.

'Who are you, really?' he asked me.

I stayed where I was, hands in my pocket as I looked around. I wasn't sure if the truth was would persuade the man to talk. 'Why do you ask?'

'You're not the first man to come looking for him recently, that's all.'

'Really?' He had my full attention.

'Owes money, does he?'

'Not to me.' I took my mobile out, ready to roll the dice. I went online searching for a suitable photograph before holding it out. 'Seen this man around here?'

'That's the one.'

The man looked confused at how I knew, but the odds were in my favour. Ian Jagger. I'd thought about Piercy's foot soldiers being used again, but figured Jagger would want to keep this one close and personal. 'Did they speak, do you know?'

'I told him the same I told you. Haven't seen him around, so I doubt they've spoken to each other.'

I pointed back to the boat. 'Any idea where I'll find him?'

'I'm not sure I should be handing out those types of details.'

We stared at each other and I got the message. I took my wallet out. 'Looks like I'll be needing to rebook my fishing trip, doesn't it?' I held two £20 notes out. 'Will this help?'

The man took the money from me and folded it before placing it in his jeans pocket. 'Maybe give your man another ten minutes. The road in from Skipsea and his caravan gets clogged up at this time in the morning.'

I knew the place, another village on the crumbling coast. A small dot on the map. He walked off with a small salute in my direction. I waited for him to jump onboard his own boat and disappear from view before returning to my car and pointing it towards Skipsea.

THIRTY-NINE

I missed the unmarked track the first time. The staff in the nearby holiday park had told me what to look out for, but it only worked if you knew the area. Spotting the entrance, I parked up and walked slowly down the track, a slight descent to the edge of the cliff. I was a couple of miles east of Skipsea, ten miles south of Bridlington, isolated enough if you wanted to avoid people. It wasn't to dissimilar to Don's decision to move out to his cottage. Glancing at my mobile, I was out of signal range. Approaching slowly, the bottom of the track opened up into a large turning space, a single caravan placed at the bottom of it, backing up against thick trees and bushes. No sign of a car. I came to a stop and looked around. Rubbish had been piled up in bin liners between the caravan and a cardboard box overflowing with empty beer bottles. The caravan had once been white, but stained by age and weather, it looked more like a dirty shade of cream.

A pile of cans sitting at the edge of nearest trees caught my eye. I walked across to them, nudging them apart with my foot. It took me a moment to figure out that the holes in them were from bullets. Beyond the pile, a further number of cans were lined up on a thick tree branch. I could see from the markings on the floor that Forrester had set up his own shooting range. It was possible the thing was entirely legal, but it still left me feeling uneasy about the type of man he was.

Moving closer to the caravan, the net curtains were too thick to see through. It had a number of Leeds United stickers in the window, all proclaiming the club to be '*The Pride Of Yorkshire.*' Stepping forward, my hand went to cover my mouth as my nose filled with the smell of dog shit. It was scattered around the caravan, a post with a lead tied to it to the side along with two empty bowls. There was no sign of a dog. It was as if Forrester had decided he wasn't going to live within normal society. The grass around the track was overlong, potholes underfoot. His entire hidden corner of the world grim, totally off the grid and he was clearly a man who didn't want to be found.

I span round hearing what I thought were footsteps behind me. It was paranoia, but the thought I was being watched struck me. Maybe Forrester was in the caravan. Maybe I'd been seen. Maybe he was weighing up making a move. I remained still, listening, but only hearing the sound of birds in the nearby greenery. It felt desolate, the still air around it suggesting it had been abandoned.

A quick glance at the lock on Forrester's caravan told me it was flimsy, easy enough to bypass. It was my decision to make. I checked my phone to confirm I was out of range. I'd have to return to the main road if I wanted to use it. Maybe the woman I'd spoken to at the holiday park would remember me, maybe she wouldn't. Putting my mobile back in my pocket, I was totally alone.

Picking the lock was quick and painless. I stepped inside quickly and quietly, closing the door behind me. Eyes blinking against the gloom, my hand went to my nose, the smell of sweat and unwashed clothes mixing with the cloying aroma of fish. I stepped into the living space, a small flat screen television in the corner, an untidy mess of items on top of the table next to the kitchen area. The sink was full of unwashed plates and mugs, a pint of milk on the side. Looking at it, it was still in date. The newspaper next to the kettle was from yesterday. I was wrong. Forrester was definitely still around.

I checked out the bedroom and the bathroom. Both rooms told me very little, the same stale smell in the air. Standing still, I heard a sound outside of the caravan, footsteps crunching on the ground. This time I wasn't imagining it. I leaned closer to the window, listening harder, sure someone was outside. Moving to the door, I nudged it open with my foot. I stepped outside quietly, staying flat to the caravan wall, edging my way along. Stepping forward, I turned a second too late, hearing someone closing in. Forrester barrelled into me, sending me crashing down. He was straight on to my back, trying to pin me down on the ground. I bucked and struggled, determined not to let him. I managed to get enough purchase and strength to throw him off me, Forrester landing on the ground next to me. He was straight up, roaring as he threw himself forward again. This time I saw it coming and managed to block his move, the struggle becoming an arm wrestle for supremacy. I managed to get a jab in to the side of his head with my weaker hand, forcing him to take an unsteady step backwards. I hadn't covered myself properly though, Forrester thrusting forward, all of his weight behind a punch into my stomach. I screamed and fell to the ground in pain. I rolled over and grabbed at a piece of wood, pushing myself upright. Forrester read the situation, realised things could quickly go against him now I had a weapon in my hand.

'Fuck you, Geraghty.' He glanced to the caravan, conflicted, trying to come to a decision. He hesitated for a moment before running away, off up the track and into the trees. Breathing hard, I didn't have the energy to chase him and knew I wouldn't find him anyway. He knew the terrain in a way I didn't. The way he'd glanced at the caravan told me there was something in there that I'd missed.

I took a moment to pull myself back together, satisfy myself that Forrester wasn't returning. I walked over to the caravan, looking around the living space again. I poked my way through the items on the table, looking at old newspapers going back over the last couple of weeks, some paperwork in relation to his boat. The mooring fees invoice I looked at was in Forrester's new name. An A4 envelope caught my eye, no details written on the front of it. Peering inside, it contained a number of photographs. I looked at the printer placed opposite the seating, a pile of photographic paper next to it.

I tipped the images out, picking them up one by one. Forrester had been busy. I looked at a photograph taken outside of Mail's business premises, Mail a blurred figure in the distance heading into the portakabin I'd seen there. Putting it down, the next one showed Peter Till talking to a customer in his car lot. There were more. One showed Ian Jagger talking to Grant Piercy in the bar on the Fruit Market in Hull. The last two gave me pause for thought. The first showed myself and Natalie Okorie in the Spring Bank restaurant we'd spoken in. It was a long lens shot taken from the other side of the road. Another photograph showed me in the reception of the hotel I was staying in. Forrester had been tracking me and had turned my hotel room over. It hadn't been Grant Piercy after all. The last photograph in the pile was the worst. It showed Don heading into his cottage. Forrester had tracked him down and now he was dead.

I captured the images on my mobile for reference before tidying them away. I quickly walked back up towards the main road, remaining on guard for trouble. It never came. Forrester was in the wind. My mobile sprung back into life, the signal returning. Natalie Okorie had left me a voicemail, wanting me to call her back. A text message arrived from Coleman, saying we needed talk and that I should get myself to Hull Royal Infirmary immediately. Pete Till was in a critical condition.

FORTY

I hurried towards the hospital entrance, knowing only bad news would be waiting inside for me. I'd missed more calls from Natalie Okorie, but she could wait for now. The outside of the building had been clad in light-coloured panels to offset the grim concrete brutality I remembered. The lack of smokers congregating around the door was a change, too. The lift took me up to the Intensive Care Unit, but I couldn't go any further as the door was locked. I sent Coleman a text message, saying I was outside.

Pacing and waiting, I walked over to the end of the corridor, looking out of the window, the city in miniature below. The sky was newspaper ink grey, rain starting to splatter against the window. I was on edge, knowing I'd fucked up. I played back the message Till had left for me the previous night. I'd forgotten about it until Coleman's call. Listening again, he said he wanted to tell me the truth about the night thirty years ago. I slapped my hand against the wall at the missed opportunity before leaning against it, forehead first, eyes closed. I turned as I heard footsteps behind me on the polished floor, Coleman walking towards me.

'You look like shit, Joe.'

'What's Till saying?' I asked, ignoring his comments.

'He didn't make it.'

Bile rose at the back of my throat. I turned away from Coleman and headed straight into the nearby toilet. Leaning over a toilet, I was sick. My eyes watering, I stayed where I was, knowing I really had fucked up. I should have called Till back, let him share his burden. I could have helped. Slowly, I straightened back up, flushed the toilet and made my way over to the sink. Splashing water on my face, I needed to focus, think it through. I couldn't look myself in the eye, though. I dried my hands, avoiding looking at the man who'd walked in before heading back out. Coleman was in the same spot by the window.

'Better out than in?' he said.

'I'm fine.' I looked out over the city again. Life went on, people and vehicles hurrying from place to place. Who found him?' I asked, wanting to keep to the reason I was here.

'His nephew first thing this morning. His wife said he was working late, catching up on paperwork. She was out of town last night, so didn't realise anything was wrong. It could have been random, someone thinking the place was empty and trying their luck for keys to the cars, or in the hope there was some cash on site. Might have just been a situation that got out of hand.'

'Wouldn't be the first coincidence to have happened around his place.' I kept my eyes forward, not looking at Coleman. He was far from stupid and knew it wasn't a coincidence as well I did. I laid it out for myself. If Till was working late, it meant a light would have been on. It meant it wasn't random, more a deliberate act. It had been a confrontation. 'Any arrests yet?' I settled for asking him, knowing what the answer would be. Coleman said there hadn't been.

'Any witnesses?'

'None that have come forward yet.'

'Cameras?'

'None that appear to be working.'

'Handy for someone.' I turned to face Coleman. 'Just don't go putting two young, inexperienced detectives on the case, especially if one of them might be corrupt.'

'No chance of that.' Coleman ignored the sound of his mobile in his pocket.

I prided myself on being able to read people, but Coleman was a tough nut to crack. He was holding back. I needed him as things threatened to spiral out of control. It was mutually beneficial to have a relationship, even if the distribution of power tipped in his favour.

'How does this fit in with your theory about John Gove's murder?' I was thinking about his suggestion that it was drugs related, tying in with corrupt detective, Reg Holborn.

'I don't know.'

Coleman looked at me. 'So what have you got for me?'

There was always an exchange, a price tag attached to information.

'Till was trying to speak to Jagger at an official event on the Fruit Market a couple of nights ago.'

'I won't ask how you know that.'

'How about if I said that what Forrester and Mail did went beyond corrupt?'

Coleman interjected. 'You'd have to have some serious evidence to back it up.'

I didn't have it, just words Don had said. It didn't matter that I instinctively believed them. It would be easier to write things off at the hands of a detective like Reg Holborn, proven to be corrupt, and more importantly, long dead. 'You can't just dismiss it because it's not what you want to hear.'

'Don't start trying to claim any moral high ground here.'

'Sure you're doing this for the right reasons?'

He stepped forward. 'What are the right reasons, Joe?'

'Nothing to do with benefitting your career?' I smiled, sure I had the measure of the man. 'Do you want to go up against someone as powerful as Jagger? That's what it's becoming.'

'Fuck you, Joe.'

'What?'

'You're giving me nothing here. That's not how it works.'

I snorted, knowing he'd only revealed what he'd wanted, just enough to keep me ticking over and doing his dirty work for him.

Coleman took his mobile out, telling me he had something else to share. 'Till dropped his mobile outside of his office. Guess what it tells me?'

I didn't answer, knowing I was in trouble. Coleman was staring at me, examining me for a giveaway sign.

He brought up a photograph and showed it to me. It showed the screen of another mobile phone, a log of recent calls made. 'Got lucky. It was outside on the floor near the door, probably fallen out of his pocket or something and he hadn't noticed. It sounded with a call when I was looking around, so I had a quick look before it was taken away.' He leaned over and pointed at what he wanted me to see. 'Look at the last call he made.'

I didn't need to. 'I didn't speak to him.'

'You're not telling me everything here, Joe. You think you can play me for an idiot? Not going to happen, but I'll tell you this. Till wanted your help, but here we are.'

'What's that supposed to mean?' I was angry; angry at myself, angry at his inference.

Coleman turned back to the window, watching the world go by. 'At least you didn't bring Okorie with you.'

'She'll find out soon enough. I'm not the boss of her.'

'Sounds like you've picked a side?'

I stared back at Coleman, wanting to be away from him, away from the hospital. 'I don't pick sides. I'm doing this because of what happened to Don.'

'You're getting close to the time when you have to decide who your friends are.'

'What does that mean?'

He took out his mobile and searched for a website before holding it out to me. 'This might help you decide. Your mate Okorie has decided to publish the story, anyway.'

FORTY-ONE

I walked out of the doors of the hospital, the rain turning to drizzle, stopped and checked myself. I leaned against the wall and tried to think what my next move should be. Coleman had subscribed to Natalie Okorie's website, leaving me feeling stupid for not doing so myself. I'd trusted her. A lone smoker trying to find some shelter nodded to me before pulling his dressing gown tighter around his body. He sneaked back under the canopy, waved his cigarette in the air and asked if I minded. I shook my head, not wanting to deny him a simple pleasure.

I registered for access to The Northern News Alliance, not bothered if Okorie saw my name or not. The story was front and centre on the website. It made sense of why she'd been trying to reach me. I hadn't returned her calls, though there was no way I was going to accept this was on me.

The headline was suggestive, laying it out that it was a fresh look at an unsolved murder, an under the radar investigation going on around the city, but one linked to contemporary players. Taking a moment, I let the anger pass, telling myself she was just doing her job. I could understand it, but I wasn't sure I could make sense of it. The story wasn't finished yet.

Okorie's piece started with the necessary background on John Gove's murder, a handful of photographs to illustrate the starkness of where he'd died, a chance to fix in place the various parties involved. Okorie had picked her words carefully. She'd made sure to name-drop individuals like Ian Jagger, ensuring his current role as an MP was front and centre, talk of his role in regeneration in the city and the Fruit Market post-City of Culture. She was also careful to highlight the link to Grant Piercy and his importance in leading the change. The report hinted at several unanswered questions and loose ends in relation to the original police investigation. She was painting pictures in the minds of readers.

Reading further, she was revealing more contemporary information. Careful not to overplay her hand, she spoke of Don's death, how he'd shown an interest in the case before dying in an unsolved hit and run. The article made it clear he'd been a detective within Humberside Police at the time of Gove's murder and knew the detectives involved. I paused after reading the next paragraph, which outlined the fact an unnamed private investigator was conducting his own review of the case and looking into Don's death. I wasn't named, but my involvement sounded salacious. I was portrayed as the glue holding the two strands together.

The piece concluded with attempts to obtain quotes from the police and Jagger, neither forthcoming. She'd taken their silence, essentially a negative, and turned it into something more. It made them sound like they had something to hide. The piece contained embedded links to further pieces about the City of Culture spending and asked questions about value for money and its ongoing legacy. I closed the screen down, done with the piece.

I glanced up at the hospital, Coleman inside working already on the aftermath of Till's murder. As much as he was pulling my strings, it changed things. Till was another person who'd reached out to me and I'd let down. I also knew there was no way Coleman could risk taking it further. It had to be someone expendable. I was the only candidate desperate enough for answers. I owed it to Don, even more so now Sarah had drawn a line underneath things. I had a feeling in my gut, slowly beginning to see where the various people fitted into the picture, but it was still just a theory. I couldn't prove anything yet and I wasn't ready to share.

The smoker next to me coughed, looking to start a conversation, but I moved to the side and took my mobile out. It had to be done now as things started to spiral out of control. It was when he might make a mistake. I punched the number in and waited, the call answered quickly.

'We need to talk again, Mr Jagger,' I said, a pause before he answered. 'Who is this?'

'Joe Geraghty.'

'I've said all I needed to. We don't have any business together.'

'Guess where I'm ringing from?' It quietened Jagger down, no answer from him. He didn't cut the line, either. 'I'm outside of the hospital,' I told him. 'Someone beat Pete Till to within an inch of his life last night.' Jagger didn't offer anything. 'They did a hell of a job, as he didn't make it.' I noticed the smoker was trying to listen in to the conversation, so I moved away, heading down the main path towards Anlaby Road. I stopped and moved underneath a tree for some shelter. I had to move the handset away from my ear, the booming volume of a sound system being tested at his end. When the noise faded away, I suggested it was time to talk, but the line was dead. Calling him straight back, I only got his voicemail, but I knew where he was.

I headed towards the Fruit Market, the rain starting to give way to drizzle, sun threatening to break out from behind the clouds. I listened to a report on the local BBC radio station as I drove, the reporter explaining that crowds were starting to assemble at the best viewing points, a buzz about the area already. Breathlessly, she estimated tens of thousands would be in the city centre for the evening, most following the parade from point to point.

Parking up, preparations for the night's parade and celebrations were well-under way. Roads were closed to traffic, numerous people with walkie-talkies directing lorries and vans into place to unload the necessary equipment walked along Castle Street and the perimeter of the marina, aiming for Humber Street. The closer I got, the busier it was, the road was at the centre of the night's programme.

A number of interested by-standers watched the preparations, one or two already behind metal barriers, reserving prime spots for the night's parade. A City of Culture volunteer stepped forward and handed me a leaflet advertising what was going to happen. I glanced through the details of the parade. It would move along Humber Street and around the marina before coming to a close in the Old Town area after heading along Whitefriargate. Other activities included a spectacular fireworks display and displays on the water. I read how a boat would sail into the marina, one that symbolised Hull and Liverpool's key positions in the transmigrant route from Eastern Europe to America, actors forming a chain of people loading and unloading, a performance for people to reflect upon how it's themes still resonate today.

I nudged my way through the activity towards Piercy's bar, sure he'd find the boat performance pretentious and excessive. I suspected he'd like the sound of his tills ringing, though. It also felt like the most likely place to find Ian Jagger. The bar was already busy, food and drink being served, a queue at the bar. A media team were busy setting up in the far corner, a news presenter waiting patiently to record her piece to camera, a path being cleared so she could walk and talk her way to the door and the parade preparations.

'This is a surprise, Joe.'

I turned to see Grant Piercy, his arm out, wanting to guide me away from the crowd. I let him have the small victory, waiting as he exchanged greetings with various people we passed. Satisfied we were out of ear shot, he manoeuvred himself to effectively pin me against the wall. He was doing his best to control the environment, but I was happy to play ball for now.

'You've come to accept the job offer?'

I smiled, having forgotten about that. 'It's not the career opportunity I'm looking for at the moment.'

'It's my loss, then, Joe. And yours. We could have done great things together.'

'Another time, maybe?'

Piercy smiled and folded his arm. 'I've been made aware of Okorie's story, in case you were wondering? My legal team are looking at it.'

'Not my problem.'

'She pretty much names you.'

'It's fair enough.' I told him I'd been busy. 'John Gove was a fan of yours. I've seen some sketches he did. He made you look like Roy of the Rovers in some of them.'

'I was the big local hero back then.'

'He wasn't so happy when you moved on.'

'That's sport for you.'

'Wonder if he used to watch you play, maybe even met you, back in the day?'

'Suppose it's possible, but who's to say? I met a lot of people back then and still do.'

'Speaking of selfless dedication to a place, I was hoping to run into Ian Jagger? I thought I might find him here.' I wanted to wipe the smug, shit eating grin off his face, but let the thought go. Jagger would have had time to make himself scarce. It had been a long shot. 'There are things I need to talk to him about. Turns out Don Ridley kept a file of his own into John Gove's murder somewhere in his cottage, which doesn't surprise me. Haven't found it yet, but I will. I was wondering if he knew anything about it?'

Piercy shook his head. 'I wouldn't think so.'

'Any idea where I might find him?'

'None at all, but it's a very busy day and evening for the city. It's important it goes well, and given he's our MP, I'm sure he's got far more important things to be doing than talking to you about your wild theories.'

'Goes without saying.' I smiled, knowing I'd rattled him. 'Tell him to call me. He's got my number.'

'Sure you want to do this, Joe?'

He was calling me out, threatening me by what he didn't say rather than what he did. 'Definitely.'

FORTY-TWO

The decision on what to do next was made for me by a call from Erin Riordan, the woman I'd spoken to at the homeless shelter in relation to Dave Bolder. She'd persuaded him to talk about what he knew in relation to John Gove and it was now or never, before he changed his mind.

I picked a table in the corner of the bar area of The Station hotel and waited. The open space was all grand Victorian design work with dark wood and ornate furnishings, soft lightning and deep carpets. The kind of place that creaked in the right places. Late-afternoon and it bustled with people heading across to the Fruit Market for that night's *Hit The North* parade and activities.

My mobile burst into life, the screen lighting up with Natalie Okorie's name. I stared at it for a moment, weighing up whether I wanted to speak to her or not. In or out. I took the call.

'I was beginning to think you were ignoring me, Joe.'

'I've seen it,' I said.

'Seen what?'

'The piece on your website.'

'It's a story, Joe.'

'I don't want it up there.'

'It doesn't work like that,' Okorie paused. 'You didn't even return my calls.'

'I've been busy.' It was a shit excuse and no mistake. I was aware people were staring at me. 'It's not even a story yet,' I said.

'It's becoming one, though, and that's the important thing. Stories are organic. Once you let some of the details out, more things come to light. It's how it works. It shakes things loose.'

I sat back in my chair, wishing I hadn't taken the call. 'What if you scare people off?'

Okorie dismissed my concerns. 'What if it forces people to take action and expose themselves?'

'What if it goes wrong?'

'You're worried about being in the firing line?'

I smiled, determined not to let her needle me with such a cheap shot. 'Last thing on my mind.'

She paused for a moment. 'Coleman scared you off from talking to me?'

I wasn't entirely sure what she expected me to say. 'I make my own decisions.'

'Would you believe DS Coleman called me. Seems he wanted to have a half-hearted go about what I was putting up on the website, but he's more worried you're going to do something stupid.'

'You don't know the half of it.' Coleman could read me like a book.

'You've been busy, Joe.'

'So have you.'

'Like I said sometimes you've got to shake things up a bit, see what falls out.'

'Here we are, then.'

'I've got more story to put up now after talking to Coleman.'

That surprised me, but he was nothing if not pragmatic. And leaking to the press was an age-old tactic.

'The trick is making sure you don't bend too much and end up snapping,' she said.

'I'm not going to snap.'

'Pleased to hear it. Never hurts to have a friend in the police, either.' She lingered over her words for a moment before getting to the point. 'You can't finish this as a lone wolf. Those days are long gone.'

'How do I finish it, then?'

'You finish it by working with me'

She knew how to push my buttons. 'Don spoke to you, not me.' The reality of it cut me deep and I wish I hadn't said it aloud.

'Easy for me to say,' Okorie said, 'but it wasn't personal. I was around at the time, I knew the back story. You didn't.'

'Even so.'

'You've got to trust someone, Joe. That's how it works. Don chose me. It was a professional decision, nothing more. Question is now, what future are you going to chose?'

'Maybe I just want to finish this and go home?'

'You're already home,' it was the simple truth of the matter. I knew she was right. 'I need to finish this too,' Okorie said.

'You didn't finish things when it came to Mo Arnott?' The silence at the other end of the line told me I'd overstepped the mark, but it felt important given what she was asking of me.

'It's about timing.' She paused. 'Whoever killed Mo will be caught. There'll be justice.'

I nodded to myself, believing her and the force of her words. We weren't so different in that respect. You had a window of opportunity with an investigation like you did with a story. Once it closed, the box had to be sealed and placed into storage. Not many stories got a second chance like John Gove, though. The problem was you had to blow the dust of history off what you found. Justice had to be done. Don had died because he carried the knowledge and was going to reveal it.

'What are you going to do, Joe?'

I didn't answer immediately. 'I'm working the case, like you say in your report.' Looking up, Dave Bolder walked in with Erin Riordan. Both looked around nervously. I told Okorie I had to go and killed the call, putting my arm up to attract their attention. Bolder immediately headed towards the toilets instead. Erin walked over and took a seat at the table opposite me.

'Thanks for doing this,' I said to her. 'I appreciate it.' I put my mobile away in my pocket, not wanting to think about Okorie.

'I've gone out on a limb for you here, so please don't spook him or we'll all end up in trouble.'

'I promise.' It was a fair point. I'd always tried to minimise the damage done, though sometimes it didn't always play out like that.

We sat in an awkward silence until Bolder appeared from the toilets and made his way slowly over. The woman encouraged him to sit down with us.

'This is the man I told you about, Dave.'

'Nice to meet you,' I said, but Bolder didn't meet my eye. Looking at him, he'd been beaten recently. Wincing as he pulled out a chair, his other hand went to his ribs.

'I'll go and get the coffees,' Erin said, leaving me alone to talk with Bolder.

I waited for her to go before speaking. 'I spoke to your sister,' I said. 'She wants you home.'

'She shouldn't have to deal with my problems,' he said quietly. 'It's not fair on her.'

It was a reasonable point, but things were rarely so simple. 'Not all our problems are caused by us,' I said. 'It's not always our fault. Sometimes things just happen. It's how we react to them that counts, I reckon.'

'You sound like you're speaking from experience.'

'Believe me, I am.' I glanced over at the bar, Erin was in no rush to come back over to us. I leaned in a little closer to Bolder. 'I was living and minding my own business in Amsterdam until Don Ridley died recently. I've no doubts now that he was murdered.' I sat back again, knowing the words had landed. Bolder was shocked, just as I had been when I'd accepted it as the truth of the situation. Bolder was on edge, maybe I'd gone too far, but he had to understand this was serious and had consequences. 'Where have you been staying?'

'Here and there.'

I nodded, letting it go. It was none of my business. Sleeping rough had to be tough at any age, never mind at his advancing years. 'Don came to your flat, didn't he?' I knew I was hitting him with a lot of questions, moving him around, but I wanted to shake something loose. He needed to unburden for his own good too.

'How do you know that?'

'The last call Don made was to a taxi firm. They took him to your address.' Bolder didn't deny it. 'He wanted to talk about John Gove?' Bolder looked away, eyes flitting around the room. 'It's better you get it all out,' I told him. 'That way, we can stop this and get you home.' I glanced around, too, looking for Erin, not wanting to be disturbed. She'd taken a seat at the other side of the room. She had a sightline across to us, but we had our privacy. I'd found the right words, though. Bolder focused back on me, a small nod of his head. 'Don was a good man,' I said.

'It was none of Don's business. Not really.'

'He made it his business, though. That's the kind of man he was.'

'Sometimes it's better to keep your head down.'

'No way to live, though, is it? Don couldn't walk past someone in trouble and I reckon you're the same.' I took a breath, ready to ask the question that counted.

'You were bedding down in that car park and witnessed Gove's murder.' I presented it as the fact I knew it was. His sister had said as much to me. Bolder's arms went out in front of him, gripping the sides of his chair. The genie was out of the bottle.

'I didn't ask for this,' he eventually said.

I nodded, said it was OK. 'Don wanted you to come forward?'

'That's why he visited me.' Bolder stared straight at me. 'He tracked me down thirty years ago and he did the same recently, told me to do the right thing. It was always easy for him to say that.'

'Why's that?'

'Who'd believe what I had to say. Who'd believe the word of someone like me?'

'Why wouldn't they believe you? It's clear Don did.'

'Powerful people wouldn't believe me. Don't kid yourself that they would.'

'The police are accountable.'

Bolder snorted, shaking his head. 'I didn't take you for an idiot, so don't take me for one.'

I held my hands up, acknowledging the point. We both knew the score.

'Don wanted too much from me,' Bolder said. 'More than I was prepared to give. It was none of my business and I didn't want to be involved. There was nothing I could do for the poor lad.'

'You could have intervened?' Bolder stared at me, the words didn't need to be spoken. He thought I was out of order for even suggesting it, but I was too far in. I needed to know what happened that night. 'If you'd done that, it would have been two against two, a fairer fight.'

'You have no idea.' Bolder shook his head. 'It was never a fair fight.'

'What did Forrester and Mail do?' I wanted him to acknowledge the names, confirm what Don had said on the recording.

'There was a third person there that night. I told Don that. That's why he came to my flat.' He took a breath, spent from knowing he'd said something that had been on his conscience for thirty years.

A third man. I placed my hands down on the table, running the calculation. 'Don had always known,' Bolder said. He abruptly pushed his chair out and didn't hesitate, heading straight for the rear door of the hotel which opened up on to the train station concourse. I stood up, shouted his name out, but he didn't stop or look back. I headed for the door, but he'd disappeared into the crowd, a train emptying out at the end of the line. Walking back into the hotel bar, Erin Riordan was waiting for me. She'd watched things unfold.

'I asked you not to upset him,' she said, her tone accusatory. 'I couldn't have been any clearer.'

'Did he mention the name of the third man to you?'

'What?'

I slowed myself down, looking again to the door. Bolder wasn't coming back. I apologised. 'He had some important information for me.'

'If he wants to share it, I'm sure he will.'

I headed outside and headed for my car, ignoring the crowds making for the Fruit Market, knowing who I needed to talk to.

FORTY-THREE

I watched as the 4x4 I'd seen previously pulled out of the yard quickly followed by a moped. It was a punt, but as I watched the gates to the yard remain open, I was sure I was right. Someone was still in there. I got out of my car and stretched before crossing the road and heading into the yard, night starting to draw in. It was quiet, no sign of life. A light was on in the portacabin. I headed over and walked in without knocking, finding it was empty. Looking around, the laptop on the desk had been shut down for the night. I glanced down at the sleeping bag in the corner before jumping as the door slammed shut behind me. I turned to stare at Gary Mail.

'You didn't reply to my text message,' I said.

'You don't get to tell me what to do.'

I took the point with a curt nod of my head. 'Dossing down in here?' I asked, pointing at the sleeping bag.

'I did suspect you weren't quite as dumb as I first thought.'

'Coming home's always the right move when the going gets tough.'

Mail moved further into the office. He closed the blinds and perched on the corner of the office desk. 'What do you want?'

I leaned against the window and folded my arms. 'Things are getting out of hand,' I said. 'I tried to speak to Forrester. Did you know he's got a new name these days?' Mail had a good poker face, not even a twitch at the mention of his old colleague's name. 'I went to his boat, but he didn't show.'

'You spooked him?'

'I tracked him down to a caravan out near Skipsea, so not that far away from here.' I took my mobile out and teed up the photographs I'd taken, showed them to him. 'It's how he lives.'

Mail swiped through them before handing it back to me. 'Grim.'

I wasn't going to argue with such an assessment. 'He's totally off the grid.'

'He wasn't there?'

'He tried to attack me.'

'Maybe you should take the hint?'

'I've never been good at that.'

'Doesn't surprise me.'

'Forrester has been watching me,' I said, explaining about the photographs he'd taken of me talking to Natalie Okorie and of my hotel. 'He took one of Don outside of his cottage just before he died.' I let that linger with him for a moment, silence settling before speaking again. 'He's got photos of you out here, too.' Mail shook his head. 'I'm not making it up,' I said, offering him my mobile again. 'Have a look.'

'You don't know anything.'

'I know more than you think,' I said. 'People are being silenced, and from where I'm standing, people like me and you are in the firing line.' I pushed myself off the windowsill and moved closer to Mail. 'Jagger's a powerful man, but he's not untouchable.'

'You're an idiot if you're thinking of taking him on.'

'Pete Till's dead.' I eased myself back a step, this time seeing a twitch from the man. I'd scored a hit. 'He was kicked to death next to his office. It's a bit like this place, really,' I said. 'Could be a robbery gone wrong, but we both that's not true, right?'

Mail shook his head. 'You really don't know anything. Forrester and Till went back years.' He counted them off on his fingers. 'School, football, socially. No one gave a shit back then.'

There it was, the connection I'd suspected was there, delivered so casually to me. I walked back over to the window, peered out of the blinds unable to see anything, the sky rapidly darkening. Don had always been right. It was a conspiracy that had held for decades. I took a breath, composed myself and turned back to Mail. 'It's time for the truth to come out. It needs to.'

'I walk away.'

'You didn't do anything?'

'No.'

I believed him when he said it was Forrester who'd led the way. I could picture the scene; one man dominating, the other going along with it. But it wasn't a free pass. 'You didn't stop it.'

'Fuck you.'

'No, fuck you.' I was pragmatic enough to accept things weren't always black and white, but this wasn't an easy one to swallow when we were talking about the actions of the police. 'You don't get to walk away, but you owe the truth here.'

Mail shook his head, a smile on his face. 'Who do I owe the truth to now, thirty years later?'

'The dead.'

'Fuck off, Geraghty.'

'Jagger's swanning around as if he owns the place,' I said, ignoring his jibe. 'Do you think that's how it should be?'

'He does own the place.'

'Forrester's running his own business. He's winning, too. Why should that be allowed to stand?' Mail had no answer for me. 'The story's out there,' I told him. 'It's on a website, The Northern News Alliance.' I looked at the laptop on the desk. 'Have a read if you don't believe me.'

'So what?'

'It means the rest of the media won't be far behind. They'll be coming for me, as I'm all but named, but they'll also come for you. If I can find you, so can they. You've got a life here, but they'll destroy all that.'

'Leave my family out of it.'

'It's not my decision to make.'

Mail pushed himself off the corner of the desk, he thought about starting up the laptop, but decided I was telling him the truth.

'Tell me about Reg Holborn,' I said.

He looked puzzled. 'Holborn? What's he got to do with anything?'

Mail was genuinely puzzled at mention of the corrupt detective's name. I watched as he walked over to his sleeping bag and picked up a bottle of water. He shrugged at me. 'I know what Holborn was, and I might have made some bad decisions in my time, but credit me with some sense.'

'Forrester wasn't so smart, though?'

'That was none of my business.'

'He made it your business.' Mail opened the bottle of water and drank back half of it without taking his eyes off me. 'Don't go down with him,' I said. 'You don't need to do that.'

'He's already ruined my life.'

'There's a way of putting it right here. Tell me what you know.'

Mail walked over to the door. 'Are we done?'

He headed outside. I followed, telling him we were nowhere near done. 'You said I was looking at things from the wrong angle when we spoke at the service station,' I said to his back.

He stopped and turned back, taking another mouthful of water before speaking. 'You'll figure it out if you're as clever as you think you are.'

I took out a piece of paper, pulled up a number in my mobile, scribbled it down, and told Mail what I wanted him to do. 'It's time to finish this for all of us.' He took it from me, but I wasn't sure if he would act on it. Every move had consequences for him. Mail looked over my shoulder, pointing at something behind me. I turned, looking at the fire in the distance.

'That's coming from Paull,' he said.

FORTY-FOUR

I drove as fast as I could to Paull, eyes on the fire at all times. I didn't know exactly where it was coming from, but I had a bad feeling about what I was going to see. Hitting Main Street, I slowed, parked traffic making the road difficult to navigate. Lights were on in the pub I'd visited to talk about Don's life in the village.

Closing in on the lighthouse, a fire engine blocked off the road. I watched the car in front of me slow and perform a three-point turn. Leaving my car parked on the pavement, I jogged across, able to see the fire was coming from Don's cottage. It had spread across both floors, a team of fire fighters working quickly and quietly, containing the damage. A small crowd had assembled close to the lighthouse, well away from the cottage. A uniformed officer kept them at a safe distance, the flashing blue lights on his car lighting the scene up. My eyes went to the ambulance beyond him, its doors open but it had reversed in, so I couldn't see what was going on inside.

I tried to break past the uniformed officer, but he was more alert than I'd given him credit for. He pulled me back by the shoulder, shouting out that I wasn't to go any closer. Coleman appeared from around the ambulance doors, wanting to know what was going on. I stared back at him, telling him to get his colleague off me. Coleman weighed the situation up before nodding that I was ok. I could come through.

Coleman took me to one side. 'He's doing his job, Joe, keeping you safe.'

'A walker on the front saw it after her dog escaped its lead and went around the back. Lucky really. Could have been a lot worse.'

'Deliberate?'

'If I was a betting man.'

I remembered the pile of timber around the back, you'd only notice it from the front if it caught your eye, and you'd need to be looking, not staring down at a phone. There wouldn't be a huge number of dog walkers out at this time so there was every chance the fire would spread quickly and was likely to remain undiscovered until it was too late.

'What's the ambulance for?' I asked, turning to look at it.

'How did you hear about the fire?'

I turned back to him. 'You didn't answer my question.'

Coleman rubbed his face, knowing it was true. I wasn't in the mood for playing games. 'Sarah tried to get inside,' he said, looking over to the cottage. 'She's fine. It's just a precaution, but you know how it is. Seems she was in the area when the alarm was raised, but had the good sense to back away after trying to get inside.'

I was rooted to the spot, heart beating faster. I'd made this happen by prodding Piercy about the missing file. It confirmed there was something worth finding, but the price of learning that had been high.

Coleman's mobile sounded. He headed off to take the call, told me to behave myself. I stayed where I was for a moment, feeling the wind coming in off the water. I took a deep breath and walked over to the ambulance, unsure if I'd be welcome or not. Sarah was sitting alone, a blanket around her shoulders to keep her warm, head down as she fiddled with her phone. I made sure to make some noise so she'd notice me.

She looked up and stared at me before she put her mobile down. 'At least this saves me the bother of deciding what to do with this place. Someone's done me a favour.'

I sat down next to her on the ambulance step, feeling like shit. It didn't feel like the chain of events I'd set in motion had done her a favour.

'What do you know, Joe?'

'I'm getting closer to the truth,' I said, knowing how to read between the lines with her, what she was really asking me. 'Feels a bit like the old days.'

'They're gone now.'

That was true. Everything had changed. 'It's heavy shit, Joe.'

'Could have been a lot worse.'

'Story of your life.'

I had to agree she wasn't wrong.

'I need a fresh start,' Sarah said to me. 'I need to get away from here. Maybe the insurance pay-out will set me up. What are you going to do when it's over? You've still got the job offer from the journalist on the table?'

'I have.'

'What about Amsterdam? What about your life over there?'

'It's not me.'

'Sounds like you're making a go of it, though?'

'Amsterdam was running away, just me kidding myself. You were right about that. This is all I can do.' I didn't need to explain further. Sarah knew exactly what I meant. Whether I worked for myself or worked for Okorie, it was about wanting justice. It was a simple word, but such a powerful one. One loaded with different interpretations and meanings. It was what fired me up.

'What about Marieke?'

'She's great, but things have run their course. It's not going to work. She deserves better than me.' I'd come close to making the call, but it was something that had to be done face to face when I returned, even if it was just to collect my things.

'You shouldn't be so hard on yourself.'

I stood up, and glanced down at Sarah, wondering if our friendship could be repaired. It wouldn't be the same as it once was, that wasn't how it worked, but there was something there worth salvaging. I knew where I needed to go, what I needed to do. I squeezed her shoulder before stepping away. 'Look after yourself.'

'You, too.' I started to walk away, thinking back to Don and his link to Holborn and my own father, how that had fucked things up. How it driven a wedge between us all. It was time to put it to bed. I didn't necessarily have to forget about it, but I could forgive, shed myself of the weight it carried. Sarah called out to me, forcing me to turn back.

'The truth will come out about the fire,' she said, 'but I don't care. Not really. I haven't got any memories here. If it needed to burn, it needed to burn.'

I looked at the cottage. 'I guess it did.'

She nodded, took a moment before speaking again. 'Thanks for coming back for the funeral. It meant a lot.'

Things were clearer in my mind. We'd said what we'd needed to. Moving towards where the uniformed officer was holding back the dwindling group of people watching the fire fighters at work, a journalist stood to the side of them, scribbling down into a notepad. I was stopped from leaving the scene by Coleman appearing at my side. Maybe my assumptions were all wrong. I pushed past me, ready to go back into Hull.

'Where are you going, Joe?'

'To finish things.'

FORTY-FIVE

'It's a good job you're predictable, Gerard,' I said, standing over his regular table in the backroom of the Anlaby Road pub.

'If I wasn't here, I'd only be at home.'

The television played out live coverage of the latest Brexit news on the rolling news channel, fixed since my last visit. Several newspapers were spread around the table, various crosswords not quite completed. Looking around as I waited, the wallpaper was coming away in the joins, nicotine yellow in places dating it instantly. The carpets were threadbare, the football trophies behind the bar reminding that the place still had a purpose. It needed some care and attention, an injection of resources that would never come. Make do and mend, what you see is what you get, no artifice. The city in a nutshell and difficult to reconcile with the brave new world Ian Jagger and Grant Piercy were trying to pioneer.

'Just you, is it?'

I nodded. 'Just me.'

'What's happened to Okorie?'

I pulled up a stool, but didn't give him the satisfaction of an answer.

'At least you've come to your senses. Better late than never.'

I glanced at the empty glasses in front of him, 'Can I get you another?'

'I'll buy my own,' Branning said.

'It's your funeral.'

He picked up his pint, toasted me. 'Feels like it'll be a sweet relief some days.'

'Have you seen the news today?' I asked, wanting him to move away from feeling sorry for himself.

He pointed to the newspapers in front of him. 'I'm old school. I'm reading yesterday's news in today's papers.'

I decided not to tell him about the fire in Paull, instead telling him I'd been busy. 'I spoke to Mail.'

'Good for you.'

'He's scared, but he's got a story to tell. It comes with strings attached, though. He wants to tell someone what he knows, but he wants out of things, a clean break.'

'Most people just want to live their lives in peace with no one bothering them.'

'Sometimes you don't have a choice,' I said. 'Sometimes other forces mean you have to act.'

Mail was far from blameless, but he could unlock things for me.

Branning snorted, didn't take his eyes off me. 'What does Coleman have to say about it all?'

'It's above his pay grade, apparently.'

Branning smiled and shook his head. 'You're doing his dirty work, right? He knows you're doing it for the right reasons, but sees a chance to claw himself up the slippery pole off the back of it. You've got to admire that kind of naked ambition, I suppose. You're on your own, Joe.'

He finished his drink, stood up and I watched him walk towards the door, knowing his analysis was on the money. We all had our reasons for wanting to know the truth about the murder of John Gove in 1989, something I was making my peace with. I could live with it, despite Branning's cynicism.

I followed him out into the car park behind the pub. 'I've tracked Forrester down,' I said to his back.

Branning turned around. 'Is that so?'

'He runs a boat out of Bridlington, but you already knew that?'

'I like to stay involved, but fair play, he's not an easy man to find.'

I wanted him to know I wasn't idiot, that I was following the trail. 'Pete Till's dead. Seems he was attacked on his business premises.'

'Till? The car dealer back in the day?'

'There's a team out, asking around, the usual resources. Nothing yet, though.' We both knew the answer wasn't going to come via the traditional route. Everything tied back to John Gove. Everything had to be looked at through the prism of his murder. 'Turns out he was connected to the story all along.'

'That's interesting.'

I told him how Till connected to Forrester, that it wasn't just chance that had seen his car dealership broken into that night, a vehicle taken. 'Till went along with it and Jagger must have known.' I stepped forward and leaned in closer. 'I want to talk to Jagger again, but he's not so keen.'

'Stands to reason.'

'I tried to get to him but couldn't get close because of Grant Piercy.' I explained the men were cousins, though there was more at stake for them now.

'I've read about Piercy in the paper. Can't miss him in the thing.'

'Jagger's got tonight's parade to use as an excuse to hide.'

'Must be another way, though? Piercy's a wanker, style over substance?'

'He offered me a job.'

Branning laughed. 'Doing what?'

'This and that,' I said. 'Consultancy services, mainly.'

'That covers a multitude of sins.'

'It pays well.'

'Seriously?'

I shook my head and said I'd walked out at the point. 'He was trying to buy my silence.'

Branning considered what I'd said, eventually agreeing. 'He wants a quiet life for Jagger so his business interests don't fall off the radar?'

'Maybe Jagger would speak to an old friend if he was to suggest a time and place?'

'Why would I want to do that?'

'For Don,' it felt like the most obvious thing to me, but Branning wasn't convinced. 'Someone killed John Gove thirty years ago and someone killed Don a week ago because of what he knew. Jagger knows what happened. Forrester and Mail have got blood on their hands and they took part in John Gove's murder..'

'That's a big accusation to make.'

'I'm not making it.'

'Who is?'

'Don is. It's all on record' There was no way of sugar-coating it. The colour drained from Branning's face. What I was saying cut to the heart of a job he'd given his life to. 'Natalie Okorie recorded an interview with him about it.'

A small smile on his face, a shake of the head. 'He went to her? That's quite something.'

Branning knew how to press at an open wound, draw some pain out. It was a shot back, a reminder that I wasn't calling all the shots here. 'She played me the recording.' I told him I had a witness to John Gove's murder.

'Stop right there, Joe. I don't want to hear it. You should be sharing that kind of thing with Coleman.'

'There was someone dossing down in the car park. He saw it all.'

'How do you find someone like that thirty years later?'

'Because it's my business to.' He didn't need to know the details. 'The man's scared of coming forward. In fact, he won't.'

'He'll have a price.'

You could always make people talk, I knew that much. You had to find their weak point, make them fear a worse outcome from not talking to you. It wasn't always pleasant, but it was the truth. I didn't want to do that. Bolder had given me the key piece of information. Anything more was bringing trouble to his door and I didn't want to do that to him. 'He gave me what I needed, it wouldn't be right to push him any further.'

'Grown a conscience?'

'There's a line. He did nothing wrong. He shouldn't suffer.'

'It best be worth it then.'

'He said there was a third man in the car park.' I let that sink in. 'It's time everyone accounted for their actions.'

'And for Okorie to get a story?'

'I don't care about that.' It was the truth. We were both doing what we thought was right, even if we had different approaches.

'This isn't a game.'

'I know.'

'How far are you prepared to go? What price are you prepared to pay?'

We both stood firm, weighing each up other. It was a situation loaded with danger, but one I understood had ramifications for a lot of people and the city. I was asking Branning to light the fuse on a potentially dangerous situation, one that had already seen people die. I was asking him to put aside whatever had fuelled his distaste for me at Don's funeral and co-operate. 'Whatever it takes,' I told him.

Branning nodded and took out his mobile. I brought up Jagger's number and held it out to him, watched as he made the call. I listened as he introduced himself, saying they needed to talk about John Gove and Don, that it wouldn't wait. Branning was good, holding his ground and remaining insistent. He repeated back the time and place so I could hear it before killing the call. 'I hope you know what you're doing, Joe.'

So did I. There was no going back now.

1989

The CID room buzzed with telephones ringing, people coming and going with sheets of paper, detectives huddled together talking in small groups. Don Ridley sat back in the chair, rocking slightly. Brooding. It wasn't where the action was. His mind went back to Dave Bolder, the man had gone to ground again, no trace.

Pushing the chair fully out, he headed out of the office, one detective smirking as he passed. The Incident Room for the John Gove investigation was at the end of the corridor, out of sight and out of mind. He wasn't meant to be there, but it was a compulsion, a need to know what was happening. Stepping inside the empty room, he breathed in the details. Blown up crime scene photographs on the wall showed John Gove inside the boot of the car parked up in the multi-storey. Others showed Gove alive, one a recent image sitting on a floral-patterned settee at home, smoking a cigarette. A flip chart had a sheet of paper with various questions on it – timings, last sightings and an attempt to build a network of associates. It was the word at the bottom of the page, circled twice, that grabbed the attention – witnesses? Bolder needed to talk about what he'd seen.

Gary Mail walked into the room, a mug in his hand. 'What are you doing here, Don?'

'What's the score?'

Mail placed the mug down on the windowsill. 'There isn't one yet and it's none of your business.'

'You must have a theory, though?' He pointed to the displays. 'The flip chart suggests so.'

'There's no theory yet.'

No theory, Don said to himself under his breath. Mail had pulled out a chair at the side of the room, busying himself with a stack of reports. It was an investigation going around in circles, asking questions, but not going to any great lengths to figure out the right answers.

'Isn't this is a surprise, if it isn't everyone's favourite failed detective.' Forrester walked in, also a mug in his hand. Spilling a bit from the top, he placed it down next to Mail's. 'That's why he should always be the one that puts the kettle on.'

Don paid the comment little attention, recognising it for what it was – a less than subtle show of the power dynamic between the two detectives.

'Haven't you got a sweet shop theft, or something, to be dealing with?' Forrester asked.

'Let the adults crack on with the real work in here?'

'You don't seem to be doing much cracking on from where I'm standing?' Forrester walked over to the flipchart, made a show of looking it over. 'It's never easy when the victim is a piece of shit. Live by the sword, die by the sword, as the DI says.'

'You think he deserved it?'

'You think he didn't?' Forrester shook his head, walked back over to where he'd placed his mug and drank a mouthful. 'Fuck off out of here, Don, before the DI returns.'

He didn't care for Jagger. 'Found any witnesses yet?'

Forrester smiled. 'There aren't going to be any witnesses to find, are there, in a place like that?'

Mail walked across the room and opened the door. 'You heard the man, Don. Off you fuck.'

Don held his ground for a moment, one last look around the room before leaving, heading for the toilet rather than back to the CID room.

Leaning over the sink, the cold water from tap cooled his face. Staring at his reflection, the person staring back needed to get a grip. He shook his head, laughed. John Gove wasn't even his problem, wasn't even his investigation. Things were being neglected at home, an early warning sign that this was in danger of becoming an obsession.

Needing a piss, all three cubicles were empty, force of habit meaning he headed into the middle one. What more could he do? The longer the investigation went on, the more people forgot and the less likely they were to come forward.

Hoofed in the back, he went flying forward, arms out against the cubicle wall to break the fall, everything spinning. Piss on his hands, a shout from behind to watch the door.

'You're becoming an irritant, Don.'

Forrester's voice. With one arm forced up behind his back, he couldn't fight back, Forester as strong as an ox. Trying to distribute his weight and find a more comfortable position, ready to retaliate, it was all he could do.

'You need to keep your nose out of my business,' Forrester hissed in his ear.

'Or what?' A blow to the back of the head sent him to the floor. Forrester quickly hauled him back to his feet, spun him around, so they were face to face.

'Or what? You haven't got many friends here, Don, and you're going to end up with even fewer. You're getting close to being out of your depth and in serious trouble.'

'You're scared?'

'Me? I've got nothing to be scared of here. Don't forget Gove was a scumbag dealing drugs. Why do you want to go into bat for someone like that? Makes no sense, does it, Don? Whatever you think you know, you don't. Whatever you think you've seen, you haven't. Am I making myself clear?'

'Fuck you.'

A punch to the stomach, forcing him to bend over, gasp for breath. 'You're going to piss people off, Don, if you don't sharpen up.'

Another blow, this time from a boot, pain shooting through his body as he struck out in an attempt to fend Forrester off. No strength to do so. 'Piss you off, or piss others off?'

Forrester leaned down to him. 'This is about picking a side, Don. We're all supposed to be on the same one here, share the benefits of our labours, but you're making it hard for everyone.'

'Tell me about Angela Howe.'

'Who?'

'Gove's former-girlfriend. She died of an overdose. Why hasn't she been linked to things? What's her part in this?'

'She doesn't have one, why would she?'

'It's a loose end you've done nothing with.'

'There's no evidence her death is linked to Gove.'

'Manchester might have something to say about that.'

'There's nothing doing there.' Another punch. 'You'd do well to remember that.'

'This should have been my investigation. I was there from the start.'

'It's not, though, is it?' Forrester jabbed a finger out and stepped back. 'Walk away and forget about it. You should never have got involved.'

'What if I don't want to do that?' Don said, struggling back to his feet. 'What are you going to do about it?'

Forrester smiled, a small shake of his head. 'You're not going to throw your career away over someone like Gove. Think about your family.' He stepped forward so they were toe to toe. 'Think about your daughter.'

Don lunged forward, fists curled, grabbed at Forrester's suit jacket. 'You don't talk about my family.'

Forrester let it happen, smiled, his words measured. 'It's nothing personal, Don. We all know each other's business, don't we? We're a different type of family here, but we're still a family. We share highs and lows, all that bollocks. But families can cause us pain, too.' Pushing Don away, he slapped him lightly on the cheek. 'Think about what I'm saying.'

Don watched Forrester go, leaving him standing there. He leaned against the door, the threat having been delivered. Seeing movement out of the corner of his eye via the mirror above the sinks, he edged forward, the angle just right. Forrester nodded to the man standing by the door ensuring they weren't disturbed. The other man was DI Jagger.

FORTY-SIX

Pushing my way through the expectant crowd lining the marina, a riot of colours and noises exploding overhead, I had two questions which needed answers. Firstly, I wanted to know who'd killed Don. Secondly, but related to that, I wanted to know who'd murdered John Gove in 1989. I was going to finish things. I was thinking about Don's death and how he knew too much but not enough, the pieces he held didn't quite fit together and were still too dangerous.

A performance was underway on the water, a series of trapeze artists lit up by spotlights, increasingly impressive feats of gymnastics drawing approval from the audience. Sound systems pumped out loud music, police officers and an army of City of Culture volunteers subtly overseeing events. The evening's main event, the parade through the streets of the area was due to start imminently, mobile phones raised to the sky ready to film as it snaked past.

Aware I was pushing against the flow of the crowd, I was aiming squarely for the new amphitheatre next to the digital enterprise centre. It backed out against the water directly opposite The Deep, an outdoor arts space used for the summer festivals. A large tent had been erected over the stage area making it the nerve centre of the parade, a space for VIPs and those the city was looking to impress. It was the venue Gerard Branning had been given for his meeting with Ian Jagger.

Closing in, the area's bars were busy, door staff trying to control the flow of customers, pop-up bars on the pavement struggling to keep up with demand. Pushing my way through the crowds and towards the entrance, I focused on what I needed to do. What I needed to extract from Jagger. I paused, watching the people in front of me give their name to the security team, wondering if I could sneak by on their blind side again, take Jagger by surprise. An arm was thrust out as I tried to do that, stopping me dead.

'I'm expected,' I said, eyeballing the two members of the security team. 'Ian Jagger.'

'Mr Branning?'

I hesitated for a moment before nodding. 'That's right.'

One of the team stepped away from me, speaking into his headset. He turned back to us and nodded. 'Follow me,' the other man said.

We weaved through the throng of people eating canapés, sipping at expensive-looking drinks and making small talk. None of them paid us any attention. We came to the far corner of the tent, a small door built into the design. Another member of the security team standing against it.

'Through there,' the man who escorted me said. 'You'll be seen.'

The guard on the door stepped to one side to allow me to enter. I had no choice. Pushing my way through, it opened into a small space sectioned off with metal fencing, deep in the shadow of the surrounding buildings. Private and out of sight. I could hear the sound of passing crowds, the sound of the parade making its way down the street.

'Joe Geraghty.'

A figure I hadn't noticed stepped forward. I turned to Jagger. 'Gerard decided he couldn't make it.'

'Of course he couldn't.' Jagger stepped forward, hands in his pocket. 'Do you think I'm that stupid? I've had no contact with him for years, decades even, but then he suddenly decides to get in touch to talk about the good old days and his mate, Don Ridley? No, it doesn't work like that. You might not think I was much of a detective, but this was obvious from the start.' Jagger had started to pace around. 'You're an irritant.'

'I'll take that as a compliment.'

'You really shouldn't. I'd say I've been tolerant of you so far, understanding what you're going through in relation to Don's death, but you need to walk away.'

'That's not going to happen.'

'We've got a problem, then.'

I smiled, watching him closely as he paced around the small sectioned-off space. If he thought this was going to be easy, he was mistaken. 'We're going to get to the truth tonight, one way or another.'

'You're not in charge here.'

I smiled and made sure I had the necessary eye contact before speaking again. 'I'm different to you. You're a Member of Parliament, so you have to play by the rules. I don't.' I stepped forward, closing the gap between us. 'The more I speak to people about what happened in 1989, the more questions I have. I've had very interesting conversations with the two officers who led the investigation for you, Forrester and Mail.'

Jagger's eyes narrowed, searched my face to see if I was telling him the truth.

'I've already told you they weren't up to the job. You think something's going to stick via them?' He shook his head. 'Regardless of what you think you can make them say, it won't work. They'll be seen as discredited by the media, if it gets that far.'

We both backed off slightly, taking a moment. I span around suddenly, sure I heard a noise behind me. It was still too dark to see into the corners. I turned back to face Jagger, the man smiling at my paranoia. I cut him off from speaking. 'Mail probably wasn't up to the job,' I said, knowing how it had fucked with him. 'Forrester was a bad lad, though? If you work with people like Reg Holborn, people will draw their own conclusions.'

'Different times, different attitudes to how the job should be done. You're reaching here and wasting my time.'

Jagger tried to push past me, but I shoved him away from the door. The security guard outside didn't react. 'How about if I said Forrester and Mail murdered John Gove?'

He took his time answering the question. 'Why would they do that?'

'Maybe they were under orders?'

'Like I said, different times, but it wasn't the Wild West back then. Have you heard yourself? The police don't go around murdering people.' Jagger smiled at me, like he felt sorry for me in some way. 'You're letting your imagination run away from.'

'I don't think I am.' I stepped towards him again, forcing him closer to the fencing, wanting him to feel like he was penned in. I wanted to ruffle the man's feathers, shake something loose. 'I tell you what isn't reaching, shall I? There was a third man with Forrester and Mail in the car park that night when Gove was murdered.' Jagger couldn't hide the look of terror on his face, the fear that I was about to bring everything crashing down around him. I'd scored a hit. He was sinking. It was the moment of truth. I heard footsteps behind me, but too slow to move, a weapon was brought crashing down on the back of my head. Everything turning black as I hit the floor.

FORTY-SEVEN

I came around slowly, pain pulsing through my head, settling at the back of it where I'd been struck. I stayed still in the hope everything would stop spinning, but to also buy myself some time to think. Looking at the ground below me, I was sure I was still in the same closed off space. My plan to take back control didn't last long. Kicked in the back, I rolled over, groaning as I tried not to vomit, eyes watering. The passing parade sounded like the volume had been turned up to maximum, the firework explosions in the sky that bit brighter, fizzing and swirling like the pain in my head.

I heard a voice say I was back with them, too indistinct to figure out who it was speaking. I tried to sit upright against the wall, stared up at Grant Piercy grinning at me. I stared back, trying to disguise the pain I was in, not wanting to give him the satisfaction.

'Interesting chat you've just had with my cousin,' he said, lighting a cigarette and taking a long drag on it.

It was Piercy's way of telling me he'd been listening in, that he'd been the one who'd knocked me out cold. 'The police are on their way here,' I said, rolling the dice. I was in a dangerous situation and needed something to change it somehow.

Piercy kneeled down, getting himself right in my face. 'The police aren't coming, Joe. You're not built that way. You're not someone who asks for help. You never have done and never will.' He straightened back up. 'You think the police will side with you over people like me?' He laughed. 'You're not that dumb.' He threw the cigarette to the floor, it's tip glowing brightly before it was snuffed out by his foot. 'No, this gets finished now.'

Piercy was a man with an ego, but there was something more there now. He was manic, on edge and unable to stay still. Cocaine I guessed. I caught sight of Jagger behind him, watched as he edged away to the side of my vision.

Piercy stepped forward and lashed out, a boot going into my stomach. 'We've worked hard for all this. Do you seriously think we'd let you bring it all crashing down over something that happened thirty years ago?' He shook his head and took a deep breath. 'Who'd miss you, Joe?'

'Fuck you.' Speaking was an effort, the act of breathing sending pain shooting through my body.

'No one will miss you, that's the truth. If you just disappeared, no one would even go to the bother of reporting you missing. That's how sad and empty your life has become.'

'Is that meant to be a threat?'

'It's a reality check, shit happens. Maybe you fell into the water, maybe I'll tell the police you were unbalanced, a danger to yourself? Who'd give a shit? You'd wash up eventually, but it would probably take time to identify you.'

'The police know everything.'

Piercy smiled and kneeled down again, grabbed at my face and twisted it. 'What do they know, Joe?'

'Don had pieced it all together.' I was reaching, but I had to land a blow, sow the seed of doubt in his mind.

Piercy spat onto the floor next to me and stood back up. 'Don didn't know anything. You've backed the wrong side, that's what happened. If you'd taken my job offer, it could have been very different for you, but decisions have consequences.'

I tried to move, push myself up on to my feet. There had to be a way out. I needed to get myself closer to Jagger, as he was clearly uncomfortable with how the situation was developing. He was a man with a lot to lose if things went wrong, if I could just get under his skin I might still have a chance.

Piercy saw what I was doing and pushed me back down to the floor. 'Behave yourself.'

I winced as I hit the floor, swallowing the pain down. Piercy struck out again, this time a boot to my ribs. I couldn't swallow, another blow, I howled out in pain.

'Let's stop playing games, shall we?' Piercy pulled me up by my hair. 'You said there was a third man at Gove's murder. Who was it?'

'Fuck you.'

Piercy hit me in the stomach and let me fall back to the floor. 'I'm asking politely at the moment.'

I closed my eyes, breathed in hard. 'You know as well as I do,' I managed to spit out, a smile on my face. Another blow cut me down.

'You're testing my patience, so I'll ask one more time. Who was third man?'

I glanced over to Jagger. 'Something you want to say, Ian?' I shouted over. I felt a blow on the side of my head.

'You're talking to me,' Piercy said, 'not him.'

I turned back to Piercy. 'Still looking out for your cousin? It's above and beyond.'

Piercy told Jagger to come closer. 'Pass me an empty bottle.'

I instinctively backed up against the fencing, ready to fight what was coming. Piercy told Jagger to hurry up. Taking it from him, he held it out in his hand.

He waved it close to my face before smashing it on the floor. 'Just remember I asked politely first.' He bent down and picked up a large shard of glass, held it up against the moonlight. A hand came out and grabbed my face, gripping it tight. 'Remember you did this to yourself, Joe.'

I felt the glass dance around my cheek, its tip sharp, before he moved it closer to my eye. He laughed before moving it back to my cheek, nicking my skin enough so that I could feel blood slowly trickle down my face.

'You best start talking,' Piercy said.

'You should ask your cousin.'

Piercy shook his head, a smile on his face. 'I've done some things I'm not proud of to get to where I am today, but I'm quite happy to do more and hurt you.'

The tip of the glass went back to my eye and it took every ounce of self-control not to scream as he traced its outline. The knife jabbed forward, breaking the skin near to my eyebrow. I launched myself forward, a cornered animal fighting for its life. I wasn't thinking, just acting. Piercy was off-balance and surprised, my lunge knocking him backwards, the shard of glass falling to the ground. Launching myself forward, we grappled on the floor, rocking from side to side, neither of us getting any traction. I rolled on to the glass, feeling it scrape down the side of my body. Piercy laughed as my face scrunched up in pain, his good fortune holding.

Feeling my strength slipping away, I made one last effort, ready to throw myself at him. I was stopped by the sound of a gunshot. Time seemed to stop, a pause, before the sound of screaming. Another gunshot and louder screaming, the sound of people running, confirmed it wasn't my imagination. Piercy released me and ran. I hauled myself to my feet and pushed my way through the crowds of people panicking inside the tent. Standing outside, the crowds were running away from the Pierhead and towards the dual carriageway and the city centre beyond it. I could hear sirens in the distance starting to grow louder.

FORTY-EIGHT

I didn't hesitate, starting to run, pushing my way through the crowds heading in the opposite direction, screaming and trying to get off the Fruit Market as quickly as they could. It was a struggle to stay on my feet, the flight instinct kicking in for the majority as they barrelled past. Some held mobile phones in the air, determined to capture whatever unfolded. Some had the sense to just get themselves to safety.

Breathing heavily, I could see the initial commotion was coming from the Pierhead. I eased off as I approached, crowds starting to thin. Coming to a stop, I heard raised voices. The wooden structure went out maybe fifty feet long heading out into the water, split across two levels, the main jetty jutting out to the left. I stood at the bottom of the steps, people running down them in the opposite direction, screaming. Grabbing the nearest rail, I headed up.

Two figures I recognised were standing at the far end. Forrester was on the floor, bleeding out, Mail standing over him with a gun in his hand.

'You really should put it down.'

'He thought I'd just roll over for him,' Mail shouted to me. 'Like I was just going to lie down and die.'

I thought about the shooting range I'd seen at Forrester's caravan, a dark feeling overcoming me. The realisation I'd helped make this happen hit me like a fist to the stomach. I leaned over the edge and vomited. This was on me. I'd chosen not to tell Coleman what I'd seen in Forrester's caravan and this was the result.

The last few people in the area for the parade pushed past me, running away. It left the three of us. I edged closer, moving to the side, making sure I made as much noise as possible on the planks of wood underfoot so I didn't spook Mail. I came to a stop, water lapping gently underfoot. 'Put the gun down,' I said to him.

'That's not going to happen.' Mail turned the gun towards me, gestured that I should move closer. 'I want to be able to see you.'

I did as I was told, scoping out the area for escape routes, wondering how deep the water was underneath if it came to it. I made sure to hold Mail's stare hoping I didn't look as scared as I felt. 'This has got a bit out of hand, hasn't it?' I took a step forward.

'Do what the man says, Gary. Put it down.'

We both turned to where the voice had come from, watched Ian Jagger step forward. He looked out to the water, hands in his coat pockets.

'This needs to stop now,' he said. 'No one else needs to get hurt here.'

'What lies have you been telling them?' Mail said to Jagger. 'I bet you haven't told Geraghty the truth.'

'He doesn't need to tell me,' I said. 'I know.'

Mail swung the gun back to me, manic. 'And what do you know?'

'I know you and Forrester murdered John Gove.' I sounded calmer than I felt. He could pull the trigger and turn everything to darkness, but I wasn't going to stop until I'd said my piece. 'There was a third man there with you,' I said. 'That's the important part.'

'Is that so?' Mail trained the gun on me. 'Who's got the big mouth?'

'You were seen.'

'Bullshit.'

'A homeless man was bedding down for the night in the car park. You didn't check carefully enough.'

Mail laughed. 'Fuck me, that's perfect.' He spun back to face Jagger. 'Don't you wish it was always that easy?'

I glanced at Jagger, who wasn't moving or speaking. 'The man's ready to go on the record with what he saw,' I said to Mail. I wanted his attention on me. The anger he was feeling towards Jagger was tangible, something that could blow up at any point. I didn't want that to happen yet.

Mail turned the gun back to me, levelled it at my head. 'I suppose we best finish this, then.'

'Forrester set things up that night,' Jagger said. 'Tell Geraghty.'

I didn't move a muscle. I glanced down at Forrester. He wasn't moving. I knew an ambulance wasn't going to make any difference. He was dead. Forrester and Mail had been living a lie, both running from their shared past. Both had been hiding in their own way. This was the tab that still needed paying thirty years later.

'Forrester made the call,' Mail said. 'I went along with it, as usual. I trusted him.' He moved the gun in his hand. 'You don't think I wasn't sold a lie, too? You don't think this fucked me up just as much? We followed the orders we were given and did our job. That's the bottom line.'

'You shouldn't have.'

'We didn't have a choice.'

'There's always a choice.'

Mail was shaking his head violently, his feet beating out a steady rhythm on the wooden floor underfoot. He moved backwards and forwards, a man on the edge.

'If I'd said no, I was finished,' Mail stepped forward. 'I'd have been as pointless as Don Ridley. No, you pick a side and you fucking stick to it.'

'Even if it costs you everything?'

'I had no choice.'

'You were complicit.' I believed him that he wasn't the prime mover behind John Gove's murder, though it didn't excuse his actions by a long way. If he wanted someone to say everything was fine, he wouldn't be hearing it from me.

Mail moved the gun back towards Jagger. I started to move, knowing I had to do something, but the timber underfoot screamed as I started to move. Mail pivoted, the gun trained back on me. 'Don had the measure of you and no mistake. He believed in justice and you let John Gove down.'

'You know fuck all about justice.' Mail moved the gun around in his hand again, feeling its weight, working out if he could use it again. 'Gove wasn't innocent.'

I stepped forward. 'What did Gove do? Did he supply the tablet that killed Angela Howe?' Mail nodded vigorously, blinking rapidly, recognising the name.

'She was Gove's girlfriend.'

'He was a piece of shit.'

'He deserved to die?'

Mail shrugged. 'For dealing a tablet that killed a young woman? I don't really have a problem with an eye for an eye under those circumstances. No one was ever going to miss him.'

'You're wrong,' I said, thinking about Gove's elderly father and his grief. 'He had a family.'

'We were doing the city a favour.'

The emergency services sirens were grow louder and closer. I stared at Mail, knowing he was justifying his own role in what had happened that night. Deep down he hadn't fully bought into the lie. It was written all over his face. 'You need to give me the gun,' I said,' or at least put it down.'

Mail stared at me, his eyes dead. 'I'm a bit sick of being told what to do. You think I wasn't expecting this night to come, one way or another?'

'It can end in different ways for you, though.'

'I can't walk away, like I wanted, can I?'

I shook my head. 'You were never going to be able to do that.' I took another step closer to him. 'I know who the third man was.' I said the name to him, watching as he nodded confirmation.

'Maybe you're better than I thought, Geraghty, but what are you going to do about it?'

'Take him down.'

'You think you can do that?' Mail laughed. 'This is totally fucked, but I've got nothing better than you.' He brought the gun up to his own head. 'I didn't see it ending like this, either.'

'Put the gun down.' I reached out to him, wanting him to hand it over. 'This can still end the right way for you.'

'You should have left well alone, Geraghty.' His eyes bored into me, his breathing deep and fast. He didn't need to say anything more.

I threw myself forward, a split-second too slow as he pulled the trigger. The gun went off, a deafening blast ripping through the night air, a scream in the distance. The gun fell to the ground, clattering on the wooden boards.

It took a moment for me to realise I was being lifted up of the floor, pushed well away from the bodies of Mail and Forrester. I couldn't focus, struggling to take in what had just happened. The area around was quiet, the last few people heading as far away as possible. The sirens were louder, blue lights approaching. Coleman was standing in front of me.

'It's over, Joe.'

I looked around for Jagger, but he was gone. 'It's far from over,' I said, turning back to Coleman. 'It's over when I say it is.'

'It's over for you.'

I went to push my way past him, but he stood his ground. 'You have to stay here.'

'No chance.'

'I'll arrest you if you try to leave.'

I laughed, possibly delirious. 'For what?'

'Take your pick, but it doesn't really matter. It's to look after you.' Coleman took a step back. 'The gun's gone. That means the situation is dangerous.'

I glanced around, my brain catching up. Jagger had the gun. I knew where he'd go. There was only one place in the area he'd feel safe. 'This needs finishing now.'

Coleman planted his feet, straightened himself up. 'You'll have to go through me.'

I didn't hesitate, throwing a punch that sent him to the ground.

FORTY-NINE

I headed down Humber Street, the last few stragglers from the parade still in the area. Grant Piercy's bar was in darkness. I tried the door, finding it locked. Cupping my hands to the glass, I could see the door which linked to the building next door, the extension Piercy had shown me, was open. I had no proof, but I was betting it was the only place Jagger would head for. Blood is thicker than water, as he'd told me.

I looked around for a suitable stone to smash the glass with. Finding one, I stood back as I threw it close to where the lock was before reaching inside and releasing the mechanism. Stepping inside, I went straight through the connecting door. The floor underfoot was bare concrete, the walls bare and harsh. Building materials and pieces of equipment littered the floor. Otherwise, the ground floor was clear. I picked up a small metal bar, weighing it in my hand as I headed for the stairs. The first floor was in the same unfinished state. I paused hearing a noise travel from higher up. I'd been as quiet as possible, but it was almost impossible to stop the echo of my steps in what was a concrete and brick box. I took my mobile out and pressed record, hoping it would pick up whatever was about to happen.

I came to a stop at the top of the stairs, ready. Staying close to the wall, metal bar in hand, I edged forward toward the window. I registered the air change too slowly, a weapon crashing into my torso. Struggling, I collapsed to the floor, working hard to breathe, the room spinning as I tried to recover. The metal bar fell out of my hand. I watched as it was kicked away from me. I took my time, eyeing up Jagger before sitting up against the wall. 'We didn't get finished on the pier, did we? Can't lie, I did feel a bit like a gooseberry, seeing as it was an impromptu thirty year reunion.'

Jagger moved forward, a smile on his face. 'Can you hear the sirens, Geraghty? What do you think is going to happen once the police catch up with you? I'm a Member of Parliament, and you, to be frank, you're the shit on my shoes. You'll be going to prison for a long time.'

'I've got nothing to lose, then, have I?' I smiled at him, rubbed at my ribs hoping for some relief before correcting myself. 'We've all got something to lose, haven't we, if we're being honest?' The time had come to get the answers I needed. 'You kept Don away from the live investigation in 1989. It's time to account for that.'

'It's the way it goes. He wanted the job, but was needed elsewhere. We don't get to pick and choose what we do at work.'

I didn't take my eyes off him. The answer was too easy, too prepared. But I wanted him to be comfortable enough to drop his guard and make a mistake. 'You let Forrester and Mail loose on it,' I said. 'They weren't capable of catching a cold at that point, never mind a murderer, but it was your call.'

'You allocate resources as best you can.'

'But you specifically put them on the job?'

The look on Jagger's face told me he was catching up with where this conversation was heading. I hauled myself to my feet, breathing in hard. 'They killed John Gove.' I laid it out for him. 'Your two detectives kicked him to death and left his body in the boot of a stolen car in a grim multi-storey car park.'

'You need some serious proof to back up your fantasies. This isn't justice.'

He wasn't wrong. The odds were still stacked against me. I was taking on a decorated former police officer and now Member of Parliament. 'What would you know about justice?'

'I know when it's served.'

'Gove's death?' I shook my head. 'Don didn't need to die.'

'You've got to let it go before it eats you up and does you some damage. Don died in a hit and run. They happen.'

'They don't happen like this. Did you know he spoke to Natalie Okorie? It was recorded. He told her everything. The evidence is there.'

Jagger smiled. 'Doesn't work like that. No one was bothered about Gove back then, no one's bothered about him now.'

Moving caused me to wince, but adrenalin was pushing me on.

Jagger pointed at me, angry. 'Don't even try and twist things to suit your agenda. It happens all the time. You apply pressure and you see if the person cracks. It shows you what they're made of, whether they can handle playing with the big boys or not.' Jagger stopped, stared at me. 'In fact, it reminds me of you. You're out of your depth here.'

I held his stare. 'I'm not the one out of my depth here.'

'You're close to drowning, Joe. It's about time you recognised that. The smart money would be on disappearing, hoping no one remembers you were ever here.'

That wasn't going to happen. The pieces were falling into place. 'Talk to me about Angela Howe.' This time there was no disguising the fear on Jagger's face. I'd scored a hit.

'There's nothing to say.'

'For a politician, you're a bad liar.'

'She's not relevant.'

'The death of Gove's girlfriend just before his own isn't relevant?'

'You're talking like there's a link between their deaths. Youngsters take drugs, some of them die. It's an unfortunate fact.'

'You suppressed it. It's in Don's file.'

Jagger moved forward, the gun coming into view. 'I'd watch your mouth.'

'We're well beyond that point.' He was looking over my shoulder, eyes darting left and right. 'I don't think Piercy is coming to your rescue. Looks like he's cut and run.' I smiled at him, telling him to focus. 'It's just us.'

'You're a loser, Geraghty, always have been. Maybe you should turn the gun on yourself like Mail, as no one's listening to you. You've got no credibility here, same as Don. A shitty office investigating cheating husbands was probably about right for the pair of you.'

Jagger was trying to push my buttons, see if he could force me into losing control. He wanted me to come for him. If I did that, he'd put me back down on the floor, but for the last time. What happened after I wouldn't have any control over. He'd spin it as an act of self-defence. It had been building to this moment. I let a wave of pain pass before speaking. 'Forrester and Mail would have gone to prison for a long time, but there's still the chance the third man present that night will. In fact, he'll go to prison for a long time.' I closed the gap between us. 'Wouldn't you agree?' He didn't respond, so I changed tack. 'Don was killed because he knew all of this. All those vast, open spaces in the area must have been tempting after learning he was going to blow the lid off things. No cameras, no witnesses and a man with a regular dog walking routine. Sounds like an absolute gift to me.'

I heard the sound of someone emerging from the wall behind me, too slow to react. Piercy took the gun from Jagger. 'You're a man with a lot to say, Joe.'

I looked at him and then at Jagger. 'I know the truth.'

He nodded to Jagger who opened a door close to us, the cold night air blowing in. It could only lead to the roof.

'Out we go, then, Joe.'

FIFTY

The low brick wall circling the edge of the roof came up to my chest. Piercy thrust me forward, bending me over the edge, a gun pressed into my back. Blue lights flashed around the Fruit Market, the sound of the emergency services at work. I instinctively tried to kick back and move, but was held down in place. I looked down, trying not to be sick. I was one push away from a fall of several floors and certain death. Piercy pushed the gun further into the back of my head, dialling up the pain. I'd poked the hornet's nest and was now cornered, the bill needing to be settled.

'You sound like you've got something you want to say?' Piercy said.

'The truth.'

Piercy hauled me around, my back to the wall. 'You best start talking then.'

I took a moment, scanning the roof top. Jagger, true to form had quietly made himself scarce so it was just the two of us now. The night had fallen silent. Maybe the police didn't know we were up here. Or maybe they were creeping closer. Time was running out. 'Let's talk about Angela Howe,' I said, knowing she was the key. Piercy kicked my legs apart and held me by the throat, starting to bend me backwards over the edge. I still managed a smile for him. 'The truth, remember?' Piercy eye's bored into me. 'She had a secret boyfriend and I'd assumed it was John Gove,' I said. He released his grip on my throat, let me talk. 'He fitted the bill, as you wouldn't want your family to meet the local drug dealer, but it never really felt right. She wanted the finer things in life, someone with a future, and why not? She was a teenager, away from home and she wanted a bit of excitement in her life.' I had his attention and needed to twist the knife in. 'But Gove was skint, a low-level dealer in it to keep himself supplied, so who better than one of the city's top sports stars? Of course, you were married, so it was just a bit of fun for you. You weren't going to flaunt her around the place too much, were you?' Gary Mail had been right. I'd been looking at things from the wrong angle.

'You best watch your mouth, Geraghty.'

I was thrust further back, my back arching over the wall, gun grinding into my forehead. 'But then she died, right?' I managed to say. 'Did you know where the pills came from? I'm betting you did.' Piercy swiped me across the head with the gun. Blood trickled down my face, the metallic taste of blood in my mouth, my right eye starting to close over. 'You knew the truth, but you couldn't prove it? You certainly couldn't let her death stand, could you?' My head being snapped back over the wall made me feel sick, but I had to press on, struggling to breathe and talk. 'I don't blame you, not really. I wouldn't let it stand, either. It must have been handy having Jagger, a police officer, on your side, though? He was no fan of John Gove, either, and wanted to take him down. It was a result for everyone involved, even if things did spiral out of control that night' Piercy aimed the gun at my forehead, but I couldn't stop. 'My bet is that Forrester and Mail were only ever meant to see he got a good kicking, what more could be done without certain truths coming to light? But it got a bit messy when a third man joined in with them at the car park.'

Piercy released me, took a step back. 'You'd need to speak to Jagger about that.'

'I've got a witness who saw everything.'

'That your best card to play?'

Too weak to resist, I was spun around, pushed forward over the edge. The gun went to the back of my head. I was in deep shit, a clung to the wall. 'You were the third man there,' I said, braced for a response. I was maybe going to die, but I wanted him to be aware that I knew the truth.

Other things made sense to me now. The sketches John Gove had done, violently scribbling over images of Piercy weren't related to his decision to leave Hull City. They were done because Angela Howe had left him for Piercy. But then Piercy had left the city, a surprise transfer to another football club. I was willing to bet Jagger had insisted he left after Gove's murder, put some distance between himself and the city. It maybe killed his professional dreams, but I doubt he'd argued, given the circumstances. I thought again about Angela Howe and her death, wondered what part John Gove had played in that. Maybe he'd passed her drugs when they'd been in a relationship and she'd taken it. Maybe her death explained the descent his father spoke about in his video interview, the darkness that followed his son. He was culpable.

I carried on speaking. 'Jagger set it up for you and you got carried away. It's why the witness didn't want to speak out thirty years ago. You were someone back then, not like now when you hang on to Jagger's coat-tails.' My words were striking home. I laughed, delirious, as Piercy tried to force me further over the wall. I had little to give as I tried to resist, digging my feet in as best I could. 'Jagger's investigation was shit, which makes sense now. It's why he didn't want

Don sniffing around it. There was too much to lose.' Staring down into the darkness below, I carried on talking. If I was going to die, I wanted to get it all out. 'Forrester and Mail fell into line for Jagger and kept their mouths shut, but it fucked them up. You fucked them up.'

'They followed their orders.'

Piercy swiped the gun against the back of my head again, my feet unsteady. I had to stay with him, stay alive. 'She had expensive tastes that someone like Gove was never going to satisfy. She wanted the finer things in life and someone with the cash and profile to give them to her.'

'Gove was a piece of shit she needed to be rid of.'

'And that was your decision to make?'

'Think what you like, but I did something about it.'

'You'll go to prison for it.'

'I've got no intention of going to prison.'

'That's definitely not your decision to make.'

'People have always come for me,' he said. 'You think I'm scared? You think I haven't seen better men then you off? I had people try to cripple me on the football pitch. I had people tell me I couldn't build this in the city, couldn't build that in the city. Fuck them all. You don't create something without putting yourself on the line. That's what people like you will never understand.'

Piercy pushed me further over the edge, as I scrabbled with my feet to get some purchase against the wall. 'I understand what makes you tick, don't worry about that. So does Natalie Okorie.' She was my last roll of the dice, the suggestion she had something on him.

Piercy leaned in close to me. 'The police might want to ask questions about what happened here tonight,' he said, 'but Jagger will smooth it over. You'll be a suicide stat, Geraghty, someone who came here spouting baseless theories, but really needed help to come to terms with his grief over the death of Don Ridley.'

'Okorie knows all about you and Jagger. She knows you're skint. She won't let it stand.'

'She's got fuck all, I'm afraid. Just another one with conspiracy theories and no real evidence. Maybe you should have taken that job with me after all? That way we could have been friends.'

Piercy made another attempt to shove me over the edge. I held on, weak, but knowing I had to keep him talking. 'Till was another loose end for you? You're in danger of becoming a serial killer.'

'Till thought he was owed. He thought I'd provide him with a nice retirement nest egg. Not how it works.'

'And you had to burn Don's cottage down?'

'Better to be safe than sorry.'

'You're lucky no one died.' Sarah had maybe turned a blind eye to what had happened, knowing I'd lied by omission. It had firmed up the link to Piercy in my mind, though, adding to what I knew about Angela Howe and his football career. The suggestion there was a file of evidence had spurred him into action. There was never anything for him to find, but he'd decided to be thorough. What made me sick was knowing Jagger would try to pick up the pieces again, make sure nothing came of the fire investigation, or Till's death. It was the price Jagger had to pay to preserve his own status, the price to pay for decisions he made thirty years ago. 'It was just business to you?'

Piercy paused for a moment, his grip loosening. 'Isn't everything? It's how winners are crowned.'

Bottom line, profit and loss, money. I got the picture. 'You're as soulless as the buildings around here.'

Piercy laughed and nudged me further forward, my leg slipping out from between his. I didn't hesitate, spinning around and bringing my knee up to crash it into his balls. With what energy I had, I followed through, making sure he collapsed to the floor, the gun falling from his hand. It was instinct as I moved, first stamping on his face so he wasn't going to move. I picked up the gun, taking a moment to compose myself. I backed off, breathing heavily, waiting. Piercy groaned and opened an eye, taking in the situation. I waved the gun in the air, so he could see I had it before gesturing to the edge of the roof. 'Your turn.' Piercy smiled and slowly did as he was told.

'It's always about winning,' Piercy said, slumping down against the wall. 'Remember that.'

'Don didn't win.'

'Don didn't have to lose, though. He made his choice.'

'He came for you and you killed him.'

'Good luck proving that.'

I stepped forward, my turn to grind the gun into his forehead, enjoy the sensation of him leaning over the wall, letting him stare death in the face. Piercy laughed, encouraged me to go further.

'Do it, Geraghty. Make a name for yourself. Shoot me, push me over the edge, do something. Be a man. If it helps, I'll tell you how it felt when I knocked Don off the road. It was fuck all, really. He didn't want to listen to reason, so it had to be done. Ian never had the balls, even when it comes to protecting what we've both built. It was always down to me. If anything, Don made it easy with his pathetic moving away to the middle of nowhere routine.' He paused for breath. 'It was a fucking thrill to do it. Really gets the blood pumping.'

I screamed out, wanting him to shut him up. Wanting to shoot him. Closing my eyes, I put more pressure on the trigger, feeling how easy it would be. I'd be doing it for Don. I opened my eyes again, Piercy staring back at me, daring me to do something.

I looked out beyond Piercy at Hull. I knew the city and its people but was also clueless about it. I wasn't going to kill Piercy. I struck out with the gun, hitting him across the face. He fell straight to the floor, unconscious. I sunk to the floor next to him, crying, an emotional release. I was done, no idea what would stick when I listened back to the recording on my phone, what Coleman could work with and build a case. I didn't know what would come next, but this was me. I looked out at the city, the sprawl of lights twinkling into the distance, knowing this was home.

The End

Also by Nick Quantrill

- Broken Dreams: Joe Geraghty Book 1
- The Late Greats: Joe Geraghty Book 2
- The Crooked Beat: Joe Geraghty Book 3

- Made In Hull: Joe Geraghty Collection
- No Direction Home: Joe Geraghty Novella

All available from Fahrenheit Press.

About the author

Nick Quantrill was born and raised in Hull, an isolated industrial city in East Yorkshire. His novels featuring private investigator Joe Geraghty,are published by Fahrenheit Press.

A prolific short story writer, Nick's work has appeared in Volumes Eight, Nine and Ten of The Mammoth Book of Best British Crime alongside the genre's most respected names.

With a growing reputation as an event chair, Nick has interviewed a series of writers on stage including Lee Child, Martina Cole, Val McDermid, Peter Robinson & Mark Billingham.

Nick is also co-founder of Hull Noir, an official 2017 UK City of Culture event. When not writing fiction, Nick interviews and writes for a variety of publications, including the 2017 UK City of Culture website and magazine.

He lives in Hull with his wife, daughter, cat and the constant fear Hull City will let him down.

You can follow Nick on Twitter @NickQuantrill

Acknowledgements

Chris McVeigh and everyone at Fahrenheit – the wider team, my fellow authors and all the readers - for the show of faith and for breathing new life into Joe Geraghty...

Nick Triplow and Nikki East for all the crime chat, Ted Lewis discussion and Hull Noir scheming...

Eva Dolan, Jay Stringer and Luca Veste for all the wise words, help and comradeship...

Joe Hakim, JE Books, Waterstones Hull, The Rabbit Hole and the city's numerous writers and poets for the support and friendship... we don't need a title to be cultured...

Cathy, my mum, my father-in-law, my cat... couldn't do it without you...

More books from Fahrenheit Press

Black Moss by David Nolan

In April 1990, as rioters took over Strangeways prison in Manchester, someone killed a little boy at Black Moss.

And no one cared.

No one except Danny Johnston, an inexperienced radio reporter trying to make a name for himself.

More than a quarter of a century later, Danny returns to his home city to revisit the murder that's always haunted him.

If Danny can find out what really happened to the boy, maybe he can cure the emptiness he's felt inside since he too was a child.

But finding out the truth might just be the worst idea Danny Johnston has ever had.

"As one would expect from a writer with the skill and experience of David Nolan, this haunting book deals with very difficult issues in an incredibly sympathetic manner while at the same time throwing a light onto one of the most complicated and shaming areas of our society - the failure to protect those who are the most vulnerable."

Know Me From Smoke by Matt Phillips

Stella Radney, long-time lounge singer, still has a bullet lodged in her hip from the night when a rain of gunshots killed her husband.

That was twenty years ago and it's a surprise when the unsolved murder is reopened after the district attorney discovers new evidence. Royal Atkins is a convicted killer who just got out of prison on a legal technicality. At first, he's thinking he'll play it straight. Doesn't take long before that plan turns to smoke—was it ever really an option?

When Stella and Royal meet one night, they're drawn to each other. But Royal has a secret. How long before Stella discovers that the man she's falling for isn't who he seems? A noir of gripping suspense and violence, Know Me from Smoke is a journey into the shadowy terrain of murder, lost love, and the heart's lust for vengeance.

"A beautifully written, brutal & brilliant slice of hardboiled crime fiction. A Knockout."

Rubicon by Ian Patrick

Rubicon has recently been optioned by the BBC with a view to making a six episode series.

Two cops, both on different sides of the law – both with the same gangland boss in their sights.

Sam Batford is an undercover officer with the Metropolitan Police who will stop at nothing to get his hands on fearsome crime-lord Vincenzo Guardino's drug supply.

DCI Klara Winter runs a team on the National Crime Agency, she's also chasing down Guardino, but unlike Sam Batford she's determined to bring the gangster to justice and get his drugs off the streets.

Set in a time of austerity and police cuts where opportunities for corruption are rife, Rubicon is a tense, dark thriller that is definitely not for the faint hearted.

'A sharp, slick, gripping and compelling novel'

www.ingramcontent.com/pod-product-compliance
Lightning Source LLC
Chambersburg PA
CBHW020611310726
48979CB00008B/1430/J

* 9 7 8 1 9 1 2 5 2 6 8 4 0 *